Choosing You

By Allie Everhart

Choosing You
By Allie Everhart

Copyright © 2013 Allie Everhart
All rights reserved.
Published by Waltham Publishing, LLC
Cover Design by Sarah Hansen of Okay Creations
ISBN-13: 978-0-9887524-4-3

CHAPTER 1
October 30

The lines on the track are like a map telling me where to go. I follow their orderly path, my arms and legs moving in a rhythmic pattern. My body repeats the motion effortlessly, leaving my mind to replay what just happened.

I see a girl at a party. She's drinking. She never drinks. Ever. But there were no other options. It was history repeating itself. Like the script had already been written and she just had to let the scene play out. For 18 years, she promised herself this would never happen. And then it did. She lost all control within a matter of seconds.

That girl was someone else. I will never be her. And I will never be her mother. I refuse.

My legs take longer, quicker strides as I become aware of my body again. I pump my arms because I'm not going fast enough. I still feel all of it. The confusion. The rage. The pain. And I just want it to go away.

The cold night air clings to my skin, cooling the sweat and sending an icy chill through me. My arms and legs ache and my lungs burn from inhaling the frigid air. But I keep going. Because I like feeling this pain. I understand it. And it keeps my mind off the pain that I can't understand.

A drop of rain hits my face. Then two, then three. Soon rain pours from the sky, stinging my skin.

"Jade, what the hell are you doing out here? I've been looking everywhere for you! Jade!"

It's Garret, the boy who made the girl live out that scene at the party. The scene that was never supposed to happen.

My eyes remain on the lines in front of me and I run past him like he's not even there.

"Jade, stop! Wait!"

I make another loop around the track as he continues to call out my name. As I approach him again, he moves into my lane and I veer to avoid him.

There's a sharp tug on the back of my shirt and I stumble forward to a stop. I'm gasping for breath as Garret turns me around and holds me against him so tight I can't move despite my efforts to break free.

"Stop." He says it quietly now as he presses my head against his chest. "Just stop running."

I give up trying to fight him and let my body collapse into his.

A minute ago I never wanted to see him again, but now I don't want him to let me go.

"Tell me what's wrong," he says. "If it's something I did, I'm sorry. I'll fix it."

The cold rain continues to pour down in a steady stream. My shorts and shirt feel heavy against my skin and I shiver as the wind blows around us.

He runs his hand along my arm. "What are you doing out here? It's freezing and you're soaking wet. Let's go inside."

My legs aren't ready to move. My entire body is aching, leaving my emotions numb, just the way I want them.

"Jade, talk to me."

I look up and see him watching me, waiting for some kind of answer. Before he can speak again, I reach up and press my lips to his. I shouldn't be kissing him so I don't understand why I'm doing this. But I don't understand anything right now.

Garret gently pulls away. "Tell me what's going on. Why are you out here? Why were you at the party? And why were you drinking?" His voice is filled with so much worry and so much concern. After seeing him at the party I don't know why he even cares. But I know he does. I can feel it and I can see it in his face and it pisses me off. I don't want him to care about me. Not now. Now after what he did.

I push away but his arms tighten around me. I won't look at him. Because when I do all I see is the image of him coming out of that room. With her. And then I see the vodka bottle and it reminds me of my mom and that letter she wrote.

It's too much. It's too many emotions. I want the numbness back.

The rain continues to pour and I shiver again.

"We're going inside." Garret's tone is forceful. He finally lets me go but grabs my hand, pulling on me to go with him. "Jade, come on. I'm not leaving here without you."

My mind is still racing, trying to make sense of things that make no sense at all.

When I don't move, he picks me up and carries me up the hill to our dorm.

CHAPTER 2
Sept. 4, Two Months Earlier

I sit on the blue vinyl seats of Ryan's car with a bag of potato chips in my hand and a 20-ounce soda wedged between my legs, my bare feet resting against the dashboard. As I reach in the bag, Ryan snatches it from me.

"I'm cutting you off, Jade." He tosses the potato chips in the back seat. "That's your fifth bag in two days."

"Yeah. So I like potato chips. Big deal." I lick the salt from my fingers, release my seat belt, and reach over the seat to retrieve my chips.

"Hey, buckle up. And if you finish those, that's your last bag. You need to start eating better."

I roll my eyes as I resume my position. "You're not a doctor yet, Ryan. You haven't even started med school, so don't start lecturing me on my health."

He wipes the sweat from his forehead with the back of his hand while his other hand grips the steering wheel. "I don't need to be a doctor to know that a diet of potato chips and soda isn't good for you."

"Potatoes are a vegetable." I chomp loudly into a chip but Ryan doesn't notice.

"Damn, it's hot." He rolls his window all the way down, blowing even more warm, humid air into the car. A semi roars past us as we go down a hill, followed by two more after that.

"Put your window up. I can't hear the radio with all that noise."

"If I put the window up, we'll suffocate." He rolls it back up halfway. "When I'm a doctor, the first thing I'm gonna do is get a car with air conditioning."

"The first thing you'll be doing is paying off your student loans." I stuff more chips in my mouth.

"That's true. I'll probably be driving this thing for another ten years." He nudges me from across the seat. "Not everyone gets a full ride scholarship to some fancy East Coast college."

I shrug. "What can I say? If some rich guy offers to pay for your college you go."

"He gave you the scholarship because you deserve it. More than anyone I know."

"Don't start, Ryan." I focus out the side window, watching yet another state go by. We're in New York now, driving past farm fields. I never realized how much farming went on in New York. Yesterday was the first time I'd ever been outside of Iowa and since then I've been to five states. From the interstate, almost every state looks the same. Big, open fields on both sides of the road. Then we hit Pennsylvania and the landscape got hilly and filled in with trees. New York is a mix of trees and fields.

Ryan rolls his window all the way up, muffling the road noise. "We're almost there and I just need to say it one last time and then I'll shut up."

I sigh dramatically. "Fine. Hurry up."

"I'm really proud of you, Jade. Most kids your age would've shut down after what happened. They would've dropped out of school. But you ended up the freaking valedictorian."

"I know. I was there. Now are you done? Because none of that matters now. That was high school. This is college. I have to start at the bottom and prove myself all over again."

"You won't have to prove anything. You're going to totally kick ass at that school from your first day on campus."

"Okay, no more pep talks. I don't need you boosting my ego only to have reality hit as soon as I get there. High school was easy. There's more competition at college. And I'll be going to school with spoiled rich kids who went to fancy prep schools and probably had private tutors their whole lives."

"Hey, don't get that attitude going before you get there. You haven't even met these people. Give them a chance before you start judging."

"Oh, please. Like they aren't going to judge *me*? I'm the Kensington Scholarship winner. Everyone knows that's for charity cases."

He rolls the window down again. "I doubt anyone there even knows about your past."

"It only takes one person to find out and tell the whole school. Then I'll be known all over campus as the poor girl from Iowa who at the tender age of 15 found her mom dead on the bathroom floor from pills and booze. They'll think I'm just as crazy as my mom. And maybe I am . . ." My voice drifts off.

"Stop it, Jade. You are *not* your mom. You're nothing like her. You've already accomplished more than she ever did."

"Can we not talk about my mother, please?" I open my soda and it fizzes out the top and all over the seat. "Shit! I'm so sorry." I hold the bottle up, wiping the soda off with my hand.

"Don't worry about it. This car is thirty years old. This isn't the first time soda's been spilled on it."

I grab a towel from the back and quickly wipe up the dark, sticky liquid running down the seat. *Dammit, Jade! Look what you did, you worthless brat!* My mom's voice is screaming in my head. I wince, preparing to feel the sting of her hand as it slaps my face.

"It's clean." Ryan grabs hold of my arm, which is furiously drying the seat.

I put the towel on the floor by my feet. Ryan lets go of my arm and gets quiet. He knows how my mother haunts me sometimes and he knows I won't talk about it because I don't want to talk about my mother. She's the past and the past is over. And although she gets in my head sometimes, it's nothing I can't handle. Ryan probably disagrees with that, but he knows that bugging me about it will only make us fight. So he remains silent.

Ryan is my brother. Well, not my real brother, but close enough. I met him six years ago when he moved into a house down the street from me. He was 15 at the time and I had a huge crush on him. He, of course, had no interest in dating a 12-year-old. So I gave up trying to win his affection and just

7

hung out with him, acting as his annoying little sister. The role stuck and I've been annoying him ever since.

I scrunch up the open end of the potato chip bag and drop it behind my seat. "There. I won't eat any more. Are you happy now?"

"I'd be happier if you ate an apple once in a while."

"Baby steps, Ryan." I return my feet to the dashboard and wipe my hands on my shorts to get rid of the salt that remains on my fingers.

"I'm getting off at the next exit. I need to get some gas and check in with Dad."

"Let me call him." I hold my hand out for the phone. "You know he'd rather talk to me anyway."

Ryan smiles. "I know he would." He reaches in his shirt pocket for his phone and hands it to me.

Ryan's dad, Frank, volunteered to be my legal guardian after my mom died. Frank and my mom went to college together but lost track of each other when my mom dropped out. Her college career ended when a one night stand resulted in me. The sperm donor took off and she never heard from him again.

After I was born my mom never managed to get her life back on track. Instead she started drinking and got hooked on prescription drugs. I can't remember a time when she was ever normal. My entire childhood was spent taking care of her. And to this day, I hate her for that.

When Frank moved in down the street he tried to be friends with my mom again, but she wanted nothing to do with him, probably because he kept trying to get her into rehab. Whenever she had one of her drunken meltdowns, I'd run off and stay at

Frank's house. Pretty soon I was staying at Frank's almost every night, so it wasn't that big a deal to move in with him and Ryan when my mom died.

"Hey, Frank," I say when I hear him pick up. "We're almost to Connecticut. And thank God, because your son is driving me crazy." I smile as Ryan rolls his eyes. "I can't take another minute in the car with him. Now he's trying to ban me from eating potato chips. Can you believe that?"

"She's had five bags," he yells at the phone as I hold it by his face. "In two days! And not the little bags!"

I hear Frank laughing as I put the phone back to my ear. "See what I mean?"

"He just worries about you, honey. We both do."

I get a lump in my throat as he says it. It's only been a couple days and I already miss Frank. He's been like a father to me ever since I became friends with Ryan and if he hadn't taken me in years ago, I probably wouldn't even be going to college.

"Has Ryan given you his lecture about college boys yet?" Frank laughs as he says it.

"No, but I'm sure he will."

Ryan takes his big brother role seriously. He's very protective of me, sometimes too much. I don't like people protecting me. I can take care of myself just fine.

"So you're almost to Connecticut?" Frank asks. "Are you getting nervous?"

"What's there to be nervous about? It's college. Big deal."

Truthfully, I'm scared shitless. I have no idea what college will be like other than what I've seen in movies, which is basically a mix of sex, drugs, and alcohol. I have no idea what the classes will be like or the homework or the professors. At this point, the whole idea of going to college is freaking me out, but there's no way I'd ever tell Frank or Ryan that.

"You're going to be great there," Frank says. "I'm so proud of you."

"Here we go again." I glance at Ryan. "I haven't even done anything yet."

"You know I'll never stop saying it. Let's talk later, Jade. I need to speak with Ryan." I hand the phone back to Ryan as he pulls up to the gas pump. We both get out and I fill the tank while he talks to Frank. He paces back and forth shaking his head as he listens. Something must've happened.

Frank has multiple sclerosis. In the past few months, it's gotten worse. He used to work as a newspaper reporter, but he had to quit last year because of his illness. He freelances when he feels up to it although lately he hasn't been able to even do that. Sometimes he loses his balance and falls so now he has a wheelchair but he doesn't always use it. Ryan hired a nurse to stay at the house while we're gone because he didn't want Frank being alone for all these days.

When the gas tank is full, I wait in the car for Ryan. A few minutes later, he gets in, still on the phone. "No, just let me call them. I'll do it right now." He pulls forward and parks in front of the gas station.

"What's wrong?" I ask him as we get out again.

"Dad's nurse quit today. I need to call the agency and get someone over there." He reaches in the car for his wallet. "Let's go inside. You need to eat an actual meal and I need to figure out this nurse situation."

We go in the restaurant that's attached to the gas station. There's a row of red vinyl booths on one side and some wooden tables and chairs scattered on the other. Displayed on the walls is an odd assortment of mismatched frames that hold photos of horses and barns.

A love song from the seventies is playing from the speakers mounted in the ceiling. I try to ignore it so it doesn't get stuck in my head the rest of the day, but I know it will. For some reason, only really crappy songs get stuck in my head, never the good ones. I wonder if that's just me or if it happens to everyone.

The waitress seats us at one of the booths and hands us each a small plastic coated menu. I'm not that hungry due to the earlier potato chip binge, but I have to eat or Ryan will lecture me again on my junk food addiction.

"I know it's short notice, but your nurse quit on me!" Ryan lowers his voice when he notices people staring. "Yes, fine. Call me back when you know." He sets the phone down hard on the table, then takes a deep breath and moves his wavy brown hair off his face. He wears his hair a little long which I think gives him an artsy look even though he's not at all artistic.

"Did they find a replacement?" I ask.

"No. She's calling around. I can't believe this happens when I'm halfway across the country." He takes a sip of water. "Sorry, Jade. This was supposed to be our fun road trip across America kicking off your new life at college and it's not turning out that way."

"What are you talking about? We played road games. We sang along to the radio. We ate truck stop food. What's not to love? This has been a great trip."

My attempt to cheer him up falls flat. His mind is focused on his dad.

"Why don't you have Chloe stop over and check on him?"

Ryan shakes his head. "Like I would ever ask her to do that. I've only dated her for a month. She hasn't even been over to the house yet."

"She seems nice. And it would be a good test. If she refuses to check in on your father, you'll know to dump her now before things get too serious."

"I need to make some calls. Just get me a chicken sandwich and fries." He takes his phone and goes outside.

I order for both of us, then sit there in the vinyl booth, my bare legs sticking to the seat. I'm still sweaty from the hot car and the ice cold air conditioning is giving me chills.

My mind wanders to the college I'll be arriving at soon. I've never been to Moorhurst College. I've only seen the brochure, which showed a photo of a big stone building surrounded by maple trees at the peak of autumn color. On the website there were photos of some of the students. They looked like rich, preppy kids who get whatever they want. I know Ryan told me not to judge, but it's hard not to when you see those photos.

I look down at my white ribbed tank top and jean shorts which together cost $15. The people at Moorhurst probably spend more than that on a pair of socks.

I'm still not sure why they want me at this school. I didn't even apply there. My guidance counselor just called me into his office one day and said I was offered a scholarship to some private college in Connecticut. He said I was awarded the Kensington Scholarship, named after a rich guy who owns a chemical company and donates a lot of money to the school. Apparently Mr. Kensington heard my story and was so inspired he offered me the scholarship. I didn't even know I had a story. But apparently, a person with my background who ends up valedictorian is a story.

Ryan comes back to the table in a much better mood. "Okay, it's all set. The agency is sending someone over within the hour."

"Why does someone have to get over there so fast? Did something happen to Frank?"

"Don't worry about it. Everything's fine now. Our road trip adventure continues."

He's hiding something. He always gets overly enthusiastic when he's keeping bad news from me. Frank must be getting worse and Ryan doesn't want me to worry. I don't ask because I know he won't tell me.

We eat dinner, then get back on the road. A little over an hour later we exit off the interstate onto a road that winds through a maze of trees. Connecticut is nothing like Iowa. In Iowa you can see for miles. The land is flat and there's nothing obstructing your view. Rows of corn and soybean fields cover almost the entire state. Here in Connecticut I can only see what's straight ahead or behind us. Tall, leafy trees line both sides of the road. I don't even see any houses. They must be buried within the trees.

"Could you check the directions?" Ryan hands me his phone. "We should have seen it by now."

I swipe through his phone. "You have a message from Chloe. Do you want me to see what it says?"

He grabs for the phone, but I hold it high so he can't reach. "Come on. Just check the directions."

"Geez. Calm down. What does she send you? Naked pictures?" He doesn't answer. "Okay, it should be right up ahead."

I look up as we pass a large granite sign that reads Moorhurst College.

"Turn around. You missed it."

"I did? Really? I swear, you can't see a thing with these trees." Ryan turns the car around and drives slowly back the other way. I show him where to turn. We drive up a hill on a long entrance road and finally reach the campus.

It looks like something from a movie. The buildings are covered in light colored stone with ivy growing up the sides. Some have big pillars in front. They remind me of those really old buildings you see in England. Not that I've ever been to England, but I've seen pictures. The buildings line the perimeter of campus forming a square and in the middle there's a large grassy area with benches and giant shade trees.

I spot a group of students hanging out under one of the trees. They're stumbling around like they're drunk, which they probably are since it's Friday night. Other than that, the campus seems pretty empty. School doesn't start for four more days so a lot of people haven't moved in yet. Ryan made us leave early in case we had car trouble along the way. Unfortunately for me we didn't and now I'm stuck being one of the first people on campus.

Ryan parks in front of Carlson Hall, the place I'll be living for the next four years. "Well, this is it. What do you think? Pretty fancy, huh?"

"It's just a bunch of old buildings. It's not that fancy." I try to sound calm but inside my stomach is a churning bundle of nerves. I don't know what I expected, but this is not it. The campus seems small and intimate. I don't do small and intimate. I prefer big and detached.

As I look around and take it all in, I'm already feeling claustrophobic.

CHAPTER 3

"Are you getting out or what?" Ryan is holding my door open. "Let's go find your RA and see where your room is."

I step out of the car, suddenly feeling like I might throw up. Where is this coming from? I'm stronger than this. Way stronger. I take a deep breath, hoping the feeling is just carsickness from driving through those winding roads.

The inside of the residence hall smells old and musty, like a museum, making the sick feeling in my stomach creep up into my throat. I keep an eye out for a bathroom just in case I get sick.

Dark wooden doors with numbers on them line the hallway. We stop at one that has an RA sign on it. Ryan knocks on the door and a tall thin girl with long black hair and olive skin answers.

She looks at me and smiles. "Hi, are you moving in?" She has a slight foreign accent, but I can't tell where it's from.

"Yeah, I'm Jade Taylor. And this is Ryan, but he's not moving in. He just drove me here."

"Great, nice to meet you both. I'm Jasmine. Welcome to Moorhurst. Let me grab your key." She turns back and takes a key from a box on her desk, then grabs a large folder sitting next to it. "This is your housing information packet." She hands me the folder. "Go through it and if you have any questions, just let me know. Follow me. I'll show you your room."

She leads us to the very end of the hall, right by the stairwell. She opens the door, then hands me the key. "The rooms are small but you'll get used to it."

I scan the room. It's not that small. But I guess if you're used to living in a mansion, like the other students are, then it probably seems like a closet. The room has white walls that look freshly painted, light wood floors, and a window covered with beige curtains. There's a twin bed, a tall wooden dresser, and a small desk with a chair. A giant basket is sitting on the desk.

"That's a welcome gift from the Kensingtons," Jasmine says.

I go over and unwrap the cellophane around the basket. It's overflowing with an assortment of items stamped with the Moorhurst logo; a t-shirt, hooded sweatshirt, keychain, coffee mug, plastic cup, shorts, sweatpants, socks, and other items. There's even a cover for the cell phone I don't own.

"Looks like they bought out the whole campus bookstore," Ryan comments.

"Well, I'll let you get settled," Jasmine says. "If you need anything, just stop by."

She leaves and I shut the door and sit on the thin bare mattress on the bed.

Ryan stands there surveying the room. "I don't think it's that small. And you hardly have any stuff so you'll have plenty of room." He sits next to me. "Jasmine seems cool, right?"

"I don't know her well enough to say. But from her name alone, she doesn't seem that cool. She's named after a cartoon princess. That speaks volumes about her personality."

"What did I say about judging people?"

"I'm just saying that I doubt we'll be friends. I don't get along with people like her. I doubt I'll get along with anyone here which is fine with me."

"Cut that shit out right now. You're never going to make friends with that I-don't-care-about-anything-or-anyone attitude. Besides you can't keep that act going for four years. You're not at all like that. You know that, right?"

"I have no interest in being friends with any of these people. I'm here to get an education. That's it."

Ryan turns to me, his lecture face on. "You can't go four years without any friends. Not everyone here is a stuck up snob. And just because people are rich doesn't mean they aren't good people. You need to get out and do stuff. Interact with other students. Go to football games. Go to some parties. That's what people do in college. Well, I don't, but I'm the exception to the rule."

"You know I don't like parties, Ryan."

"Yes, I know. But you don't have to drink. Just go there and hang out. And if it gets out of hand, just leave."

"It always gets out of hand. If it didn't, I wouldn't be here."

He stands up and faces me. "Dammit, Jade. You keep saying you want to forget your past and then you keep bringing it up.

You're not your mother. You don't drink. You don't do drugs. You don't do any of the stuff she did."

"You're right. I shouldn't have said it. I'm done talking about her. Let's go unpack the car." I take his hand and drag him out of the room.

"Did you just say that I'm right? That's a first."

"First and only. Don't get used to it."

We go outside and start unpacking the trunk, which holds a few boxes and some garbage bags stuffed with clothes, sheets, and towels. As I'm picking up one of the bags, it splits open on the bottom and clothes start seeping out.

"Shit, I knew I should've got—"

"Can I help?" The voice seems to be coming from a guy, but I can't really see him because the bag I'm holding is blocking my view. I peer around it to see him picking my clothes off the ground. "Here, you take these and I'll take the bag. It looks heavy."

"I can handle heavy." I snatch the tank tops he's holding, then turn my back to him and maneuver the torn bag a different way so it doesn't tear even more. I feel the guy watching me. "You can go now. We don't need any help."

Ryan clears his throat. "Um, Jade, why don't you introduce yourself?"

Every part of me wants to kill Ryan right here and now. This make-a-friend kick he's forcing me into is beyond annoying.

I turn around, the bag still teetering in my arms and extend my hand. "Hi, I'm Jade. Nice to meet you." The bag is blocking my face again.

"I think you're in there somewhere. You sure you don't want some help with that bag?" The guy slowly takes the bag from me, holding onto the torn end. I give up and let him have it.

He's really tall, like 6'3 or 6'4, and has broad shoulders. The bag looks tiny with him carrying it. He holds it with one arm and extends his hand with the other. "Hi, I'm Garret."

It's dark out, but the campus lights provide enough illumination for me to check out this Garret guy. He's not bad. Okay, he's hot. Like extremely hot, which means he's probably a complete ass who uses girls, then tosses them aside. Guys that good looking always get what they want, then move on.

"She's right on the first floor if you want to follow me." Ryan motions the guy to the door. I quickly grab another bag and slam the trunk shut, making sure to give Ryan the evil eye as I walk past him.

"Are you a freshman?" Ryan asks Garret once we're in my room.

"Yeah, I moved in this morning. I actually live right upstairs."

"Do you know anyone here?"

I give Ryan a look to shut up and let the guy leave, but he ignores me.

"I know a ton of people. Half my prep school ended up here. It's almost like we're just continuing high school."

"Isn't that great, Jade? He knows a ton of people. He can introduce you around."

"Yeah. Great. I'm going back to the car." I start to leave, but Garret stops me.

"Where are you from?"

I turn around and look at him. It's hard not to stare. He's that good looking. "Iowa. Des Moines, Iowa."

Garret doesn't say anything.

"It's in the middle," I explain. "East of Nebraska. West of Illinois. South of Minnesota. North of—"

"Yeah, I know where it is," he says. "You're the Kensington Scholarship winner, right?"

How did he know that? Did they include my bio in the orientation packet? Or did the garbage bag suitcases give me away?

"Yeah, that's me. Anyway, I need to unpack so I'll see you around."

"Let me help. I'm not doing anything."

"No, that's not—"

"That'd be great," Ryan says. "Thanks!"

I scowl at him once again. He smiles back.

With the three of us carrying stuff, it only takes a couple more trips to get everything inside.

"Okay, well, thanks for the help," I say to Garret, praying that Ryan will finally let the guy leave.

"Sure. If you need anything else, just come upstairs. My room is about halfway down the hall."

Once he's gone I slam the door shut. "What the hell was that about?" I whisper-scream to Ryan.

"I was helping you make friends. He seemed okay, didn't he?"

"I didn't notice. It's late. I'm super tired. And look at me!" I pull on my tank top. "I've been stuck in these sweaty clothes all day. I stink. And you thought now was a good time to introduce me to people?"

"That guy didn't care. And it's like 100 degrees outside. Everyone is sweating."

"I need to shower and go to bed." I dump one of the garbage bags out on the floor and begin searching for pajamas.

"I'll guess I'll head to the motel. I should call Chloe and check on Dad. I'll come by around 8 and we'll go to breakfast."

"And then you're leaving?" My voice sounds sad and a little desperate. I didn't mean for it to come out that way. The last thing I need is for Ryan to think I can't handle being alone.

"I'm sorry I can't stay, but I have to start heading back. It's a long drive and I need to get home to take care of Dad."

"I know. I was just giving you a hard time. Go call your girlfriend. I'll see you tomorrow."

He leaves and the sick feeling gnaws at my stomach again. A shower will help. Once I'm clean and get some sleep I'm sure I'll feel better.

I dig through a box for my shower supplies, then grab my pajama shorts and a t-shirt and head to the communal bathroom. I thought it was bad having to share a bathroom with Frank and Ryan, but this is way worse. There's no privacy at all. And I'm all about privacy. Luckily nobody's in there.

Halfway through my shower, I hear some girls come into the bathroom. Living on a floor full of girls will take some adjustment. I've never had many female friends and the ones I did have I only saw when I was at school. There was no way I would invite anyone over to my house with my mom there.

"Did you see Garret?" one of the girls says. "He was just on our floor. God, he looks even hotter than when I saw him in Cabo. I told you I saw him there, right?"

"Did you two hook up?" another girl asks.

"No. He said he was dating some girl he met during his internship in DC."

"Are they still going out?" the other girl asks.

"How should I know? I ran into him like 5 minutes ago. Why don't you ask him tonight? I'm sure he'll be at the party."

I wait for them to leave, then hurry back to my room. I grab my comforter and wrap myself in it like a sleeping bag. I'm too tired to make the bed and the comforter reminds me of home.

As soon as I'm situated, I hear a knock on the door. "Jade? Are you in there?"

What the hell? Who could possibly be knocking on my door? I don't know anyone here. I ignore it, but the knocking continues.

"Jade? It's Garret."

What does he want? I've been here less than two hours and already have some crazy guy stalking me? Those girls in the bathroom were looking for him. He should go bother them instead. I get up to answer the door, my hair sopping wet, the comforter still wrapped around me.

I open the door just a little. "Hi, Garret. What do you need?"

He looks surprised. "I didn't know you were sleeping. It's kind of early, isn't it?"

"It's 10. It's not that early. And I'm tired from the drive." I'm staring at him again. I can't stop myself. He has on a white t-shirt and dark jeans, my favorite combo. His skin has a golden tan and his eyes are this really cool shade of aqua blue. He has a strong jawline that's covered in a light layer of stubble. His dark brown hair is short on the sides but longer on top, spiked up a little in front. His body is lean and muscular, like he might be an athlete. And he smells good. Really good.

"I just wanted to invite you to this party I'm going to. I was heading over there and thought you might want to come with me and meet some people. Is your boyfriend still here? Because he can come, too."

I hear the silence around us and realize that it's my turn to speak. "My what?"

"Your boyfriend. That guy I met earlier?"

A short laugh escapes as I think of Ryan as my boyfriend. "Ryan's not my boyfriend. He's more like an older brother. He just drove me here. He's heading back tomorrow."

Garret smiles which draws my attention to his mouth. He has a nice smile. Full lips and straight white teeth. "Then what do you say? You want to go?"

He glances down at my comforter-wrapped body. I follow his gaze and notice that I've let the comforter slip down to my waist exposing the skimpy t-shirt I'm wearing—without a bra, of course. I quickly pull the comforter up to cover myself.

"No, I'm really tired. But thanks for asking."

"Come on. You can't spend your first night on campus in this crappy dorm room."

"Yeah, actually I can." It sounds rude. I can hear Ryan scolding me in my head, telling me to act friendly. "I mean, I'm just really tired from the drive. Maybe some other time."

"How about tomorrow? There's a party just down the street from here."

"Sure. See you then." I don't like parties, but I agree to go just to get rid of him. I'm sure by tomorrow night he'll forget he even asked me.

"Great. Well, goodnight."

I close the door and lock it. I can't figure out why this guy has declared himself the one-person welcome committee for Moorhurst College and why he's zeroed in on me of all people. There's got to be other new students he could harass at this hour.

I lie in bed exhausted but unable to sleep. I hear some girls running down the hall, laughing. I'm used to sleeping in silence. Ryan and Frank never made a sound at night and my mother was usually passed out drunk.

"Kristen, I need to borrow your red stilettos," I hear a girl say. It sounds like she's in the hallway next to my room.

"No, you ruined the last pair. Plus you'll spend the night at Craig's and he's got that stupid dog that chewed up the last pair of shoes I let you borrow."

Why do these girls insist on having this conversation right outside my door? Do they not understand that people are trying to sleep?

The one girl raises her voice. "Don't be such a bitch. Your mom will buy you new ones. Plus, you've got more shoes than you could ever wear."

"Forget it. You're not borrowing them. I have to grab my purse. I'll be right back."

I hear loud footsteps stomping down the hall, stopping abruptly at my door. "Hey, babe. Get that hot ass in the truck. We're leaving."

I assume it's the hot ass' boyfriend. She giggles like a little girl as something smashes into my door. I hope to God they're not pressed up against my door making out, but it kind of sounds like that's exactly what's happening. After a few minutes, I hear them finally leave.

It's quieter now, but I can't sleep knowing that I'm stuck here for the next four years. I'm not sure how I'll survive given that I've barely been at Moorhurst three hours and I already hate it. Just a few weeks ago, the thought of going far away to college sounded like the perfect plan. I'd get away from all the crap of my old life and start fresh. But now I feel lost and alone. I guess this is why so many people drop out of college after the first or second week.

You wanna give up? Then give up! You'll end up just like me! Is that what you want? You wanna end up like me? I hear my mom's voice in my head again. Those were the words she said when I was crying on the first day of kindergarten. She repeated those words every time I cried or showed the slightest sign of weakness. At least I can give her credit for that. Those words stuck with me all these years. They're the words I live by. Because I *don't* want to end up like her. I can't let it happen. I *won't* let it happen.

I will not give up. I will not drop out and go running home. I'm strong. I can do anything. I repeat the phrases over and over again until I finally fall asleep.

Ryan arrives at 8 a.m. sharp. I've been up since 6 when the morning sun started filtering through the useless curtains on my window. I watched the minutes on the clock tick slowly by waiting for Ryan's familiar face to show up. I'm dying to see a familiar face.

"I'm ready. Let's go." I push past him and shut the door, locking it. I just want out of that room and out of that dorm. "Where do you want to go? Did you see any restaurants on your way here?"

He grabs my arm. "What's with the crazy rush? Are you trying to hurry and eat so you can get rid of me?"

His statement couldn't be more untrue. I desperately want him to stay. At least until my first day of class on Wednesday. It's only Saturday. What am I going to do with all this free time before school starts?

"I'm not trying to get rid of you. I'm just starving. Let's go eat."

"But I thought we could walk around campus first. You didn't even get to see it last night."

"I'll see plenty of it later. Let's just go." I pull on him, trying to get out of there as fast as possible.

We find a restaurant a couple miles away. It's loud with screaming kids and clanking dishes. I don't do well with loud noises. I get very anxious and feel like I can't breathe. When my mom was alive, she would yell and throw things or bang pans

27

together to get my attention. When I got older, I'd run out of the house to escape the noise.

"How was your first night at college?" Ryan asks. He's way more excited about the whole college thing than I am.

I hesitate, wishing I could tell him the truth. But I can't. Over the years, I've learned that people really don't like the truth. The truth is ugly and painful. It's uncomfortable. It makes you question things. It creates uncertainty. People don't want that. They want to hear a version of the truth that meets the expectations they've already conjured up in their own head. And Ryan has conjured up the idea of me living this picture-perfect happy life at a prestigious private college.

"It was great," I say, smiling but also cringing as the toddler in the seat behind me lets out a high-pitched scream.

"Did you meet anyone last night or did you go right to bed?"

"I met some girls when I was in the bathroom," I lie. "They were really friendly and they live on my floor."

"See? I knew you'd make friends right away."

"And that Garret guy stopped by again. He thought you and I were dating. I almost couldn't stop laughing."

"Huh. So he's trying to see if you have a boyfriend." Ryan gets his overprotective look. "I want you to be careful around these college guys. Keep practicing those self defense moves I taught you and don't be afraid to use them."

"Okay, Dad." I roll my eyes.

"I'm serious. Remember, bony parts meet soft parts equals pain. Jab an elbow in his eye or a knee in his groin."

"Yeah, enough of that. I'm trying to eat breakfast."

28

"I'm just saying. It works. You may need it someday, especially if you've got pretty boy knocking on your door all the time. What did he want anyway?"

Pretty boy? I guess Garret is kind of a pretty boy. Like a male model for one of those preppy clothing brands.

"He invited me to a party tonight. I told him I'd go, but I'm sure I won't."

"You should go. But go with a group of girls. You shouldn't get in a car alone with a guy you just met."

"He said it's close to campus. We'll probably just walk there."

The toddler behind me screams again making me nearly jump from my seat. The screaming doesn't stop. It's too loud. Way too loud. My feet start nervously tapping the floor under the table.

Ryan doesn't seem to notice the noise. "Still, just go with those girls you met. It's safer." He pours more syrup on his pancakes.

"You worry way too much. You're like a 50-year-old stuck in a 21-year-old's body."

He keeps his eyes down on his plate and I realize I shouldn't have said that. I know Ryan doesn't want to be that way. He wants to be a carefree college student like other guys his age. Instead he's been forced into this caretaker role for his dad. I suppose that would've been my future, too, if my mom hadn't died. I'd be the responsible caretaker of my drunk, pill-addicted mother.

I kick his foot under the table. "Hey, I didn't mean anything by that. I like that you're responsible. I was just kidding."

He sets his fork down and looks at me across the table. I know that look. And I know I won't like whatever he's about to say.

CHAPTER 4

"I have some bad news. I was going to wait until after breakfast but I might as well tell you now. My dad—" Ryan stops for a moment as the bus boy cleans the table next to us, banging dishes together. When he leaves, Ryan continues. "Dad went to the hospital in the middle of the night in an ambulance."

"Why? What happened?" I swallow hard as my feet continue to anxiously tap the floor.

Before he can answer, the toddler behind me goes into total tantrum mode, stomping repeatedly on the seat of the booth and screaming even louder than before. I can't take another second of it. It's so much noise and I need it to be quiet right now.

I whip around and glare at the parents who don't seem to notice the excruciating sounds coming their child. "What the hell? Can't you make that thing be quiet? I mean, seriously? Are you not hearing this?"

They stare at me as if I'm the rudest person on the planet. I turn back around. Ryan's red with embarrassment, trying not to make eye contact with the people behind me. Meanwhile the kid continues to scream.

"Let's just leave. I'll be at the car." I get up and storm out the door, not waiting for him. I'm doing all I can not to break down into a sobbing mess. I can't handle Frank being this sick. I can't handle something bad happening to him. He's my family. He and Ryan are all I have. They're the only people in the world who care that I even exist.

I take some deep breaths and wipe away the liquid that has pooled on the inside corners of my eyes. Ryan meets me by the car and unlocks the doors.

"My freaking allergies are acting up with all these trees everywhere." I reach down and grab a tissue from the box on the floor of the car. "God, can you believe that kid? And what the hell is wrong the parents?"

Ryan doesn't answer. He remains quiet as we drive back to campus. I wish he'd just finish telling me about Frank and get it over with. His silence makes me worry even more.

"Do you want to go sit somewhere?" he asks when we're back on campus.

"Yeah, but let's stay outside."

I feel like I might throw up the pancakes I just ate, so there's no way I could go in my residence hall with its old, musty stench.

I lead Ryan to the open grassy area in the middle of campus. We take a seat on one of the benches under a giant oak tree. It's a beautiful late summer morning. The humid air has been replaced by a light, almost cool breeze, as if fall has decided to make a brief appearance before summer finishes up.

"So how bad is it? Is he going to die?" I blurt it out. It's completely selfish of me to mention Frank's possible death like that. I know it's the last thing Ryan wants to hear or even consider. But I hate bad news and if it's bad news I want to be told quickly. Like a bandage being ripped off, not slowly peeled away.

"No, it's not like that. He got dizzy and fell when he got up to use the bathroom in the night. He wasn't using his wheelchair."

"So why is he in the hospital?"

"It was a bad fall. He bruised his ribs and has a stress fracture in his arm." Ryan takes a deep breath and lets it out. "The doctors said his disease is progressing faster than they expected. Plus he has some other health issues and the MS only complicates those."

"I don't understand. What are you trying to say? That Frank won't be okay?"

"They're running some tests today and tomorrow. They should know more after that. They're keeping him in the hospital until at least tomorrow afternoon."

I get the feeling Ryan's only telling me part of the story. He always worries about his dad, but he seems even more worried than normal. I don't know what to say to him. I'm terrible at comforting people. Probably because nobody ever comforted me.

He leans forward resting his forearms on his knees. "I did some thinking last night and I decided to take this semester off."

"But, Ryan, that'll mess up your plans for med school. You'll have to wait another whole year to start."

"Med school might be on hold indefinitely now. I have to take care of my dad. As you witnessed yesterday, I can't count on those home health care people. And I can't afford it. We have medical bills that—" He stops. "Never mind. It's just that med school is expensive and I need to take care of my dad. I'll finish college later. Maybe I'll go back in the spring. I just need to take this semester off and get a job to help pay bills."

"Have we always been in debt like this? Why didn't you tell me? I would've got a job and helped out."

He sits up and lays his arm along the back of the bench. "You had a job. Going to school, getting good grades, and getting into college."

"I mean a real job. A paying job. Sacking groceries or waitressing. Anything."

"Enough talk about money. Let me worry about that. I want you to have a normal college experience. Have fun. Don't even think about this. I'm sure everything will work out."

"Not if Frank doesn't get better," I mumble.

Ryan gets up. "I really hate leaving you so soon, but I need to get on the road. I have to pick up Dad when he's released tomorrow."

"You'll have to drive all night in order to make it there. That's like 22 hours hours of driving."

He laughs. "I know. I just drove it. Don't worry. I'll be fine. I'll stock the car with caffeine on my way out of town. Do you need anything before I leave?"

"No, I don't need anything. But you'll call me later, right? Let me know how he's doing?"

"Yeah, I will. Set up the voicemail on your room phone so I can leave a message if you're not home."

"I'm sure I'll be home but I'll get it set up."

"I'm really sorry I can't get you a cell phone, but I can barely pay for this one."

"It's okay. I don't need one." My eyes are pooling with liquid again, infuriating me.

Ryan waits for me to get up, then pulls me into a hug. "I'll miss you, Jade."

Dammit! Why did he have to say that? And what the hell's with this hug? We never hug! I feel more tears building. My face hurts and my throat burns as I try to hold them back. Ryan starts to pull away, but I don't let him. I have to get control of myself first. I close my eyes and think of my mom yelling at me, telling me I'm weak and how weak people never go anywhere in life. Thinking of her shuts off the tears completely and I'm finally able to let him go.

He smiles. "You annoy the hell out of me, but I'll still miss you."

I punch him. "Like you're not annoying with your constant safety reminders and junk food bans?"

"You know you love me, even when I nag you about shit." He reaches into his pocket and pulls out his wallet. "Here." He hands me a stack of twenties. "When you need more, just call."

"I'm not taking this!" I shove it back in his hand. "You just told me you had no money. You need that for gas to get home. I don't need money here. Everything's paid for."

He takes my hand and places the money in it, forcing my fingers to close around it. "You should always have cash. What if you need to take a cab or a bus somewhere? Or maybe you'll need it for laundry or to feed your potato chip addiction."

My stupid eyes get watery again as I look down at the wad of cash in my hand.

"Thanks, Ryan." Now my voice is shaky. God, I hate this. I hate people being nice and I hate saying goodbye. A tear escapes my eye and runs down my cheek. I pretend it isn't there, but I know he sees it.

He puts his arm around my shoulder. "Hey, I know it's tough being so far from home, but you'll get into a routine and everything will get better. Call me whenever you want, okay? Even if it's the middle of the night."

We walk slowly back to the car. I want to act like that toddler at the restaurant and scream and cry at the top of my lungs, begging him not to leave me here. But I can't, so instead I say, "Have a safe trip."

"It won't be as fun without my travel companion, but at least I can pick the radio station now." He gets in the car and rolls the window down. "Go to the party tonight. It'll be good for you. Don't hide in your room, okay?"

"Yes. I know. Bye, Ryan."

"Bye, Jade." He backs out and I watch as he drives away.

I'm left feeling empty and alone and completely out of place. My chest is so tight that just the simple act of breathing is difficult. I look around at the open quad, focusing on the lush, green grass, trying to relax.

It's only 10 in the morning. I have the whole day left in this strange place with nothing to do and no one to talk to. And even more days after that. Maybe I shouldn't have gone to school so far from home. I can't handle it. Maybe I *am* weak, just like my mother said.

I go back to my room and dump all of my garbage bags out on the floor. I find some running shorts and a t-shirt and put them on, then head back outside. There has to be a track somewhere on this campus.

I run past the buildings down a small hill and there it is, next to the gym and the tennis courts. I breathe a sigh of relief. I need to run. It's the only thing that will make me feel better. When I run, I almost go into a trance. I listen to the rhythm of my breath and the sound of my shoes hitting the ground and together they form a pattern that's oddly soothing.

I usually don't like to run on a track, but today it's exactly what I need. I like how predictable it is. Straight then curved, then straight, then curved.

As soon as I start running, I feel the calmness I was craving. I get lost in the repetition of my movement around the oval track and I lose all sense of time. After a while the sun is really hot and I realize that it's probably way past noon. I take a break and sit at the side of the track, completely soaked in sweat.

"Have a good run?"

I turn to see Garret walking toward me in navy athletic shorts and a gray t-shirt. It looks like he's been running, too, although he's not nearly as sweaty as me.

"It was all right," I say. "I don't usually run on a track."

"You should've come with me. I ran a couple miles around campus."

I shake my head, sweat dripping off me like a wet dog. "That's not far enough. I usually run 8 or 9 miles."

He sits down next to me. As in *right* next to me. Can he not see how sweaty I am? I'm sure he can smell me from 10 feet away. *I* can't even stand the smell of myself.

"Eight or 9 miles? You must be a serious runner. I'm a swimmer. I only run to improve my cardio for the pool. I do a couple miles at a normal pace and then I do sprints on the track."

So that's why he has that body. He's a swimmer. That explains the broad shoulders and narrow waist V shape he's got going on.

"Go ahead." I point to the empty track. "It's all yours."

"Why don't you do them with me?" he asks in a challenging tone. "Let's race."

I never turn down a challenge. Well, sometimes I do, but it's rare. "I'm a distance runner, not a sprinter. But a distance runner can beat a swimmer any day. This should be easy." I stand up, stretching my legs which are stiffening up after my short break.

"You think you can beat me, huh?" He stretches as well. "So what's with the insults? You don't like swimmers?"

I shrug. "Swimmers are okay. I just don't think they have to work that hard. I mean, the water makes you basically weightless. It's easy to go fast when you don't have to drag your body weight around. You don't get that benefit with running."

His jaw basically drops to the ground. I've just insulted both him and something that's near and dear to his heart. Apparently this has never happened to him before. Pretty boy must be used to only getting compliments.

"Are you shitting me? Did you just say swimmers don't work hard?"

"Yeah, why?" For some reason, I'm really loving insulting this guy.

"Game on, Iowa girl. Get your ass in position."

He sets himself up in lane one of the track. I take my sweet time walking over to lane two, yawning just for added effect.

"Do you need a head start?" I ask him, stretching my arms behind my back.

"Damn, you're annoying." He smiles when he says it. "We do one lap around. Ready? Three, two, one. Go!"

I take off down the lane, my eyes straight ahead pretending he's not there. I quickly round the first end of the track and hit the straightaway. I imagine myself running far away from that place. Running back home and seeing Frank and Ryan again. I round the next end and keep running.

"Stop! We're done!" I hear Garret's voice and slow down, noticing that I'm already halfway through a second time around the track. I finish the loop and meet up with him again. He's bent over, hands on his knees trying to catch his breath.

"Okay, I admit it. You're fast," he says, panting as sweat drips off his face.

"Fast? That was my normal pace."

He glances up at me, trying to figure out if I'm kidding. Then he stands up straight and wipes the sweat off his forehead.

"Remind me never to do that again." He walks over to the edge of the track and gets his water bottle. "You should sign up for cross country or track. You're really fast."

"Nah. I ran cross country in high school. Now I just run when I'm stressed." It's true, but I wish I hadn't said it. It makes me sound weak and I hate sounding weak, especially around a guy.

"What are you stressed about? School?"

"No. I didn't mean that I only run when I'm stressed. I run for all kinds of reasons. Like today I ran because it's nice outside and I'm bored."

"You want some?" He offers me the water bottle. I'm a little hesitant to drink out of it, assuming pretty boy has herpes or some other contagious STD. But I'm dying of thirst, so I take it from him. "If you're bored, let's do something. I'll show you around and we can grab lunch somewhere."

"I can't. I have stuff to do. I need to unpack and make my bed." It sounds really pathetic, but I don't have any other excuse. I gulp the water and hand him the bottle back.

He takes a drink and a drop comes out. "You drank the whole thing! What did you do that for? I'm dying here."

"You didn't say how much I could have. You should really be clearer next time."

He stares at me like he's never come across someone like me before.

"Fine. Give it here." I hold my hand out. "I'll go fill it up for you."

"Forget it. I'm heading back now anyway. I can't do any more sprints after that." He starts to leave the track, then turns back. "Aren't you coming?"

What is *with* this guy? He won't leave me alone. "You go ahead. I'll stay here and stretch."

"We're having lunch. Come on. Let's go."

I find myself following him as he walks up the hill. Why am I following him? It makes absolutely no sense. And I don't like it. I never follow. I lead. But for some reason I'm intrigued by this guy, even if he is a swimmer.

CHAPTER 5

"I never said I was having lunch with you," I say, catching up to him.

"You need to eat, right? And you're bored? So we're having lunch. What do you like? Mexican? Italian? Burgers?"

I grab his arm, making him stop. "Hold on. Why do you keep trying to get me to do stuff? Coming to my room last night. Finding me at the track. Making me go to lunch. Are you stalking me or something?"

"Do you feel like you're being stalked?"

"No, I guess not."

"Then I'm not stalking you." He turns and starts walking again. "I was just trying to be nice. But you're making it very difficult. I thought people from the Midwest were supposed to be friendly. I'm not getting that vibe from you at all." He says it jokingly although I'm sure he agrees with the statement at least somewhat. I definitely haven't been friendly to him.

"The friendly thing is a myth. We just say that to attract tourists." I race to keep up with his fast pace. "Why are you making such an effort to be nice? You don't even know me."

"Because I know it sucks to be in a new place where you don't know anyone. My dad sent me to boarding school in London back in seventh grade and I hated it. I didn't like any of the people there and I hated being so far from home. I started sneaking out at night hoping they'd kick me out of school. It didn't work so I set my room on fire and within a week I was back home."

"So where's home?"

"About a half hour from here." He opens the residence hall door for me. "That's why I figured I'd show you around town. I know everything about this area." He stops at the door to my room. "Don't take too long. I'm starving."

"Want to meet back here in 15?"

He looks confused. "You mean like 15 minutes? You can get ready that fast?"

"Uh, yeah. Why? Didn't you just tell me to hurry up?"

"I've just never met a girl who can get ready in 15 minutes. I was thinking you'd need at least an hour."

"An hour? Who takes an hour to get ready for lunch?"

"I guess not you. Okay, 15 minutes. I don't even know if I can get ready that fast." He takes off through the door to the upstairs.

I shower and quickly dry my hair, then throw on shorts and a white t-shirt. To keep things simple, I only wear black or white shirts. Years ago, I realized that trying to keep up with the latest colors in fashion was both stupid and expensive. So I decided to just go with the classic black and white. I could have gone all black but then I'd get a reputation as some goth chick and I didn't need people talking about me more than they already did. That's why I mix it up with white.

Seventeen minutes later Garret comes racing out from the stairwell. I'm standing outside my door, waiting for him.

"Damn, you weren't kidding," he says. "You really can get ready that fast."

"So what took you so long? Had to style your hair or something?" I can't seem to stop hurling insults at this guy. Maybe because I know I'd never date him. First of all, I've already decided that I'm not getting into a relationship in college. And second, a rich, popular, pretty boy like Garret would never date someone like me.

"I'm going to ignore that," he says, walking down the hall without me. He seems a little mad. Maybe I took it too far. I catch up with him when we're outside.

"Hey, I didn't mean to piss you off. Sorry."

He stops and smiles at me. "So you *can* be nice. You just choose not to be."

I smile back. "Exactly. So you might want to bail on lunch. I used up all my niceness just now and you may not be able to handle whatever I say next."

"I can handle it." He walks up to a black BMW in the parking lot and opens the passenger door for me. "So what do you want to eat?"

"I thought we were eating on campus."

"The dining halls aren't open yet. Didn't you read your housing packet? They don't open until Tuesday."

Shit! What am I supposed to do for food the next few days? I'll have to take a cab or the bus to a grocery store. Good thing Ryan gave me money.

"Are you getting in or are we going to stand here all day?"

"Oh, um, can't we just walk somewhere? I can't get into cars with strangers."

He laughs. "You sound like my little sister. She's six."

I feel my face getting hot. "Yeah, I didn't mean to say it like that. What I meant is that I don't know you that well, so I don't trust you to drive me somewhere."

"Really? Am I that scary?"

I look him up and down. He doesn't look scary. He looks hot. White polo shirt, light-colored shorts, sunglasses, deep tan.

"Do you want references or something? Because I know Jasmine, your RA. She'll tell you that I'm perfectly safe to be around." He stands there waiting for me, the door still open. "Come on. I thought Midwest people were trusting."

"Trusting is just a nicer word for stupid or naive. And I'm neither one of those things." I hesitate, not sure what to do. He seems all right but I've seen plenty of pretty boys tried for murder on the news. And around here, he could easily dump my body in the woods and nobody would ever find it.

"Hey, Garret." Jasmine walks by, waving at him.

He calls over to her. "Jaz, wait. Come here for a minute." She walks over to us. "Tell the new girl I'm normal and not some crazy psychopath."

She looks confused. "What?"

"She's afraid to get in my car because she doesn't know me well enough. She wants references and you're it."

45

"Um, okay." She turns to me. "I've known Garret since middle school. Sometimes he can be an ass, but the majority of the time he's a good guy." She turns and walks away.

"What the hell? I'm not an ass," Garret yells at her.

She yells back, "The ass part's for breaking up with my sister."

He shakes his head. "I went out with her sister one time. I didn't ask her out again and Jasmine's been pissed at me ever since. Anyway, you got your reference so can we go now?"

"I guess. But I know self defense, so if you try anything you're going to be in some serious pain."

"I'm not going to try anything." He waits for me to get in, then shuts my door.

As we're driving away from campus I remember that I don't have any money. "I forgot my cash. Go back and I'll run in and get it quick."

"It's on me. Don't worry about it." He keeps driving.

"No, I don't like people buying me stuff. Then I owe them and I don't like owing people. Turn around."

"You won't owe me anything, Jade. It's just lunch." He turns onto the main road. "I was thinking we could go to a deli and grab some sandwiches to take to the park. There's a lake there and some picnic tables."

"Yeah, sure, so you can take me in the woods and kill me and throw my body in the lake." I can't believe I just said that out loud! The image was in my head, but I wasn't supposed to verbalize it!

"Are you serious? Where do you get this stuff? Do you watch a lot of horror movies or something?"

I realize that I'm the one who sounds like a deranged lunatic. If anyone should be worried about their safety, he should.

"Never mind," I say, trying to act normal. "We can go to the park."

"Are you sure? Because we can go somewhere else if you're that uncomfortable."

"Just accept it before I change my mind."

We get some sandwiches, chips, and drinks from the deli and head to the park. It's full of people, but he finds an open table under a tree. The lake is off in the distance. It has a small beach where kids are playing.

"Still scared?" he asks, making me feel like an idiot.

I ignore the comment. "Thanks for lunch. It might be the last time I eat until the dining halls open on Tuesday."

"Shit, you don't have a car, do you? Well, I can take you to the store so you can get some stuff for your dorm fridge."

"I don't have a fridge." I take a sip of my soda.

"You don't? Are you sure?"

"It's not that big of a room. I think I would know."

"You need a fridge. I'll get you one."

"No, don't do that. Lunch is enough. I told you I don't like owing people."

"You're on scholarship, right? Room and board is paid for? The people who are paying for that can pay for your fridge. It's like $80. That's nothing. I'm sure they'd pay for it."

"How do you know? Do you know the people who gave me the scholarship?"

"Sort of. I know who they are. Don't worry about it. I'll take care of it."

"I really don't need one. I just need some bags of chips and a two liter of soda. That'll last me until Tuesday."

"You can't live off that for two and a half days. We'll get you some snack stuff for your room, but you're coming out with me for meals. Do you like Thai food? Because I know this great place we could go for dinner."

"No, really, Garret. I don't eat that much. In fact this lunch will last me until tomorrow."

It's not true at all but the $100 Ryan gave me will be almost gone if I eat out every meal from now until Tuesday. And I refuse to ask Ryan for more money.

A frisbee lands on our table knocking over my soda. Garret goes to grab it but it rolls off the table to the ground. He picks it up, then tosses the frisbee back to the kids who threw it.

"Here. You can have mine." He hands me his soda.

I don't understand why this guy's being so nice to me. And I can't figure out why he wants to waste his Saturday hanging out with someone he just met. If he's from this area, he must have a ton of friends to do stuff with.

We sit there for the next hour, gazing out at the lake and enjoying the weather. He asks me what classes I'm taking, but other than that we don't talk much. That would normally be uncomfortable but for whatever reason, it's not.

"We should go," I say, getting up. "I need to unpack and put stuff away. My room's a total mess."

He tosses our trash and we go back to the car. Instead of driving to campus, he takes us to a grocery store.

"What are you doing?" I ask him. "I told you I didn't bring any money."

"That's okay. I'll pay for it." He turns the car off and releases his seat belt. "Go ahead and load up on chips or soda or whatever you said you wanted. It's on me."

"What the hell? I'm not your charity case! I don't need you to buy me stuff. Let's just get out of here."

"Calm down. I wasn't trying to piss you off. I'm just trying to be a friend."

"You're trying to *buy* my friendship."

Now *he's* getting angry. "Yeah, like I'm really going to buy your friendship by spending a few dollars at the grocery store. Why are you getting so mad about this? It's just money. I don't even care. And I promise you, I'm not expecting anything in return."

He waits for me to make a decision. I really do want to get some food for my room and I don't want to pay for a cab to take me there later. "Okay, fine. You can pay, but I'm paying you back as soon as we get to campus. This is just a loan."

He agrees and we go inside. I buy the store brand potato chips and soda and they're still more than the name brand versions back home. I grab a bag of oranges that's on sale in an attempt to be somewhat healthy.

We don't talk on the way back to campus. I think he's still mad at me for accusing him of trying to buy my friendship. But I don't care. He shouldn't be paying for my stuff. It's not right. And he's lying when he says I wouldn't owe him. People don't give stuff away for free. They always want something in return.

As we're driving back, I check out Garret's expensive car. It still has the new car smell. The beige leather seats are buttery soft and the air conditioning is icy cold. I've never been in a car that nice.

Back at the residence hall, Garret stands outside the door to my room. "Are you going to dinner with me or not?" He really does sound mad. I thought he'd be over it by now.

"Let me get your money. Wait here." I go in my room and grab a twenty from the desk. I meet him back at the door and hand him the bill. I need the change back, but I'm too embarrassed to ask.

Luckily he starts fishing through his wallet and hands me the exact amount he owes me. "I'll see you later, Jade." He walks away.

"Is the place expensive?" I ask, standing in the hall still holding the money he gave me.

He's in the doorway to the stairwell. "What?"

"That Thai restaurant you mentioned. Is it expensive?"

"I think it's like 10 bucks a meal."

"Okay. I can go. Does 7 work?"

He hesitates, like he's trying to figure out what just happened. "Sure, 7 works. See ya then."

I hope he doesn't think I was asking him out. I'm just being social like Ryan told me to be. And I *do* need to eat dinner. Plus I'm starting to think Garret's not that bad. In fact I might even say that I enjoyed his company in the brief time we spent together.

For the remainder of the afternoon, I put my clothes away and set out the few possessions I brought from home. Around

4, someone knocks on my door. It's a guy in a maintenance uniform holding a mini refrigerator.

"Where do you want it?" he asks in a gruff tone.

I lead him to an open space along the wall near an outlet. Part of me is irritated that Garret took it upon himself to get me a fridge when I told him I didn't need one, but it will be nice to have cold soda.

When the maintenance guy leaves, two girls walk through my still-open door.

"Hi. I'm Sierra and this is Ava. We saw your door open and thought we'd stop by. We live down the hall."

"Hi. I'm Jade."

They both look me up and down, then survey my sparsely decorated room.

"So where are you from?" Sierra asks. She's tall and really tan with long blond hair, wearing a yellow sundress and strappy sandals.

"Iowa."

I can tell by their expression they have no idea where that is. Why do people on the coasts never know what's in the middle? Do they never look at a map?

"Is that near Colorado?" Ava asks. She's a few inches shorter than Sierra with an even darker tan and shoulder length brown hair streaked with golden highlights. She's very thin and the tight v-neck shirt she's wearing shows off her very large, abnormally round breasts that have to be fake. There's no way those are natural.

"Um, yeah, it's close to Colorado," I say, not in the mood to give either one of them a geography lesson.

"So I saw you with Garret earlier." Sierra gives me a look like she thinks I'm trying to date the guy.

"Yeah, I met him when I was moving in."

"I saw you leave with him."

I don't like what her tone is implying. "We just had lunch. That's it."

"You better watch out for that one. He's a real heartbreaker."

Ava and Sierra laugh, as if they share some inside joke about Garret.

"Okay, well, nice meeting you. I need to finish unpacking." I pick up a t-shirt and start folding it, hoping they'll leave.

"There's a house party tonight a few blocks from here. You could come with us if you want."

"I think I'm already going there with Garret." I cringe as I say it. Now for sure they'll think I'm trying to date him.

"Garret's taking you?" Sierra glances at Ava. "I guess we'll see you there then."

They walk off and I'm left wondering what they're hiding from me. There's something they're not telling me about Garret. And why did Sierra call him a heartbreaker? Does he use girls? Maybe Jasmine's sister really did get hurt by this guy. I don't know, but it reaffirms that I need to make sure Garret is a friend and only a friend.

CHAPTER 6

At 7:10, Garret's knocking on my door. As I open it, I prepare to comment on his lateness, but I forget all about it when I see him.

I don't know how it's possible but he looks even hotter than he did at lunch. He's wearing dark jeans and a light blue polo shirt that makes his eyes an even richer shade of ocean blue. The shirt hugs his muscular shoulders, drawing my attention to his body again, which I can't seem to take my eyes off of. I'm sure under that shirt he's hiding some ripped abs developed through all those hours in the pool.

"What are you all dressed up for?" I ask, trying to sound cool.

"I'm not dressed up. I'm wearing jeans and a shirt."

He's also wearing some really great cologne.

"Yeah, I can see that."

"What's wrong? You don't like it?" He looks at himself as if he's questioning his choice.

I love that I'm making him self-conscious. I don't know why. I have no reason to keep picking on the poor guy.

"Why do you care if I like it?"

"I don't." He stands up straighter and crosses his arms across his chest. "So do I get to critique your outfit now?"

"Sure. Go ahead."

He looks me up and down. "Classic black t-shirt and jeans. It looks good on you."

"Not that I care what you think, but thanks. Can we go now?"

He smiles. I think he's starting to enjoy my insults.

We go to a Thai restaurant in a strip mall near campus. It's nothing fancy, which is good. And the meals are $8-10. Also good. Garret says nothing when I pay for my own meal. He wouldn't dare after the earlier grocery store incident.

After that, we go to the party I've been dreading. I went to a few parties in high school but never liked them. I couldn't be around all that alcohol. It brought back too many memories of my childhood.

The party is in an old, run-down house. We walk into an open room that has a couple beat-up couches and a coffee table sitting off to the side. That's it for furniture. It's almost like the house is only used for parties, not to live in. Or if Moorhurst had a Greek system, this place would make a great frat house.

It's 8:30, so it's not too crowded yet, but the people who are there are already drunk. A makeshift bar is set up in the back of the room; a long folding table topped with stacks of plastic cups and bottles of hard liquor. Seeing it brings back flashbacks of my mom and the vodka bottles that were always on our kitchen counter.

I direct my eyes away from the bar and back to Garret, who now has two guys standing next to him.

"Jade, this is Blake," he says. "Blake, this is Jade."

I shake hands with a tall, lanky guy with wavy blond hair and a dark tan. Wearing board shorts and a t-shirt, he seems to be going for the surfer look which is odd given that we're in Connecticut.

"Blake's a total ass but for some reason we still let him hang out with us," Garret says.

The guy standing next to Blake speaks up. "That's not always true. Sometimes when Blake's really drunk we lock him in a room. He's an angry drunk."

An angry drunk. Just like my mom. I can't be around angry drunks. I'm thinking less of Garret now that I know he's friends with an angry drunk.

"I'm Decker by the way." The guy extends his hand. He's barely taller than me with short brown hair and black-rimmed glasses. He's wearing baggy plaid Bermuda shorts, a bright green button-up shirt with the sleeves rolled up, and leather sandals.

"Decker may look smart with the glasses, but don't let that fool you," Garret says. "He practically flunked out of high school."

Decker turns to me to explain. "They didn't understand me there. Math and science aren't my thing. I'm a writer. An artist of the written word. I was far too creative for that school."

"So what's *your* story?" Blake asks me. I can already tell I don't like this guy. He seems to have a permanent smirk on his face and his woodsy cologne is giving me a headache.

"I just got here. I'm from Iowa."

"Iowa? Is that in the middle somewhere?"

"Yeah. It's in the middle," I say, rolling my eyes.

Blake doesn't notice or care. Instead his attention wanders to the bar. "I'll catch you guys later. It's time to get wasted."

"I think I'll grab a beer," Decker says, eyeing the keg in the corner.

"You want something?" Garret asks me.

"No, I don't drink."

He gets this confused look on his face. "Really? Like not at all?"

"Why are you so surprised? We're underage. It's illegal."

"I know, but everyone does it."

"Obviously that's not true because I don't."

"Okay, well, they probably have some soda. You want that?"

"Sure. Any kind but diet."

I wait as he goes to a cooler near the keg and gets a can of soda. He fills a plastic cup with beer for himself.

"Do you drink a lot?" I ask when he returns.

"Hmm. Do I drink a lot?" He takes a swig of beer. "Define a lot."

"If I have to define it, then you definitely drink a lot." The smell of his beer is making me anxious and a little sick to my stomach.

"Okay, I admit it. I drink a lot. But I try to limit it to the weekends. And maybe two or three weekdays."

"Then our friendship ends here. I don't hang out with people who drink. I need to go." I start heading to the door and hear Garret right behind me.

"Wait. You're seriously leaving? We just got here."

"Yeah, and I don't want to be around you when you're drinking. Or around any of these people."

"That's what a party is, Jade. A bunch of people hanging around drinking."

"I know. That's why I never go to parties." I go out the front door to the outside with Garret following behind.

"Hold on. I'll drive you back if you really want to leave."

"You've been drinking, Garret. You really think I want you driving me home?"

"I had like two sips of beer."

"I can get back on my own." I start walking down the sidewalk.

"Just wait." He grabs my wrist, forcing me to stop. "I'll make you a deal. I won't drink the rest of the night, okay? Just stay for a few hours. It's your first Saturday night in college. You don't want to spend it sitting in your room, do you?"

I hear Ryan's voice in my head, nagging me to be social. "So if I stay, you won't drink? Even what's in your hand?"

He eyes the plastic cup. "I can't finish this?"

I stare at him, not answering.

"Okay, fine." He dumps his beer out on the grass.

"And I'm not promising I'll stay for more than an hour."

"Whatever. Let's just go."

When we get back, more people have arrived. Music is blaring from some speakers in the corner. Blake is doing shots by the bar with some blond girl.

"So are you guys close friends?" I ask Garret as I nod over at Blake.

"I wouldn't say that we're close. We don't sit around having meaningful conversations. We just hang out. We were on the swim team together in high school and now we're both on the team at Moorhurst."

"Does he drink like that all the time?"

"Yeah. That's why he got a place off campus. He knew he couldn't get away with drinking every night in the dorms."

"Hey, Garret." A girl in a short white dress with long black hair and a golden brown tan walks up to him. She wraps her arm around Garret's. "I just got back from Italy. I called you several times but you never returned my calls."

"I've been busy." He seems completely disinterested in her. He doesn't even look at her.

"What did you do all summer? Did you go to your place on Martha's Vineyard?"

"No. I had an internship in DC."

"I thought you hated politics."

"My dad made me do it. I was working for one of his senator friends." Garret moves over slightly to get some distance from the girl which only makes her tighten her grip on him and move closer. "Courtney, this is Jade. Jade, this is Courtney."

"Hi." She glances at me, then turns back to Garret. "You need to be at my parent's house next Saturday at 2. Don't be late. And for dinner wear that light gray suit with the blue tie. I'm wearing a blue dress and we need to coordinate."

He yanks his arm away from her. "Yeah, I got it, Courtney."

"God, what was that for?"

He doesn't answer her.

"You're such an ass sometimes, Garret." She storms off toward the bar.

"So you two have a date next week?" I ask him.

"Her parents always have this huge end of summer party. It's next Saturday and I told her I'd go."

"Is she your girlfriend? Or ex-girlfriend?"

"I don't want to talk about her, okay?"

Before I can ask more, Sierra, the girl I met earlier, comes up behind Garret. She puts her arm around him and kisses his cheek, leaving pink lipstick behind. "Haven't seen you since Cabo. You should've called me when you got back. Or are you still dating that boring chick from DC?"

"She's not boring. And no, we're not dating anymore."

"So you're single again?" She leans in closer. "What are you doing later tonight?"

He pushes her away. "Shouldn't you be with Luke right now?"

"Luke cheated on me with Kelsey. You didn't know that? God, I thought the whole town knew."

More people are arriving at the party. Everyone seems to know each other and I feel completely out of place. "Garret, I think I'm gonna leave."

Sierra notices me standing there. "Oh, hi. What's your name again?"

"Jade. You came to my room earlier."

"Yeah. You're from Ohio, right?"

"No, Iowa." I really should carry a map around.

"How did you end up at Moorhurst? It's such a small college and it's so far away from Ohio, or Iowa, or whatever."

"I'm here on scholarship. The Kensington Scholarship."

Sierra's bright pink lips slowly curve upward as she turns to Garret. "Aww, that's so sweet of you."

Garret's jaw tightens. "Shut up, Sierra. Just go."

"I didn't know you were so attentive to the scholarship winner." She looks back at me and switches to a condescending tone. "Has he given you a tour? Shown you his room?"

Garret takes my hand. "You're right, Jade. This party sucks. Let's go."

Sierra continues to talk, raising her voice so she'll be heard above the music. "Where are you going, Garret? You can just take her in one of the rooms here."

Garret pulls on me to leave and we exit out the front door, which now has a small cooler holding it open, probably so the drunk people don't have to work so hard to go in and out. I try to pull my hand away, but he holds on even tighter.

"What was she talking about?"

He keeps walking fast toward the car. I finally yank my hand free. "Garret, she acts like we're going to have sex or something. Like you're *using* me for sex." I stop walking but he continues. "Is that why you're being nice to me? Is this all some game you're playing? Get the naive new girl to sleep with you?"

He whips around and walks back to me. "Seriously, Jade? Why would you listen to a bitch like Sierra? You barely know her and now you believe her over me? Sierra makes up shit all the time. She does it to cause problems. Her parents even made her see a counselor when she was 12 because she made up this story about a teacher flirting with her. She'd never even met the guy. She's a total liar."

I'm not sure if I should believe him. I want to, but I don't trust him. Then again, I don't trust anyone.

"I think I should walk back."

"Jade, no." He takes my hand again, this time gently holding it. "It's dark and it's not safe to walk alone. Plus there's no sidewalk. You could get hit, especially wearing that dark shirt." He leads me over to his car and opens the door. "Please. Just get in the car. It's still early. We can go somewhere else. You want some dessert?"

I take a moment to think about it. I really don't want to go back and sit all alone in my dorm room. And for some crazy reason I do want to spend more time with Garret even though part of me is screaming to stay the hell away from him.

I agree to go and he takes me to a small diner that's in a renovated old train car. There are small, high-backed wooden booths along each side of a narrow aisle and the ceiling and walls are covered in dark wood panels. The floor has black and white checkered tiles and short, red drapes hang on all the windows.

As I'm reviewing the dessert section of the menu, the waitress arrives.

"We'll have the Boxcar Bonanza," Garret says to her. "Two spoons." She takes off without even asking what I want.

I slam the menu shut. "Did you just order for me?"

"No, I just ordered for *us*." He sits back in the booth. "I used to love this place as a kid. They have great burgers."

"Excuse me, but going back to what just happened. I don't care for the way you just ordered without even considering what

61

I wanted. It's rude. Maybe I won't like the Boxcar whatever it was."

"Boxcar Bonanza. And you'll like it. Everyone likes it. It's their special dessert."

"And we have to share it? Maybe I wanted my own dessert."

"It's huge. You have to share it." He sips his water. "So tell me about yourself, Jade. This whole time we've been hanging out you haven't said one word about home."

"There's nothing to say."

"Tell me about your family. That guy, Ryan. What's he like?"

"I don't want to talk about Ryan." Hearing his name reminds me that I haven't heard from Ryan all day. He should've called with an update on Frank. "We have to eat fast. I have to call him as soon as we get back."

"Why? Is something wrong?"

"I don't know. Never mind. Talk about something else."

"Jade, I can tell you're worried about something. Go call him right now."

"I don't have a phone. It's okay. I'll call him later."

"You don't have a cell phone?"

"No. I don't need one."

"I don't think I've ever met someone who doesn't have a cell phone." He pulls out his phone and sets it on the table in front of me. "Here. Use mine."

"It can wait. Really." I slide it back over to him.

Our dessert arrives; a giant orange bowl that contains eight scoops of different-flavored ice cream topped with broken up chocolate chip cookies, chocolate syrup, and whipped cream. It's the largest dessert I've ever seen.

"What do you think?" Garret asks, taking a bite using one of the oversized spoons that came with it.

"I guess it's all right." I taste the cookies. They're incredible. Definitely homemade. "Okay, it's good. Really good."

It takes us a half hour to finish the whole thing. As we eat, Garret tells me more about the area and what there is to do there. When the check arrives, he insists on paying, saying it's his punishment for ordering for me without asking first.

When we're back on campus, he walks me to my room. I get my key out and unlock the door. "Well, thanks for dessert, but I still feel like I owe you."

"You don't owe me. Can't a person be nice without expecting anything in return?"

"People always expect something in return."

I'm not sure why he's waiting there. It's not like I plan to invite him in.

The phone in my room rings. "That's Ryan. I have to go. I'll see you later."

Garret leaves and I hurry inside my room to answer the phone. "Ryan?"

"Hey, Jade. How's college?"

"Who cares about that. How's Frank?"

"I just talked to him and he said he's sore from his injuries, but that he's starting to feel better. Now tell me about your day."

"Where are you calling from?"

"I'm at a restaurant somewhere in Ohio. I needed a break from driving. So what did you do all day?"

"I ran on the track and then I had lunch at the park. Oh, the dining halls don't open until Tuesday. Can you believe that?"

"See? It's a good thing I gave you money. What park did you go to? I don't remember seeing a park near campus."

"It's not near campus. We had to drive there. We got sandwiches from a deli and ate at the park."

"So you already made friends? That's great. Did you go out with those girls you met last night?"

"Um, no. I went with that guy, Garret. He helped us unpack the car, remember?"

"Huh. Yeah, I remember. Pretty boy. So you went with him in his car?" Ryan asks in his overprotective tone.

"Yes, but you don't have to get all worried about it. My RA, Jasmine, knows him and she said he was okay."

"Still, I want you to be careful. You just met the guy. And maybe Jasmine doesn't know him that well. So you had lunch and then what? Did you meet some other girls on your floor?"

"I met a few of them. Not everyone has moved in yet."

"Did you go to that party?"

"Yeah. I ended up going with Garret. We went for dinner and then to the party."

"You spent your whole day with that guy? I don't like this, Jade. He's too aggressive, taking up all your time like that. I don't trust him."

"He's just a friend. That's it. And so far he's the only nice person I've met here."

"Guys that age aren't just friends with a girl. Hell, guys at *any* age aren't just friends with a girl."

"Well, that's all we are. Now tell me what the doctor said about Frank."

We talk for a few more minutes, then Ryan says he has to get back on the road.

I get into bed feeling much better than the night before. Frank's improving and Ryan isn't so stressed out. And my first full day at Moorhurst turned out to be not so bad. I might have even liked it a little.

Maybe I *can* survive four years here.

CHAPTER 7

The next morning, I sleep until 10, then go to the bathroom to shower and dress. As I'm walking back to my room, I notice a girl moving in. She has a natural, outdoorsy look with long blond hair pulled into a ponytail and a toned, athletic body. She has no makeup on but she doesn't need it. She has perfect skin.

"Hi, I'm Harper," she says, stopping me in the hall.

I set my basket of shower supplies down and shake her hand. "I'm Jade. I live at the end of the hall."

"You're the first person I've seen here other than the RA. People must still be asleep or something. So where are you from?"

"Iowa. And you?"

"California. Malibu."

"And you wanted to come *here* to school? Seems like California would be a lot better than Connecticut. At least weather-wise."

"I'm here on a tennis scholarship."

"I'm here on scholarship, too. Otherwise I'd never be able to go here."

"Oh, I don't need the money. I just wanted to be on the team. Plus I do like that I'm paying for part of this myself, you know? It's not a full scholarship, but it's something. At least I earned it."

"You must be really good at tennis."

"I'm okay. At least good enough for this school's team. Hey, do you want to grab lunch? I just brought in the last of my boxes and I'm starving."

"Sure, but I need to take my stuff back to my room."

"Just come down whenever you're ready." She smiles and gives me a quick wave as she goes back in her room.

Even though we just met, I like Harper. She seems friendly and easy to talk to—way better than Sierra and Ava.

I drop my shower supplies in my room and grab some money. I'm hoping she likes fast food because that's all I can afford.

When I stop by her room she's putting her clothes away. Her room looks like a wad of bubble gum exploded in it. It's piled high with everything pink; her comforter, sheets, towels, pillows—all pink.

"You really like pink," I comment.

"Yeah, since I was little. It's my favorite color. I have two sisters and we all love pink. Do you have any sisters?"

"Nope. It's just me."

"I have to use the bathroom quick. Watch TV if you want." She tosses the remote at me. She has a huge flat screen TV on her dresser. I turn it on and the picture is almost 3D. I'm used to watching Frank's old TV which doesn't have cable. I always had to adjust the antenna whenever I wanted to watch something.

I start flipping through the channels. It's Sunday so there isn't much to watch but I stop when I see the skyline of Des Moines on one of the news channels. If they're in Des Moines, it must be a show about politics.

My hometown is the center of the political universe this time of year. Next year is an election year and Iowa is the first state to vote on who should be the presidential nominee. They call the actual voting event a caucus. Since it's the first big event in the nominating process, it gets a ton of press in the months leading up to the vote, which is usually in January. Journalists from all over the world descend on Des Moines and other towns in Iowa, following rich old men and the occasional woman as they make speeches and try to convince the public to vote for them.

"It's a beautiful day in downtown Des Moines," the show host says. "Later this afternoon, Fisk Callaway, the current frontrunner, will host a barbecue at a park just south of the capital for 300 of his supporters. The event will feature—"

"You ready to go?" Harper is standing by the door, car keys in her hand.

I turn off the TV and follow her out to her car, a white Lexus SUV.

"Do you think we could get fast food?" I ask. "Like maybe some tacos or a burger?"

"Sure, I don't care, but you'll have to tell me where to go."

"There's a taco place a couple miles from here."

"I've actually been craving tacos, so that's perfect."

When we get to the taco place, which is just a roadside stand, Harper seems to really like it, which surprises me. Most people would think this was place was a dump.

After lunch we go back to her room and I help her unpack. She tells me that her dad is some bigwig director at a movie studio in LA and her mom does charity work. Her two sisters are older than her. One is a model and the other one is an actress who's had a few minor movie roles.

Harper wants to study communications and hopes to be a sportscaster some day. Turns out she really likes sports; not just tennis, but all sports.

"Do you have a boyfriend?" I ask as I unpack her box of hair products. She has enough hair products to open a salon and they're all expensive brands.

"I did, but we broke up last year. He played basketball at UCLA and got drafted by the NBA. As soon as that happened, he dumped me. I don't really like to talk about him. How about you?"

"Nope. I'm single and I'd like to keep it that way. I want to focus on school. I can date later when I've got the rest of my life figured out."

We hang out and talk until 4, when she has to meet up with her tennis team for a welcome dinner.

As I head back to my room, I run into Garret. Literally. As in I'm walking down the hall with my head down and I bump right into him. His muscular chest feels like a brick wall hitting my head.

I feel his hand on my back. "Whoa. You okay there, Jade?"

"Sorry. I was just . . . I don't know what I was. Out of it, I guess."

"What have you been up to all day? I came by your room a few times and you weren't here."

"I met this new girl from California and we hung out all afternoon."

"I was just heading out for a run. You want to join me?"

My eyes do a quick scan of him. Freaking gorgeous even in workout clothes. It's annoying and yet so damn appealing. Add in that perfect smile and those beautiful blue eyes and I find it impossible to turn him down.

"Do you mean like a real run or one of your lame 2 mile runs that swimmers do?"

"I'll ignore that. How far do you want to go?"

"Let's see. If I'm going easy on you I'll say 5 miles."

"Five miles, huh? I told you how much I hate running, right?"

"Five miles isn't that far. Are you afraid you can't make it 5 miles?"

A cocky grin crosses his face. "I can make it 5 miles. Get changed. And I get to pick the route."

"Let me guess. No hills, right?"

"Real funny, Jade. Now get in there and change."

I put on my running shorts and tank, then we head outside and run a loop around the campus. After that he takes off toward a path that leads into the woods.

"Wait." I grab his t-shirt. "I don't think I want to go in there."

"There's a trail the whole way. A lot of people run on this trail." He takes my hand. "Come on, let's go."

I hesitate. The trail goes deep into the woods and nobody seems to be on it. I normally would play it safe and insist we run on the track instead, but there's something about the way Garret looks at me that makes me feel like I can trust him. I don't know what it is. It's almost the same look I get from Ryan when he's being protective of me.

"If you don't want to go on the trail, we can go back to the track," he says, keeping hold of my hand. "Or we can drive into town and run there."

"It's okay. We won't be in there very long. I'll race you." I rip my hand away and take off, running as fast as I can.

"Shit!" I hear him yell. "Jade, wait!"

I keep running, the warm breeze rushing past me. The soft ground feels good under my feet, much better than the hard surface of the track. I hear Garret behind me, racing to catch up. After about 2 miles, I slow down.

"Had enough yet?" I take a seat on a fallen log on the side of the trail.

His face is dripping with sweat. "That's it," he says, trying to catch his breath. "You're going on my turf next."

"What are you talking about?"

"Pool," he says as his breathing returns to normal. "You and me. In the pool. Tomorrow night."

"I'm not a swimmer."

"You don't know how to swim?"

"Of course I know how to swim. I'm just not a swimmer."

"I'm not a runner and I've raced you twice now."

71

"I can't beat you in swimming. I swim for fun. I'm not very fast."

"So you're afraid to try?" He stands in front of me, arms crossed over his chest. "Afraid of a little competition?"

"All right. You're on. Tomorrow night." I agree more because I want to see him in swim trunks than because of the challenge. "Wait. I can't. I don't have a swimsuit."

"They have extra suits in the girls' locker room. Got any other excuses? Like you don't want to get your hair wet or have your mascara run?"

I get up and punch him hard in the arm. "You just earned yourself another mile, jackass." I take off down the trail. When I stop and turn around, I find him running a slow jog.

"You gave up awfully fast," I say joining up with him. "We can go back now. I think you've had enough."

"Thank, God. Give me a minute to stretch." He leans against a tree to stretch his calves then does some quad stretches.

"Done yet?" I ask, pretending to be annoyed.

He smiles and comes up right in front of me, so close we're almost touching. "You know what, Jade?"

"What?" Having him this close to me makes my heart pump even faster than when I was running.

"I like you. I really like you."

I don't respond because I'm not sure what to say. It makes no sense for him to like me. I do nothing but insult the guy.

"That said, I still think you're rude and sarcastic and extremely difficult to please."

"Aww." I tilt my head to the side, smiling. "That's the nicest thing anyone's ever said to me. Just for that, I'll run back with you at your barely-moving pace."

When we get back to the residence hall, he follows me to my room. "Do you have plans tonight?"

"Yeah, I'm booked solid, from now until morning," I say proving his sarcasm comment.

"You want to go out for dinner? Catch a movie?"

"Dinner and a movie? Are you asking me out on a date or something?"

"Call it whatever you want. Do you want to go or not?"

I do a quick calculation in my head. Dinner and a movie will eat up at least $20 of my dwindling cash reserves. "No, I can't."

He looks disappointed.

"But we could get takeout and watch a movie here," I suggest. "There's that room down the hall with a TV."

"I have a 42-inch flat screen in my room. It's way better than that old TV down the hall."

"You want us to be alone in your room together? Yeah, I know where that leads."

He rolls his eyes. "Jade, have I tried anything this whole time we've been together?"

"No, but—" I stop, realizing that being alone with him in his room actually sounds appealing. "Okay. Come back down here in 10 minutes. And we have to eat cheap. Fast food burger and fries. All this eating out is using up my laundry money."

"Would you just let me pay for it? An athlete like yourself should eat something other than greasy burgers and fries."

"Don't start with the money thing again. I pay for my own stuff." I check my watch. "You just wasted a minute. Now you've only got 9 minutes to get back down here."

While he's gone, I shower quick, then throw on jeans and a t-shirt. I'm a master at getting ready fast. Growing up, I never knew when my mom would go into one of her drunken fits. Over the years, I learned to get out of the house whenever it happened, even if it was in the middle of the night. That meant I had to get dressed and out of there before she could find me.

Garret's back in 12 minutes, not 9, so of course I give him a hard time about it. He takes me to a local burger place. It's not fast food but it's cheap. And it has outdoor seating, so we bring our food to a table under a yellow umbrella that shields us from the slowly fading sun. Tonight is a perfect early September evening. Not too hot but not at all cold.

Garret keeps his eyes on me all through dinner and listens to every word I say, even though I'm not saying anything remotely interesting. Or maybe he's just staring at me and not listening at all. The thought makes me self-conscious and I start to worry that I have food on my face or in my teeth. He really shouldn't stare. It's rude. But to be fair, I'm kind of staring at him, too.

After dinner, we go back to his room. It's the first time I've been to the second floor. The hallway stinks like beer and sweat. Luckily Garret's room doesn't have that odor and it's much cleaner than I imagined it would be. He has a ton of electronics, including the big TV he mentioned along with a surround sound system. And there are at least 100 movies sitting in a big cardboard box on the floor.

"Pick whatever you want," he says as I flip through the movies.

"You have quite a setup here. It's like your own movie theater. I don't even have a TV."

"You don't? You need a TV, Jade."

"No, I don't. If I want to watch something I'll just use the one down the hall."

"That one barely works. If you want to watch TV, come up here."

"I'm not going to do that. I hardly ever watch TV anyway. Here. Let's watch this one." I hold up a cartoon, trying to keep a straight face. "It says it's about some dogs that solve crimes."

"How did that get in there? That's my little sister's movie."

"It's okay, Garret. I don't care if you like cartoons."

"That is *not* my movie. She must've stuck it in the box when I wasn't looking."

I laugh. "Yeah, sure she did."

"Give it here." He reaches for it, but I won't let him have it. I quickly stand up, holding it behind my back with one hand while putting my other hand out in front of me trying to keep him away.

He quickly backs me up against the wall, forcing my outstretched hand against his hard chest. I lower it to my side as he leans his hand on the wall near my head. Then he slowly reaches behind me with his other hand to get the movie. Our bodies are now touching and our faces are just inches apart. My heart is beating erratically and I struggle to keep my breathing steady as I feel his body against mine.

"Jade." He gazes down at me with this incredibly sexy smile. "Give me the movie, please." I try not to stare at his lips but they're so close and so inviting.

The movie is still in my hand wedged between my lower back and the wall. I push my hips forward slightly to release it, which positions me even closer to him. As he goes to take the movie, I accidentally drop it and he catches it, right behind my butt. I feel his hand there and I freeze as my face heats up. He slowly takes his hand out from behind me and rests it on the wall by my head. I realize I've been holding my breath and I force myself to breathe again.

I look up and our eyes meet. "For the last time, the movie is my sister's. But if you really want to watch the crime-fighting dog cartoon, we'll watch it. Or," he pauses and that sexy smile reappears, "if you want to do something else, we'll do something else."

I know from his tone what 'something else' is and I really, really want to do 'something else' but I promised myself I wouldn't get involved with a guy at college. Unfortunately, I've never been very good with promises.

CHAPTER 8

"Let's find another movie," I say. "I'm not in the mood for a cartoon."

He moves away slowly as if hoping I'll change my mind about the 'something else,' but I don't.

I search through the cardboard box and pick out an action film. After living with Frank and Ryan, I've seen a ton of action films and have even come to like some of them.

As Garret puts the movie in, I try to figure out where to sit. Other than his bed, the only seating options are his desk chair or his oversized navy blue bean bag chair on the floor. I pick the bean bag chair.

"Care if I sit there, too?" Garret asks standing over me.

"No, not at all." I scoot over.

"Do I smell or something?" he asks.

I notice the large gap I left between us and realize that I'm so far over I'm practically falling off the chair. "Oh. I was just making sure you had enough room."

"I have plenty of room, Jade. You can move over."

I scoot back toward the middle. He smells so damn good. I don't know if I can be this close to him, especially after he pressed me against the wall like that. I still have this intense urge to kiss him, which I shouldn't do because we're just friends. That's it.

About halfway through the movie, Garret's phone rings and he gets up to answer it. "What do you want, Blake?" He turns away from me. "No, I'm not going over there. You're not even making sense. How drunk are you right now?" He listens. "Yeah, well, keep them for yourself. I gotta go."

"Are you supposed to be somewhere?" I ask as he puts his phone away.

"No. Blake's just drunk dialing everyone trying to keep the party going at his apartment." Garret sits down again, closer to me than before. The weight of his body causes the chair to sink in between us, pushing me into the side of him. I'm not sure if I should push away or stay in this position. I stay and try to act normal.

"You know, if you want to go out with Blake, I can leave."

"I don't want to go anywhere. I'm in the middle of a movie. And I have a guest." He puts his arm up behind me, a classic guy move that's usually awkward and makes me laugh. But Garret's completely confident with the move, like his arm is supposed to be there, which I find kind of hot.

His arm maneuver has pushed me even farther into the sinking chair, my hip now wedged against his thigh. I sit there stiffly, completely still.

"Would you like me to move, Jade?"

It seems like a simple question, but the answer says a lot. If I tell him to move, it says I'm not interested. But if I tell him *not* to move, it'll expose the fact that I actually like him. I decide to do what I always do with guys and try to confuse him.

"You might as well stay there." I act annoyed. "If you move again I'll sink even farther into this stupid chair and I may never get up."

"You don't like my chair?"

"It's fine, but I'm finding it hard to get comfortable."

"Well, go ahead and do what you need to do to get comfortable."

I adjust myself next to him, but I can't figure out where to put my head with his arm up there like that. It either has to go on his arm or against his chest—both options that will bring us even closer together. Or I could scoot down really far so that I'm underneath his arm but not touching it which would really look stupid. I try a few variations of those options and finally decide to just rest the back of my head against his chest.

"Are you good now?" he asks, laughing at me.

"Yes. Now stop talking so I can hear the movie."

His arm slides down around me and we watch the rest of the film.

I don't know why I'm trying to pretend I don't like him. We both know this friendship is starting to go somewhere. I'm just not sure where that is.

On Monday morning, which is also Labor Day, I take the campus map that was in my housing packet and get familiar with the buildings. It's not a big campus, but I don't want to end up going to the wrong room on the first day of class.

I'm taking a mix of subjects because I haven't decided on a major. I'm still not sure what I want to do after college. I've always been good at math and science, but I don't know what that means for a career. I've kind of been thinking about going to med school like Ryan but it's too early to decide that yet. I haven't even told anyone I'm considering it.

When I get back to the dorms, I knock on Harper's door but she's not home. I go up to Garret's room and he's not home either. I return to my own room and call Ryan. He answers right away.

"Jade, where were you last night? I tried calling several times."

"I was watching a movie. Sorry. How's Frank?"

"Good. He's back home and seems to be doing better. He's sleeping now but I'll have him call you later."

"So if he gets better can you go back to school?"

"No. I start job hunting tomorrow. I haven't told Dad, yet. He'll kill me when he finds out, but we need the money."

"I'll get a job, too. There has to be something on campus I can do. I'll send you whatever money I make."

"No, Jade. This isn't your problem. Your job is school and that's it. Now tell me what's new with you. Did you say you went to a movie?"

"No, I stayed here and watched a movie."

"With one of the girls on your floor?"

"Yeah." I don't like lying to Ryan but I know he wouldn't like the truth. "I met this new girl from California. She's on the tennis team. We spent the whole day together."

"Good. I'm so glad you're meeting people. Listen, I gotta go. But I'll call you later this week to see how classes are going. And Dad will probably call you tomorrow, okay?"

"Yeah, bye, Ryan."

After we hang up, I grab an old blanket, a book, my potato chips, and some soda and go find a big shade tree to lie under. After a few hours of reading, I drift off to sleep.

"Jade. Wake up." I feel someone nudging me. It's Garret, sitting beside me on the blanket. "How long have you been out here?"

"I don't know. What time is it?"

"Six. We have a swim date in an hour. You should stretch a little before we go."

"Nah, I don't need to stretch. I'm ready." I sit up, checking to make sure my book is still there.

"You should at least eat something. What did you do for lunch?"

I hold up the empty potato chip bag and my almost empty bottle of soda. "Lunch."

"That's it? Let's go get something quick."

"I don't need anything. Besides, they say not to swim right after you eat."

He stands up, holding his hand out. "That's a myth. Come on, my car's right over there."

"No, I'll get something later." I grab his hand, letting him pull me up. "Why do we have to wait until 7? Can't we just do this now and get it over with?"

"I guess we could." He watches as I finish up my soda. "You know, maybe you could act a little more excited. After all, you get to see me practically naked."

I stare at him. "Did you seriously just say that?" I shake my head when he doesn't respond. "Well, someone's full of himself. Now I'll make sure I look the other way. Like I really want to see that."

He gives me a cocky grin. He knows damn well I want to see his nearly naked body. Every girl on campus would like to see that.

I pick up my book and take my garbage over to the trash while Garret shakes the grass off my blanket. We go to my room and I realize that he hasn't been in there since the night he helped me move in.

"You don't have much stuff," he says, surveying the room.

"I don't need much stuff. I think most people have too many things. It just ends up being clutter."

"My parents have a TV you could have. It's just sitting in storage if you want it."

"I don't need one." I go over and wait for him at the door. "Okay, let's get this over with."

He laughs. "You could at least pretend this'll be fun." He goes out in the hall and waits while I lock the door. "Don't you want to bring anything?"

"Like what?"

"Change of clothes, shampoo. I don't know."

"*You're* not bringing anything."

"All my stuff is already over there in my locker."

"We're coming back here after we swim, right? I'll just change clothes when I get back."

The pool is in a building down by the track, next to the fitness center. We go to the locker rooms to change. In the girls' locker room, there's a plastic bin full of black, one-piece suits. I find my size and put one on, then grab some towels and wrap one of them around my waist.

When I get to the pool Garret's already swimming laps, moving effortlessly in the water. He stops when he sees me. As he stands up, I gaze at his chest and abs which are pure muscle, each one defined. His arms are equally chiseled. The boy could be on the cover of a men's fitness magazine. I look farther down into the water and see that he's wearing black swim trunks. They're short and tight but they cover more than those skimpy ones guys wear in the Olympics.

"Get in." His voice echoes in the large open room. "It's cold at first, but you'll be okay once you start moving."

I peel my towel away, feeling self conscious. I haven't worn a swimsuit since gym class junior year.

I sit on the edge of the pool, dangling my feet in the cold water.

Garret swims over to me. "You gotta get in all at once. It's easier that way."

"Maybe this was a bad idea. I don't really like swimming."

"And I don't like running. But I did it."

He reaches up and puts his hands around my waist, picking me up. Before I can protest, he dips me slowly into the pool until the water is just under my collarbone. I grab the edge of the pool, holding myself up.

"How's that?" He lets go of me, but part of me wishes he hadn't. I really liked him holding me like that.

"Still cold." My feet search for the bottom of the pool. I can't find it. It's not that deep, but I'm not very tall. If I let go I know the water will be at least chin deep, maybe deeper.

Garret dips his hands in the pool and runs them over the tops of my shoulders, wetting them. "You just need to get used to it. Now go all the way under."

"I'm not ready yet." Actually I *was* ready, but then I lost focus when his hands touched my skin. His gentle touch caused a tingling sensation to coarse through my entire body, distracting me.

"Afraid to get your hair wet?"

I look at him annoyed, then dunk deep into the water and burst up to the surface, tipping my head back to keep the water out of my eyes.

"That's better," he says. "Do you want to do a few laps before we race?"

"Sure." I get in position, then kick off the wall doing a basic freestyle stroke as Garret watches. I make sure to go super slow so he'll assume I'm a horrible swimmer.

"Okay, I'm ready," I say after I return from my painstakingly slow lap.

"We don't need to race. We can just swim." I can tell he feels so bad about my lack of swim skills that he's now completely given up on the idea of racing me.

"Why wouldn't we race? I went to all the trouble to get here. You're racing me. Now get in position."

"All right, but just out and back one time, okay? Ready. Set. Go." He calls it off then waits a few seconds to give me a head start. I take off, going faster than I've ever swam, letting my true swim skills come out. I used to race people in gym class and win, but they weren't on the swim team. Still, I can hold my own in the water. I reach the end of the pool before Garret, then turn to swim back. I catch a glimpse of his stunned face as he sees me pass him. I feel him start to catch up, but I still beat him.

"Nice play," he says, catching his breath.

"I don't know what you're talking about."

He swims up closer to me. "So now that I know you can really swim, how about we try this again? Only this time I don't give you a head start and we repeat that loop three more times. A runner like you has good endurance, right? So a few extra laps should be no problem."

"Nope. No problem at all." I get in position.

He counts off and we go again. Garret doesn't hold back this time. I give it my all trying to keep up, but in the end I'm a lap behind and he wins.

"That was good, Jade. Really good." Garret stands up in the pool, clearing the water from his face.

"I was way behind. That wasn't good."

"I've been swimming my whole life. I've been trained by Olympic coaches. So for you to be that close behind is really good. You did way better with swimming than I did with running."

"You want to go again?"

He laughs. "Damn you're competitive. You'd stay here all night trying to beat me, wouldn't you?"

"Probably." I hang my fingers on the edge of the pool, bobbing up and down. "Okay, yeah, I would. So you want to go again or what?"

Garret's arm reaches around my waist and my heartbeat returns to the rapid pace it was at when I was swimming.

"I like that about you, Jade. That whole competitive edge thing." He moves closer.

I release my fingers from the side of the pool, forcing him to tighten his grip on me. He wraps his other arm around my lower back and presses me into him. My chest rises and falls between us as my breathing gets faster. I notice that Garret's completely calm, his breathing steady.

"What else do you like about me?" It comes out in a flirtatious tone that surprises even me.

His eyes lock on mine and my heart pounds even faster. "I like that you give me shit. Because nobody gives me shit. Ever." He pauses. "I like that you ignore me, making me work my ass off to chase you down. I like that you don't care what people think, including me." He moves his face to the side of mine and his lips brush my ear, his warm breath sending a chill through me. He speaks so low it's almost a whisper. "I like that you're incredibly hot and don't know it. And that you're completely turning me on in a way I didn't think was possible."

"Anything else?" I ask, now completely breathless.

He comes back to face me. "I like that I have no idea what you're gonna do after I do this."

He leans in and gently kisses me, then waits for permission to continue. I slowly kiss him back, feeling the wet slick of water that still graces his soft, full lips. I secure my arms around his neck and my legs around his waist. He smiles at my response, then tightens his arm around my lower back, pressing us even closer together. His other arm slides up between my shoulder blades under my hair, his hand grasping the back of my neck guiding me to his mouth again. I part my lips and feel his breath as his tongue mingles with mine.

His kiss goes deeper and I get lost in the feel of it. And of him. And of the way we feel together, his chest pressed up against mine, our lower bodies fused together with only the thin fabric of our suits between us. It wakes up parts of me I didn't know could feel this way. Sensations are firing off inside every cell. I tighten my grip on him, wanting to be even closer.

The cool air begins to dry the water droplets on my chest, making me shiver. He notices and lowers me deeper into the water, his eyes not leaving mine. Then he dips his face in the pool and runs his lips lightly along my neck, leaving a trail of cool liquid behind. He dips in the water again and wets my lips with his, then licks the water away and slips his tongue past. I love how he tastes. How he feels. All of it.

My body is begging for him to keep going. To do more. I've never wanted that before. With other guys I'm anxious, afraid of what they'll do next. I don't trust them. My muscles tense up at their touch as I prepare to fight them away if things go too far. But I feel safe with Garret, completely at ease as his strong arms hold me up and the cool water streams around us.

Men are liars, Jade. They tell you what you want to hear. They get what they want and then they leave.

My mother's voice enters my head like a lightning bolt, jarring me out of my blissful state. I try to ignore it, pleading for it to go away. *Let me have this*, I say back to the voice. *Let me have something I can feel. Something that's all mine. Something that's not ruined by you. I'm not you, Mom. I'll never be you.*

I notice my legs have loosened around Garret's waist and I'm falling deeper into the water. His hands move under my thighs and he hoists me up. Warmth floods my core and I arch back as he kisses my chest. I tighten my legs around him and feel his hand slide up behind my neck again, bringing me back to his lips. His other hand slips under my butt, holding me up but also lingering as if questioning whether it has permission to venture under the fabric of my suit.

My mother's voice shouts within my head again. *You'll end up like me, Jade. It only takes one man. One time. And your whole life is over.* I can almost smell the liquor as the words echo in my mind. *I'm not you*, I shout back to the voice. *No matter what happens, I'll never be you!*

Shit! Why is she doing this to me? Why now? Everything in this moment feels so right and so perfect. I don't want it to stop. Why can't I have this? Why does she take all the good things away from me?

Anger shoots through me like a canon. It erupts from within and I lose all control of it. I shove Garret away and kick at him with my legs.

He lets go, a look of complete shock and horror at my bizarre behavior. "Jade? What is it? What did I do?"

I feel guilty when he says it. He thinks he did something wrong. But he didn't do anything wrong. In fact what he did was exactly what I wanted him to do, even though I had no idea that's what I wanted until just a few minutes ago. I had no idea I could feel that connected with someone. That safe with someone.

But she ruined it. She made me feel like it was wrong. Like it will only lead to the path she ended up on. Drunk and alone and dead before the age of 40.

I swim to the edge of the pool. "I have to go." My voice is shaky and I shiver from the cold air. I push up hard with my arms, balancing my stomach on the lip of the pool, then swing one leg up and use it to help get the rest of me out of the water. I'm sure I look like a complete idiot trying to climb out of the pool that way but I'm too far away from the nearest ladder.

"Wait! I don't understand." Garret meets me at the edge of the pool. He lifts himself out with practically no effort at all. "Jade, wait!" He catches my hand as I try to walk away. "I'm sorry. I thought you were telling me it was okay. I guess I misread the whole thing."

I turn my back to him, my hand stuck in his tight grip. Tears are running down my face but there's no way in hell I'm letting him see them. I'm so mad at myself I could scream. But I don't. Instead I stand there, just trying to breathe.

"Jade, you should've said something. I would've stopped. I won't do it again, okay?"

His words only make the tears come harder. I don't want him to *not* do it again. I want him to do what he just did over and over again. I want those feelings, those emotions, the desire—all of it—again. But she won't let me have it.

CHAPTER 9

I rip my hand away from Garret's and run into the girls' locker room.

"Jade, come back!" I hear his voice echoing behind me.

I turn on the shower and sit on the cold tile floor, letting the hot water warm me. I wrap my arms around my bent knees and let my head hang over them. My tears meet up with the running water that's flowing around me. I watch as the water swirls before it hits the big metal holes of the floor drain. It hesitates, like it doesn't want to go down that dark hole. I know exactly how it feels. Every time something good happens in my life, I hesitate, thinking it can't be real. Knowing it won't last. And then it doesn't and I end up right back down that dark hole.

Why do I let her get to me this way? Why does she have this power over me? I'm not her. I was the freaking valedictorian. I got a full ride scholarship to a prestigious private college. I'm not going to get knocked up from a one night stand and spend the rest of my life drugging myself until I end up dead on the bathroom floor.

I remember the day a boy came to my house looking for me. He was in my class and was just bringing me a book I left at school. But my mother assumed he was there for sex. She was so determined to prevent any possibility of an accidental pregnancy that she put me on the pill the second I got my period. I was 13 for crying out loud! I hadn't even kissed a boy!

Even if I did get pregnant, which I would never allow to happen, I would still never end up like her. What kind of person starts drugging herself with hard liquor and prescription pills as soon as she has a baby? And then keeps it up, getting more addicted every year? Only a sick, selfish, horrible human being who lacks any kind of compassion for the tiny, helpless person who never wanted to be born into those conditions.

Steam from the shower engulfs me as I sit there on the floor. My tears have slowed but rage is still seething inside me. I hate her. I hate her so much. But I can't let her words keep controlling me like this. She's taken too much from me already. She can't take the rest of my life away.

I stand up slowly and turn the shower off. I dry off and put my shorts and tank top back on, shivering from the air conditioning. My wet hair makes me even colder, but I'm too tired to dry it.

When I get back outside, I hear a voice behind me.

"Hey." Garret speaks soft and low. I stop and feel his hand gently slip into mine. Every cell in my body wants to run, but for some unexplained reason I turn to him, keeping my head down. He steps up right in front of me, then releases my hand and wraps his arms around me without saying a word.

I close my eyes and take a deep breath, still smelling the chlorine on our skin. My arms remain at my sides as I bury my head in his chest and listen to his heart beat. It's beating fast, probably because he was scared shitless to approach me again. It slows as we stand there in complete silence. I savor how it feels to be this close to someone because I'm not sure I'll let him, or anyone, ever be this close again.

Eventually I pull away from him, but his arms remain around my waist. I keep my head down, too embarrassed to face him. "I'm sorry for how I reacted in there."

"It's okay. I shouldn't have pushed it. I didn't mean for that to happen, Jade. That wasn't my intention when I invited you to swim with me."

"I can't do this. I'm sorry, but I can't."

"Because of what just happened?"

"No. It just won't work."

"You don't like me that way, right?"

Don't like him that way? Is he serious? If he only knew how much I like him that way. My outburst must have really freaked him out for him to think that.

"I just can't be in a relationship right now. I need to focus on school."

He lets go of me, but takes hold of both my hands as they lie at my sides. "Then I'll just be your friend. Everyone needs friends, right?"

I look up at him. "I don't know. I'm not a very good friend. You might want to choose someone else."

He smiles. "Nope. I'm choosing you. Only you can help me polish off one of those Boxcar sundaes. Other girls would take one bite and leave the rest. And only you know that I secretly like cartoons. Don't you dare tell anyone that, by the way."

The comment makes me laugh, which doesn't seem possible after how I felt just minutes ago.

"And someday, even if we're the best of friends, I'm gonna beat your ass on that track."

"You're never gonna beat me. You'll always be at least a lap behind."

"Then I'll just keep chasing you until you let me catch up." He waits for me to look at him. "What do you think? Can we be friends?"

I want so badly to be more than friends with him, but if that's all my broken soul can handle, I'll take it. I don't want this boy out of my life.

"I guess. But I'm not going to treat you any differently. It's not like I'm gonna be nice to you all of a sudden."

"No, of course not."

"We should go. We've got orientation first thing in the morning."

He lets go of one of my hands, but keeps hold of the other as we walk back up the hill.

The campus is much busier now. Almost everyone has moved in. People and cars fill the area outside our residence hall. I jump when someone blasts their car radio as I walk by. Garret watches me, probably rethinking the friend agreement with someone as crazy as me.

"I don't like loud noises," I explain. "Especially when they come out of nowhere."

"You can't really get away from noise on a college campus, Jade."

"I know. Doesn't mean I like it."

He stops before we reach the door to our residence hall. "I almost forgot. You haven't eaten all day. Dry your hair and we'll go out."

"That's okay. It's too late to eat."

"It's not even 8. You need to eat something. Chips and soda aren't enough."

I don't have much of an appetite but my stomach does feel empty. "There's a taco place just down the road from here. Let's go there."

"That shitty stand?"

"Yeah. I ate there the other day. It was good."

"No way. Everyone who eats there gets sick. We call it Taco Hell."

"I didn't get sick. I felt fine."

"I can't take you to Taco Hell. Anywhere else but there." He pauses to think. "How about The Burger Hut? It's fast and cheap."

"Sounds good to me." When we get inside I spot Harper in the hallway coming out of the bathroom. She's in her pink bathrobe walking with her head down.

"Hi, Harper. This is—"

She puts her hand up, briefly glancing up to see it's me. "I'm sorry, Jade. I can't talk now. I'm so sick. I think it's from that food we ate the other day."

"The tacos?" I ask cautiously.

"Oh, God. Please don't say that word." She turns and runs back to the bathroom.

Garret gives me the I-told-you-so-look.

"Fine," I mutter. "I'll never go there again."

"I'm going upstairs to change quick. I'll be right back."

While he's gone, I go in my room and throw on jeans and a long sleeve shirt. As I'm drying my hair, I start to wonder if Garret will even come back to my room. By now, he's gotta think I'm a complete nut job. He was probably just being nice back at the pool so I wouldn't blow up at him again.

Ten minutes pass and he still hasn't come downstairs. How long does he need to change clothes? He knows how fast I am. Another 5 minutes pass. I sit on my bed and wait. I've never waited for a guy. I'm not that girl who gives the guy all the control. So why am I waiting for him? He's never coming back. He's probably upstairs right now telling his entire floor about the crazy girl on the first floor.

"Forget this," I say out loud. As I open my door to leave, Garret's standing there.

"Were you going somewhere?"

"What took you so long?"

He steps aside and Blake appears, in neon green board shorts, a navy blue t-shirt, and flip-flops, his messy blond hair hanging like a mop on his head.

"Hey, Ohio." He pushes past me into my room and plops down on my bed, putting his feet up and placing his hands behind his head like he plans to stay a while.

Garret mouths "sorry" to me, then goes over to Blake and shoves his feet off the bed. "Get up, Blake. And get out of her room."

"I need to rest a minute." He yawns and puts his feet up again.

"I mean it. Get up. Now." Garret stands above him, waiting for him to move.

"I'll get up when I'm ready to get up. And it's not even your room so shut the fuck up. Ohio's not telling me to go."

"My name is Jade. And I'm from Iowa. Not Ohio."

"Same difference," he mumbles.

"Uh, no. They're two different states. They're not even next to each other. Never mind. Just get out of here."

He sits up on his elbows. "You're not very friendly, Ohio. I thought people in the middle were supposed to be all friendly and shit."

"Get off her bed," Garret orders, getting impatient.

"What are you doing here anyway?" I ask Blake. "I thought you lived off campus."

Blake stands up and drapes his arm over Garret. "I'm visiting my buddy here. Ever since you came to town I never see this guy. We were supposed to spend these last few days before class getting wasted and instead he's hanging out with some chick from Ohio."

Blake's been drinking. I didn't notice it at first because of that disgusting cologne he bathes himself in. But now that he's in front of me, I can smell the liquor when he opens his mouth.

"It's Jade," I say forcefully. "And I'm not from Ohio."

"Whatever, bitch."

Garret shoves Blake's arm off his shoulder, then grabs hold of it and twists it back. "What did you just call her?"

Blake yanks his arm away from Garret and rubs his shoulder. "What the fuck did you do that for?"

"You'll never call her that again. Understand?"

A disgusting grin crosses Blake's face. "So you're sleeping with his girl? That's why you're never around?"

I can feel the tension in the room as Garret's temper rises. "I'm seriously gonna hurt you if you don't get the fuck out of here."

"Fine. I'm going." Blake stumbles into the hallway. "I should go anyway. I've got some tequila waiting for me at home."

"Is he driving?" I whisper to Garret. "He can't drive like that."

Garret sighs. "I'll go drop him off and be right back, okay?"

"I'll go with you." I grab my purse and follow him out into the hall.

"We're taking you home, Blake," Garret says.

"I can drive." He yawns. "I'm just tired."

"You had too much to drink. You're not driving." Garret and I walk past him.

"I need my car to get to orientation tomorrow."

"Then Jade will drive it and I'll take you in my car. Give her the keys."

"Shit, no! I'm not letting Ohio drive my car. There's no fucking way. No girl drives my car."

Garret gets up in his face. "Then give *me* your keys and she'll drive *my* car. Now let's go."

"You're really pissing me off." Blake reaches in his pocket and gives Garret the keys. "Ohio better be worth it."

We walk down the hall and outside to the parking lot. Garret tosses me his car keys. I stare at the keys like I'm not sure what to do with them. I've never driven a BMW. I'm almost too scared to drive it. What if I wreck it?

"Just follow me, Jade," Garret says. He's standing next to a red Porsche. Blake is already inside. "His place is just a few minutes from here."

I get in Garret's car and adjust the seat. Then I search for the lights and put on my seatbelt. I can't believe he's letting me drive his BMW. He barely knows me. This car is worth more than the house I grew up in.

The Porsche starts driving off so I hurry up and follow it. We go down the main road then turn off onto a dark narrow side road lined with trees. It's so dark that I need the brighter headlights, but I can't figure out how to turn them on.

We come to a stop at a gated entrance and Garret says something to the guard. When I get to the gate, the guard waves me through. Garret parks in front of a two-story condo. I was imagining a tall building filled with tiny, crappy apartments. But rich boy, Blake, wouldn't live in a place like that.

Garret gets out of the Porsche and slams the door shut, tossing the keys to Blake. Drunk boy can't catch and searches the ground for his keys.

I get out of Garret's car and get back in on the passenger's side.

Blake stands up again, shoving his keys in his pocket. "Wait 'til your dad hears about this," he says to Garret. "You can kiss that trust fund goodbye."

Garret ignores him and joins me in the car. He backs up, then speeds off, stopping abruptly to wait for the gate to open.

"Is something wrong?"

"It's nothing," he snaps.

"You seem really mad. We can just go back to the dorms if you want. We can skip dinner."

"We're not skipping dinner. Blake just pisses me off. I'll be fine in a minute or two."

"If he pisses you off, why do you hang out with him?"

Garret adjusts the rear view mirror which I moved when I was driving. "Just forget about it, okay?"

"What did he mean about your dad?"

"Jade. I asked you to stop talking about it. Just drop it."

I turn away and stare into the darkness. We go to the burger place and Garret insists on eating there instead of taking it back to our rooms, but he doesn't say anything all through dinner. He seems distant, like his mind is somewhere else. I don't ask him about it because I'd rather not know what's causing this. I'm hoping it's just Blake and that he'll get over it soon.

People are right about first impressions. From the minute I met Blake I knew I didn't like him. And this just confirms it. Even Garret doesn't seem to like the guy. I wonder why they're even friends.

CHAPTER 10

On Tuesday morning the dining halls are finally open. As I'm getting ready to head down there for breakfast, the phone rings.

"Jade, it's Frank. How's it going?" His voice is strong which I take as a sign he's getting better.

"Hey, Frank. How are you feeling?"

"I'm good, but I called to ask about you. Are you doing okay out there in Connecticut?"

"Yes. I'm fine. Everything's fine."

"We sure miss you. It's just not the same without you around."

I wish he wouldn't say that. I miss them, too, but I can't keep thinking about it. "I'm sure Ryan's keeping you company."

"Yes." Frank hesitates. "But he and I aren't really speaking right now so—"

"You're fighting? Why?" I ask, although I'm pretty sure of the answer.

"Ryan dropped out of school. Did he tell you that?"

"Yeah, but it's just for a semester."

"He made it sound like he's taking the whole year off. He's ruining his future. I tried to tell him that, but he won't listen. He's stubborn, like me. I was thinking maybe you could talk some sense into him."

"I already tried to talk him out of it. He wouldn't listen to me. I'm sure he'll go back in the spring."

"So classes start tomorrow?" Frank's tone brightens.

"Yeah, I have orientation this morning. I was gonna grab some breakfast quick. The dining halls are finally open."

"Ryan mentioned they've been closed. He said some boy has been taking you out a lot."

"Just a few times."

"Be careful, Jade. I want you to have fun, but just be careful, okay?"

"Yes, Frank. I'll be careful." For crying out loud, the way Frank and Ryan lecture me you'd think I was going to college with a bunch of criminals. They act like every guy I'll ever meet will try to harm me in some way. And that I'm some helpless female who can't defend myself. It's really getting annoying.

"Well, it sounds like you've got a busy morning, so I'll let you go. We'll call you later in the week to see how classes are going."

We hang up and I hurry over to the dining hall. I was expecting a crowd, but the place is almost empty. Apparently I'm the only one who's excited about the arrival of on-campus dining. I grab a tray and get a couple donuts along with a hard-boiled egg for some actual nutrients. Then I fill a glass with soda and sit down at a table by myself.

"Jade." Harper appears, looking much better than the night before. "Can I join you?"

"Of course. How are you feeling?"

"My stomach's still a little queasy, but I thought I should try to eat something."

"I'm sorry about the taco—I mean I'm sorry about making you go to that restaurant."

She laughs. "It's okay. You can say the T word now that I'm feeling better. And it wasn't your fault. I'm gonna get some food. I'll be right back."

Moments later she returns with a plate full of fruit and some dry toast. "So who was the hot guy I saw you with last night?"

"That was Garret. I told you about him."

"Yeah, but you didn't say he looked like that." She takes a bite of her toast. "He's freaking hot, Jade. And he's on the swim team, right? I only got a quick look at him but it seemed like he has a good body."

I peel my hard boiled egg. "He definitely has a good body."

She reaches over the table, stopping my peeling. "Wait. Are you saying you've seen him naked? Already? You just met him. I didn't even know you two were dating."

"Relax. We didn't do anything. And we're not dating. I just went swimming with him so I got a good look at his body."

I go back to peeling my egg.

"And? What about it?" She sits there staring at me, waiting for a description.

"He's hot, okay? All muscle. Six pack abs. The works."

She smiles like she's imagining him naked. "When are you going swimming again? I might have to go with you guys."

Just the idea that she's interested in Garret irritates me. I know it shouldn't but it does.

"So what's the deal with you two?" she asks as she cuts her strawberries in half. "Has he asked you out?"

"We're just friends. I really don't want a boyfriend right now. I need to figure out college first."

"What's there to figure out? You go to class and study. That's it. If you like this guy, you should date him. A guy that hot won't be single for long." She takes a bite of her strawberry. "And if he gets a girlfriend you guys won't be able to hang out anymore."

I hadn't thought about that but she's right. If I don't date Garret someone else will and our friendship will end. The thought depresses me which is concerning because I shouldn't even care. I barely know the guy.

Harper gets up from the table. "We should get over there. It's almost 10."

We put our trays away, then walk over to the Student Services building for orientation. People are already lined up inside to check in and get their orientation packet. Harper and I go to the back of the line and wait, the low roar of idle chatter all around us.

The building is hot and stuffy, like they don't have the air-conditioning running. I'm already sweating.

"Are you signing up for any activities or clubs?" she asks as she takes an elastic from her wrist and puts her hair up.

"I don't have time for that stuff. I need to find a job. Are you joining anything?"

"Probably. It's a good way to meet people. In high school, I was in show choir, drama club, French club, cheerleading, student senate, prom committee."

We inch up in line. "And you still got your homework done?"

"It doesn't take as much time as you'd think. Plus I like being around people. I'm a total people person. I hate being alone."

I gather my hair into a ponytail and hold it away from my neck, trying to get cool. "Do you have another hair elastic? It's so hot in here."

"Sure." She digs one out of her purse and hands it to me. "You have great hair, Jade. I'd kill for thick hair with natural waves like yours."

"Really? Because I'd rather have your straight hair."

As I'm putting my hair up, she turns me around. "Check out the hot blond who just got in line."

The guy she's referring to is Blake, who I don't find even the tiniest bit hot, but at least he cleaned himself up for orientation. His hair isn't a shaggy mess and he's got on light-colored shorts, a navy polo shirt, and preppy canvas loafers instead of his usual board shorts and flip-flops.

"That guy's a total jerk. Don't even think about dating him."

"Why? How do you know him?"

"He's Garret's friend. He lives off campus, but he was hanging out here last night and he was so drunk we had to drive him home."

"But you like Garret, so how bad could his friend be?" She continues to stare back at Blake.

"I don't know why they're friends but I'm telling you, Harper. Just stay away from the guy."

Almost an hour later we're finally at the front of the line where four women are seated behind tables with signs listing different letters of the alphabet. I go to the "S-Z" section for Taylor and Harper goes to the "A-F" section for Douglas.

A woman takes my name, crosses it off a sheet on her clipboard, and hands me a large binder that has the school logo emblazoned on the front.

"This is for your computer." She hands me a bright green piece of paper that has my name and student ID number on it. "Take it to the bookstore any time after 1 today."

The college provides laptop computers to incoming freshman, which is good considering I have no money to buy one.

As I turn to walk away, the woman calls after me. "One more thing. It looks like this is for you." She holds out a red square envelope. "Jade, right? You're the Kensington Scholarship recipient?"

"Um, yeah," I say, taking it from her.

I meet up with Harper. "What's that?" she asks, eyeing the envelope. "I didn't get one of those. Was I supposed to?"

"I don't think so. Let's get out of here. It's too hot and stuffy."

When we get outside we see students gathered in large groups in the open quad. "Did you see that you're in my orientation group? We're supposed to meet over there." Harper points to a group of students standing in front of the science building.

When we get to our meeting spot, her phone rings. She answers it while I open the mysterious envelope. There's a note inside. *Jade, We're looking forward to meeting you at dinner tonight. A car will arrive at 6:30 to bring you to our estate. You can expect to return around 10. Sincerely, Mr. and Mrs. Kensington.*

Crap! I completely forgot about this dinner. Back when I accepted the scholarship, I received an invitation but that was so long ago. It hadn't even crossed my mind since then. What am I supposed to wear? I'm sure jeans and a t-shirt aren't appropriate. I do have one black sleeveless dress and some black shoes with a slight heel. I wore the dress to graduation, so it has to be good enough for dinner.

Harper's still on the phone. Our orientation leader is shaking hands and getting our names. In the open quad ahead of us, I see another large group of students. Garret is in the group, standing off to the side with a couple guys. I decide to walk over and say hi. When I'm almost there, his phone rings and the other guys walk away as he answers it. I know I shouldn't, but I listen in wondering if it's Blake calling. I'm sure he saw me in line. He's probably asking Garret if he knows anything about the cute blond girl I was with. If Harper ends up dating Blake, I'll have to reassess our friendship.

"I told you I'm busy," I hear Garret say. "I don't have time." He listens. "I don't need to—" He turns toward me and I duck behind a tree to hide. "It's one time. Let me out of this and I promise I'll—" He stops again to listen. "Yes. Fine."

I peek from behind the tree to see him sitting on a nearby bench, the phone clutched tightly in his hand. He's bent over with his forearms on his knees staring at the ground.

"Hey." I take a seat next to him on the bench. "How's it going?"

He pops upright and smiles, but it's not his usual smile. It seems forced. "Hi, Jade. Did you get your orientation packet yet?"

I hold up the giant binder, which he had to have noticed. "Yep. Got it right here. So do you wanna have lunch later?"

He has this strange look on his face like he's about to break up with me even though we're not even dating. "I can't. I'm busy."

"Oh. Okay. Well, we could go on a run this afternoon. I'll even go slow." I smile, hoping to wipe the serious look off his face.

He gets up. "I'm sorry. I can't. Maybe some other day. I have to go. My group is leaving."

I look back at my own group which is now walking away.

"Bye, Garret," I say, but he's already gone.

I don't understand any part of what just happened. Yesterday he wanted to be best friends and now he wants nothing to do with me. Was it because of Blake? Did he say something to make Garret reconsider our friendship? Or did Garret already find some other girl to hang out with? After my outburst in the pool, it wouldn't surprise me if he did.

As I join up with my group, I tell myself that I don't care if he found someone else. But I do care because over the past few days I've come to really like Garret. He's one of the few people I actually don't mind being around. I even look forward to seeing him, which is especially strange given that I've never looked forward to seeing anyone, other than Ryan and Frank who don't really count.

The orientation takes all morning. Afterward, Harper and I have lunch, followed by a trip to the bookstore to get our laptops. Then I go running to ease my nerves about the dinner tonight. I have no idea what to expect but I'm not looking forward to it. I've seen photos of Mr. and Mrs. Kensington. They looked uptight and almost scary. They did not look at all friendly.

A black luxury sedan arrives promptly at 6:30 to pick me up. I have on my black dress and more makeup than I normally wear. My hair is down and I even went to the trouble of straightening it.

A half hour later, the driver pulls up to a large iron gate attached to stone pillars. The gate opens to a flawless lawn topped with large shade trees and manicured bushes. The long driveway leads to a mansion that seems to go on forever. I guess that's why the invitation called it an estate. House doesn't do it justice. The mansion is covered in light colored stone and has white trim, black shutters, and a large black front door. Four chimneys line the roof.

Off to the right I notice a smaller house. Small is relative in this description. It's way bigger than Frank's house but compared to the mansion next to it, the building looks like a small cottage. It's probably where the hired help stays.

The driver opens my door and takes me to the front entrance. The door immediately opens and a thin woman with straight blond hair and deep blue eyes appears. She has on a short sleeve black dress that looks much nicer than the black dress I have on. My eyes focus on her diamond necklace and earrings. I've never been that close to that many diamonds.

"Jade, welcome to our home. I'm Mrs. Kensington. Please, come in."

I enter into a large open room with shiny white tile floors and tall white walls. The room is so big it looks like a hotel lobby but I think it's technically called a foyer. On each side of the foyer there appears to be a room but the doors are closed so I can't see what's in them. The area ahead of me seems to branch off into the many different sections of the house.

"It's nice to meet you, Mrs. Kensington. Thank you for inviting me for dinner."

"Certainly. We always enjoy having the scholarship recipients over to the house. Let's go to the sunroom. My husband is still at the office so dinner will be in a half hour or so."

She takes me to a room that has windows along three walls. It's cloudy outside so the sunroom isn't exactly living up to its name but I'm sure on a sunny day it does. I sit on a small white sofa. The cushions are so stiff I feel like I'm sitting on a wooden bench. Mrs. Kensington sits across from me in a high-backed white upholstered chair. She looks like a queen sitting on her throne.

I glance out the back windows and see a massive in-ground pool surrounded by black metal patio furniture with white cushions. I'm sure just one of those chaise lounges costs more than all the furniture in my old house. There's a flower garden behind the pool that is so perfect it could be featured in a magazine.

"Would you like a soda or some water?" Mrs. Kensington asks.

I notice a woman dressed like a maid standing next to me. "Oh, uh, yes. A soda would be great. Any kind is fine."

The maid leaves and I'm left there with nothing to say. I should have made a list of things to talk about. Luckily, Mrs. Kensington starts telling me about the history of the college and what a wonderful school it is, leaving me free to sit there and listen.

Just as she seems ready for me to talk, a man appears in a butler's uniform. "You may sit down for dinner now," he says.

"Excellent. Right on time." Mrs. Kensington gets up. I stand up, too, my drink still in my hand. I'm not sure what to do with it. Do I take it with? Leave it there? I feel like there's a proper protocol I'm supposed to follow. She nods at me to leave the glass on the table by her chair, then watches as I set it down.

We walk down a long hallway to the dining room and I think about what a nightmare it would be to live here. Everything looks so expensive that I wouldn't dare touch anything. And the house is spotless. Eerily spotless. I check behind me as I walk. Heaven forbid if a piece of dirt from my shoe lands on the white tile floors. They'd probably send me right home or take my scholarship away.

"You can sit there, Jade." Mrs. Kensington points to a chair in the middle of the long dining table. "My husband will be arriving shortly."

She stands at the end of the table but doesn't sit down so I remain standing as well.

Mrs. Kensington makes me very nervous. When she speaks her tone never changes. Even when she went on and on about how great the college was, there was no emotion at all. No excitement. Nothing. And her expression never changes. The whole time I've been here she's had this half smile on her face that seems to be hiding something. Anger. Depression. Mid-life crisis. Who knows. But she doesn't look happy, at least not genuinely happy.

She seems to be analyzing everything about me. My hair. My dress. My posture. I'm sure she'll be judging me all through dinner. Knots form in my stomach as I imagine how awful this dinner will be. It's 7:30 and she said I'd be home by 10. So I have to make it through two hours. That's not that long. I can handle two hours. We'll be eating for part of it.

My internal pep talk isn't working. I feel my palms start to sweat when I look down at the array of silverware on the table. I'm not at all familiar with the correct usage of different-sized forks and spoons. I'm sure I'll screw it up.

"Jade. Welcome." Mr. Kensington walks in wearing a dark gray suit and tie. He's handsome for a man who I'm guessing is in his late forties. Thick, dark hair and dark brown eyes. He's a big man. Not fat, but tall with broad shoulders. He's at least 6'5, maybe taller. He towers over me as he comes to shake my hand. "It's nice to finally meet you."

"Thank you. Nice to meet you, too."

He motions me to sit, then takes a seat at the head of the table while his wife sits at the other end. I'd read that Mrs.

Kensington is his third wife. She's younger than him. Probably around 35. I think they have a kid although I don't see any signs of children around this place.

"Should we begin?" The butler is standing next to Mrs. Kensington.

"No, we need a few more minutes, please." Mrs. Kensington shoots an angry look at Mr. Kensington. I guess she *can* show emotion, if necessary.

"Are we waiting for someone?" I ask.

"I don't know. Are we?" she asks Mr. Kensington, a harsh sting to her tone.

I hear fast walking in the hallway.

"Sorry I'm late." I look up to see Garret standing there.

CHAPTER 11

"Son, please sit down," Mr. Kensington says. "We were just about to begin."

Garret sits directly across from me not making eye contact. He's all dressed up in a suit and tie and freshly shaven.

I try to act normal as my mind races to figure this out. Garret is a Kensington? As in the people who are paying for my college? As in the people who know my whole life story? A story I was hoping to hide from Garret and everyone else at Moorhurst?

"Jade, this is my son, Garret," Mr. Kensington says. "He's also a freshman at Moorhurst. Garret, this is Jade."

"Hi, Garret," I say staring right at him.

"Hi." Garret glances at me for a second, then looks down at the table.

His dad clears his throat. "You could be more friendly, Garret. I'm sure you'll be seeing Jade at school. We're counting on you to introduce her to some people. Make her feel welcome."

He's made me feel welcome, all right. Pretending to be my friend. Trying to be more than that. Why was he doing that? Was he spying on me for his parents? Making sure their money wasn't being wasted? Making sure I wasn't an addict like my mom? They wouldn't want to waste their precious money on someone like that, now would they?

"Have you two already met?" Mrs. Kensington asks. "You've been on campus a few days now. I suppose it's possible you ran into each other."

Garret keeps his head down, but his eyes turn up slightly, meeting mine across the table. "No, we haven't met."

His tone is telling me to go along with the story. I'm not sure if I should or if I want to. I have no idea why he insists on hiding the fact that we know each other. You'd think his parents would be happy about it. I guess he's just a pathological liar. He's lying to his parents and he's been lying to me since we met. I can't believe I was starting to trust this guy!

I should've seen this coming. I knew a guy like him would never be interested in someone like me and yet I let myself believe it was possible. Damn, he's good. I really believed he wanted to be friends. I actually thought he was just being nice, taking me out, going running with me. But the whole time he had some ulterior motive.

The more I think about it, the angrier I get. My left leg starts tapping uncontrollably under the table. When I get angry I have to do something physical to get rid of it. And now I'm stuck here, sitting in this uncomfortable chair, unable to move for the next two hours.

Mr. Kensington starts talking to his wife. I'm not even listening and Garret doesn't seem to be either. I feel his foot bump my leg under the table. He holds it there and stares at me, urging me to stop the incessant tapping. My leg stills and I tuck it under my chair.

The servers start bringing in the food. During dinner, Garret's dad asks him questions about his class schedule and Garret answers with a short sentence or two. Then his dad starts asking me about school and growing up in Des Moines and how I like Connecticut. They're all topics I can easily talk about so the dinner isn't nearly as bad as I thought it would be. In fact, the dinner would have been fine if it weren't for the surprise visit from Garret.

At 9:30, we finish dessert and the driver comes into the dining room. "Are you ready for me to take her home now, sir?"

Mr. Kensington stands up from the table. "Yes. We promised her she'd be home by 10."

Everyone else gets up as well. "It was truly a pleasure meeting you, Jade." Mr. Kensington shakes my hand. His wife joins him and does the same. "Let us know if you need anything. Garret can give you our phone number."

Garret stands there, saying nothing.

"Thank you. And thanks for dinner." I go over to where the driver is standing.

"I can take her back," Garret says.

I freeze, hoping his parents will tell him not to bother.

"That's a wonderful idea," his dad says. "That way you can get to know each other. I didn't even think of that. Thank you, Garret, for offering."

"It's no problem. Right this way, Jade." He walks past me, not even looking my direction. I reluctantly follow him out to the car. I get in and slam the door shut, turning my back to him.

Garret speeds off not saying a word. He continues to drive for 15 minutes in total silence, then pulls off the road into the parking lot of a scenic overlook. It isn't scenic at night so nobody's there. I'm not sure what's scenic about it during the day either. There's just a bunch of trees in front of us.

"Jade, I'm sorry about what just happened back there. I'm sorry I didn't tell you. And I'm sorry that—"

"Take me home, Garret. I'm doing all I can not to explode right now and I would really like it if you just took me home."

"Let me explain."

"I don't want to hear whatever excuses you're going to tell me. You lied to me. And don't say that not telling me technically wasn't lying. Because it IS lying. It's lying by omission and it counts as lying." I turn to face him. "I don't understand. Were you spying on me for them? Did they tell you to do that or did you just do it on your own?"

"I wasn't spying on you. I just wanted to get to know you."

"Why? So you could sleep with me? Did you think I'd be easy because I'm an orphan from a crappy home? Jasmine was right. You *are* an ass. I'll just walk the rest of the way."

I get out of the car having no idea where we are. The road is pitch-black but I start walking down it anyway. I'm so angry at him and I don't know what to do with all this negative energy. I

117

could scream, but it wouldn't be enough. So I try to walk it off in my uncomfortable dress shoes.

"Jade, get back here." He races to catch up to me. "You can't walk on the road. It's dangerous."

"My safety is not your concern. Now get the hell away from me."

I keep walking. He stays behind, but I hear his voice. "There are all kinds of wild animals out here. Coyotes, raccoons, fox. They all come out at night."

Shit! I hate wildlife. I'm scared of mice for crying out loud. I'm pretty sure I'd have a heart attack if I ran into a raccoon or a coyote.

I hear some rustling in the dark wooded area next to the road. It's probably nothing, but now Garret's put these images of rabid raccoons in my head and I'm scared to death of every little noise. I turn around and walk quickly back to the car. Garret's waiting inside.

"Let's go," I say, slamming the car door.

He reaches over to put on my seat belt, purposely hesitating before he clicks it in place. "I swear to you, Jade. I wasn't trying to spy on you or sleep with you or whatever other evil plots you've conjured up in your head. I just wanted to get to know you. That's it."

I look into his eyes. He looks so damn sincere that I almost believe him. Maybe because I want to believe him. I want whatever we started to keep going. I don't want it to end. But it has to end because he lied to me.

"Why didn't you tell me?" I grab the seatbelt from him and click it in place.

He sits back in his seat. "I'm embarrassed by my family, okay?"

"You're embarrassed to be part of one of the richest families in America? Yeah, I'm sure it's a real hardship for you."

"Just because people have money doesn't mean they have happiness or that they get along. My dad and I barely speak to each other. And when we do, we fight. And I hate my stepmom. She feels the same way about me."

"Great. So you don't get along with your family. I don't know what that has to do with me."

"It's complicated. Being part of the Kensington family comes with responsibilities. And consequences." He sighs. "And rules. Lots of rules. Rules that don't even make sense."

"I have no idea what you're talking about and I really don't care. Can we go now?"

"No, because I'm trying to explain and you're not listening."

"What are you talking about? You haven't explained anything! Why did you lie to me about who you really are? Why did you act like you didn't know me at dinner? You haven't explained any of that, Garret!"

"I told you. My family is messed up. I didn't want you involved with them."

"I'm already involved with them. They're paying for my school. Why are you so freaked out about me knowing your family?"

He gets quiet for a moment and I wonder if he's trying to come up with even more lies.

"How do you think people like my dad and stepmom get the kind of money to afford that house? And all the other houses they own? We have six houses, Jade. We also have a private plane. And a yacht. And at least 10 very expensive cars. Maybe more. I've lost count."

"I don't know. Your dad owns a big chemical company. The company makes a lot of money."

"It's more than that. You don't get that rich from a single company. At least not from ours." His hands tighten around the steering wheel and he stares straight ahead into the darkness. "They do things besides run the company. And those things result in secrets that have to be kept and then they have to protect those secrets. It's messed up. And sometimes it's dangerous. That's why I wanted to keep you away from all that. As far away as possible. That's why I acted like we didn't know each other tonight."

"You're making no sense. Your parents just told you to get to know me. And as for your true identity, it was just a matter of time before I knew your last name."

"Yes, but I wanted you to get to know me before that happened. I knew you'd think differently of me when you found out I was a Kensington. And I was right. Look how you're acting."

"Don't put this back on me! I'm only acting this way because you lied! If you would've been honest with me I wouldn't have cared about your last name."

He shakes his head. "Yeah, right. You would've said a quick hello and then kept your distance."

"Well, I guess we'll never know because you never gave me the chance. You just assumed what would happen and took it upon yourself to lie to somehow protect me from your scary rich parents. Ooh, I'm so scared of them. Their money might come and attack me in the night. Is that the best excuse you can come up with, Garret? You're just like every other spoiled rich kid. You get caught in your lies and then expect everyone to forgive you. But daddy can't buy your way out of this one."

Garret slowly nods and looks down, then starts the car and drives back on the road. He doesn't say another word. I can't tell if he's mad or offended or what. He almost seems hurt, but I refuse to feel guilty about it. His lame explanation did nothing more than leave me more confused. When we get back to campus, he doesn't bother walking me back to my room. He just goes straight up to the second floor.

It's late but I'm not ready to go to bed. I have to release this anger that's been building inside me all night. I'm angry at Garret but I'm even more angry with myself for letting my guard down and trusting him. For letting myself have feelings for him that I never should have had.

I change clothes and run sprints up and down the long road that leads to and from campus. It's about a half mile each way and I run it back and forth until my legs give out.

After a long shower, I try to sleep but my mind keeps thinking of Garret. I keep remembering how he looked when he tried to explain everything. He was almost panicked, like he was desperate for me to believe him. Maybe he wasn't lying. Maybe his parents do have these deep dark secrets that he doesn't want me involved in. If so, it's just another reason why I need to stay away from him, even though it's the opposite of what I want.

CHAPTER 12

Wednesday morning marks my first official day of college. My first class is Psych 101, which I find ironic given that lately I can't explain the psychology behind my own behavior. Like why I can't stop thinking about a guy who lied to me since the day we met. And why I'm thinking about a guy at all when I told myself I wouldn't get into a relationship until after college.

Hoping to get some type of explanation, I examine the syllabus only to find that the whole semester will be spent learning basic theories of well known psychologists. That's not at all helpful. I need an in-depth psychoanalysis course in order to figure out what's going on in my head.

Next is biology, which was not my favorite subject in high school and I'm already predicting will not be my favorite subject in college. The class itself isn't so bad but I hate the lab part. Biology labs always have that weird smell. To make things even worse, the lab partner I've been assigned to informed me that he has no interest in biology and doesn't care if he gets a bad grade. So I'll be doing all of the work and he'll get an A for doing nothing.

I meet up with Harper for lunch. She's all smiles and full of energy, which I've figured out is just her normal disposition. At first I thought she drank too much caffeine or was taking some type of prescription medication that made her that way. But nope, it's all natural.

"How was class?" She sits across from me eating the biggest salad I've ever seen one person attempt to eat. It has more green stuff in it than I've eaten in my entire life and she plans to eat it at all in a single meal.

"It was okay. No major disasters."

She eyes my tray of food, which consists of a plate of French fries, a sugar cookie, and a glass of chocolate milk. "I don't know how you eat that way and stay so skinny."

"I run a lot. But I probably do need to eat a little better."

"So I ran into that Blake guy this morning on my way to class. You're right. He's a total jerk."

"Did he use one of his disgusting pickup lines to try to get you to sleep with him?"

"No. Just the opposite. I went up to say hi and introduce myself and before I could get a word out he said, and I quote, 'Sorry, babe. I had a blond last week. Brunettes only this week. Try again in a month.'"

"Yeah, that sounds like Blake."

"Why would Garret be friends with a guy like that?"

"They're not close friends. They went to high school together and they're both on the swim team."

"Speaking of guys, I met this really hot guy in sociology and he asked me out for Saturday night. Can you believe that? And it's only the first day!"

It isn't that hard to believe. Harper is gorgeous. "Guys must ask you out all the time."

"Are you kidding? I hardly ever get asked out." She opens a bottle of some type of green juice drink that I'm guessing is supposed to be good for you. "In LA, everyone's super hot. They all have work done. Add in the fake tans and the ultra white teeth and guys out there don't even notice a girl like me."

"That's completely messed up." I dip a wad of fries in my ketchup. "You're one of the prettiest girls I've ever seen."

"Thanks, but you should see my sister. She's way prettier, which is why she's a model. But between you and me, she's had some work done. My dad said I'll never make it in broadcasting unless I fix my nose and get my eyes lifted so they're not so tired looking."

"Are you serious? That's insane."

She shrugs as she tosses her salad with her fork. "That's what I say. My talent should get me the job, not my looks. It's so sexist, you know? Just think about all the ugly men on TV, especially on the sport shows I want to work on someday. Anything's better to look at than the guys they have on there now."

I take a bite of my cookie as I get up to leave. "I have to run to class but we should have dinner tonight unless you have plans."

"I don't have plans. But I might see if some other girls can join us, if that's okay."

"Sure, I don't care." Truthfully I kind of do care. I'm more comfortable talking one on one than in groups. But I suppose I need to meet some more people.

"You should invite Garret, too. I still haven't met the guy. I saw him in the hall that day I was sick but we didn't actually get introduced."

"I don't hang out with Garret anymore."

"Why? What happened?"

"He forgot to mention his last name when we met. It's Kensington. As in the people who are paying for me to go here. It's too weird to hang out with him now."

She chomps on her lettuce. "I don't think it's weird. Why would it be weird?"

"It's not just that. He lied about it. He didn't tell me who he was and I don't like people who lie."

"Everyone lies, Jade. In fact, I just heard that the average person lies seven times a day. Seems like a lot doesn't it? Anyway I wouldn't be mad at him about that. Besides, the Kensington name doesn't have the best reputation after that fire a few years back."

"What fire?"

"There was a fire down in Texas at one of their chemical plants. I only remember because they made a big deal about it on the news. More than 30 people died and the Kensingtons wouldn't pay any damages to the families because they said it wasn't their fault. Garret is probably embarrassed to be associated with them. I'm not surprised he lied about it."

I swig the rest of my chocolate milk. "I really need to go so I'll see you tonight, okay?"

"Okay, but bring Garret to dinner. He's super hot. We could use some man candy at the table."

I laugh. "Man candy? Seriously? Is that how people talk in California?" I leave before she has time to answer.

Art history is my only afternoon class and then I'm free for the rest of the day. Now I get why people want to go to college for five or six years instead of the traditional four. There's so much open time to do whatever you want. But I need to fill that free time with a job.

After art history, I stop by the Student Services building where the job board is located. There's almost nothing on it. Where are all the job postings? My question's answered when a girl walks in front of me holding a designer purse that I know costs $5000. I remember seeing it on a morning talk show last summer. Students with money don't need jobs. Hence, the almost empty job board. I spot a job at the library but then notice the listing was posted last year.

"Looking for work?"

I glance over to find Garret's friend, Decker, standing there in red pants, a white button-up shirt, and a plaid bowtie, staring up at the job board. His clothes, along with his black rimmed glasses, almost make him look like a professor.

"Hey, Decker. I *was* looking for work but there's nothing here."

"Jade, right?" he asks, turning to me.

"Yeah. I'm surprised you remembered my name. Your friend keeps calling me Ohio."

"Ohio? Aren't you from Iowa?"

I knew I liked this guy. He's a thousand times better than Blake. "Yes. But Blake insists on calling me Ohio."

"That's because he knows it bugs you. Just ignore him."

"So you're trying to get a job, too?"

"Internship. I don't need money. I need experience. Something in journalism. Or basically any place that lets me write. I was hoping to find an internship at one of the local newspapers. If I don't find something soon, my dad will make me intern at his law firm. And believe me, anything's better than that."

"Can't you do writing at a law firm?"

"Contracts and letters. Totally boring. There's no way I could do that. Plus my dad's one of those ambulance chaser lawyers. The kind everyone hates."

"There's a billboard down the street for one of those law firms. Is that your dad?"

He rolls his eyes. "Yes. It's so embarrassing. Like he couldn't put his billboard somewhere else? He had to put it a mile from my school?"

"Now that I think about it, you do look like him. I didn't put it together before. It said the firm's in New York City. Is that where you're from?"

"No, we have a house about 30 minutes from here. But my dad's office is in New York so he has an apartment there. He's never home." Decker searches the job board again.

"Well, there's nothing here that pays so I'll see you later, Decker." I start to leave.

"Hey, before you go, I wanted to tell you something."

"Yeah, what is it?"

"I saw Garret in class this morning and he didn't look good."

"Maybe he's sick."

"He wasn't sick. He was upset. Like really upset. He said you two had a fight."

"We had a disagreement over something, but I'm sure he's forgot about it by now. He's probably upset over something else."

"No, I'm pretty sure he was upset because of your fight. He really likes you, Jade. I don't know what he did or said to piss you off, but maybe you could give him another chance."

"Did he put you up to this? I can't believe he's making his friends do his—"

"He didn't put me up to this. In fact, if he knew I was even talking to you about this he'd kill me. I get that you don't know him that well, but I've known him for years and he's a good guy. Yes, he's done his share of partying and drinking, which he said you don't like, but he hasn't done any of that stuff since he met you. And that's huge, Jade."

He waits for me to say something but I keep quiet. I like Decker but this whole conversation is making me very uncomfortable.

"Listen, you don't have to date the guy, but maybe just don't shut him out completely. At least not yet. That's all I'm saying."

"I should get going. I'll see you around."

I race out of there before he can give me more advice about Garret. I don't trust Decker. He could easily be doing Garret's dirty work, although I'm not sure how he knew he'd run into me in the Student Services building. It doesn't matter. I still don't trust him.

At dinner, Harper is disappointed that I show up alone and not with the "man candy" she requested. The girls she invited to eat with us are on her tennis team and live in a different residence hall. I wish they lived on our floor. They're way better than the girls Harper and I have to live with every day. I've now introduced myself to almost every girl on our floor and Harper is the only one who seems interested in being friends.

Later that night I talk to Ryan and Frank. They both seem to be getting along better. I don't know what happened to make them stop fighting and I don't ask. Ryan found a temp job at a hospital lab. It has flexible hours so he's able to take his dad to doctor's appointments. Frank doesn't say much on the call. And when he does talk, he sounds tired. He says he feels okay, but I'm sure if he didn't, he wouldn't tell me.

My Thursday class schedule is easier than Wednesday's because I only have two classes. Thursday morning is calculus, which doesn't sound easy but for me it is. I've always done well in math. I like the order and structure of it. I like that it makes sense and that each problem has a clear answer.

In the afternoon I have English. I arrive on time, but when I get there almost every seat is taken and I'm stuck sitting in the last row. It's not like I wanted the first row, but something in the middle would've been nice.

I reach down to pull my laptop out of my backpack and my pens fall out all over the floor. I tend to pack a lot of pens, just in case.

"I'll get them," a voice says. I look over and see Garret picking up my pens. "Here." He hands them to me, then takes the only seat left, which is right next to mine.

"So you're in this class?" I stuff the pens in the front pouch of my backpack.

"That's why I'm here," he says staring straight ahead.

He's being really cold. If he wants me to forgive him, he could be a little nicer.

"Welcome, everyone, to freshman English. I'm Professor Hawkins." A gray-haired wiry man wearing khaki pants, a plaid dress shirt, and a navy tie stands at the front of the class, chalk stains on his hand from writing his name on the board. "I expect your full attention in this class and that means no texting, no emailing, no note passing, and no talking unless you are asked to speak."

As the professor talks, I can't help but glance over at Garret. Harper's right. He's super hot. Definite man candy as she would say. An image of us back in the pool pops in my head. His wet lips on mine. His nearly naked muscular body holding me close. His hand on my . . .

I feel a foot lightly kicking mine from the side.

"Jade? Jade Taylor?" The professor is calling my name.

I raise my hand. "Yes. Sorry, I'm here." The professor continues to read off names. "Thanks." I whisper to Garret, owner of the foot who woke me from my daydream.

He gives me a brief smile, then focuses on the front of the room again.

At the end of class, the professor hands out notebooks to each of us. "These are your journals. I expect you to write something in them at least three times a week, or daily for you overachievers. You can write anything you want, but it must fill half the page or more. In the past, some students have written about their reaction to a movie, song, or even a simple quote. It's a free flowing writing exercise so write about whatever you want but I still expect proper grammar and punctuation. This is English class after all."

"Are you grading these?" someone up front asks.

"You will get points for completing it and those points will go toward your final grade. Also you will not be turning these in until the last class of the semester. I will not be reading each page but I will flip through to make sure you did the assignment."

He finally passes the notebooks to the last row. "Inside your notebooks, you will find a list of your classmates. You have each been paired with someone. This person is expected to read your journal each week and add a short comment after each post offering suggestions or just general thoughts. And you will do the same in their journal." He returns to the front of the room. "You should begin writing in these this week. That's it for today. I'll see you all next Tuesday."

Inside the notebook is a loose sheet of paper with a list of names on it. I find my name and who is listed next to it? Garret Kensington.

CHAPTER 13

"Guess we're partners," Garret says as he puts his laptop in his bag.

"Did you do this?" I hold the piece of paper up.

"Do what?"

"Did you tell him to make us partners?"

Garret shakes his head. "No, Jade. I would never *force* you to read my stupid English journal." He walks out.

"Hold on." I follow him outside. "So what's the plan? Do you want to exchange notebooks on a certain day or how do you want to do this?"

He stops for a moment. "Whatever you want to do is fine with me."

I catch a whiff of his cologne as the breeze blows. He smells as good as he looks. "Maybe we could meet on Saturday and go over them."

"You want to meet? I thought you just wanted to exchange them."

He seems totally confused by my request. I'm confused by it, too. I was so mad at him the other day, but I'm having a really hard time *staying* mad at him. I don't know if it's because it's been a couple days since our fight, or if it's because of what Decker said, or if his hotness is affecting my judgment. Whatever the reason is, I want to talk to him again, even if it's just about our English assignment.

"I think we should meet," I say. "That way if we have questions, we don't have to email or call each other. Could you meet on Saturday?"

"Yeah, but it has to be in the morning. I'll be gone in the afternoon and won't be back until Sunday."

"Then let's say 9. Stop by my room and we'll go outside."

"That's kind of early for a Saturday, but okay." He walks off.

If I wasn't so stubborn I would stop him from leaving and demand that we talk right now. I want things to go back to the way they were before all this happened. I want to hear how his classes are going and I want to tell him about mine. I want us to go on another run and have dinner together. I want us to be friends, just like he wanted. And yet I refuse to let it happen. I'm supposed to be punishing him for lying, but I feel like I'm punishing myself.

On Friday, as I'm walking back from my last class of the day, I realize how much better I feel than last Friday when I arrived. I'm way more comfortable with the campus, I've mapped out a few different running routes, and I'm quickly learning what foods to avoid in the dining hall.

I still haven't made any friends other than Harper. I'm starting to think it's too late now. People are already pairing off and forming cliques, just like in high school.

I haven't seen Garret since English class. He's just one floor above me and yet we never run into each other. I sent his parents a note thanking them for dinner. I wouldn't have even thought to do that, but Harper said it was a must, especially for people like the Kensingtons who appreciate good social etiquette.

After dinner I stay in my room and do homework feeling like a total loser. My entire floor is quiet and empty. I always thought people partied in their dorm rooms, but they don't here at Moorhurst. Everyone, including Harper, goes off campus to a house party somewhere.

Part of me wishes I could just go out like everyone else. But I'm too afraid of what could happen. I'm afraid I'll take a drink and that one drink will turn into another and another after that. And before I know it, I'll be my mother.

I hate that my mom still controls me like this. I just want to be normal. Go to parties. Date. And not worry so much about school. But I can't. I want to be different from her. I *have* to be. And that means staying away from the temptations that made her the person I hated for all those years. The person I still hate even though she's dead.

Saturday morning I wake up feeling so nervous about meeting with Garret that I can't even eat breakfast. I have no idea what to say to him. My anger toward him is long gone, but he still lied to me and I never got a good answer why.

I take a quick shower and put on a tank top and shorts. The summer heat has returned and it feels like the middle of July.

Garret knocks on my door right at 9. He's wearing khaki shorts and a white t-shirt that highlights his tan skin and muscular arms. He hasn't shaved yet and although I normally like a clean shave on a guy, I find the light layer of stubble on his face extremely sexy. I'm staring again. I don't mean to, but damn he's hot. It's very distracting.

"Do you still want to go outside?" he asks. "I don't mind the heat, but if you do we can stay here."

He waits for me to answer. The silence wakes me from my distracted state. "Um, no. Let's go outside. I have an old blanket to sit on."

We find a spot on the edge of campus near the track. I didn't want to be in the open quad by our dorms where people would keep walking past. I'm not sure where this conversation will go and I don't want to be interrupted.

I set the blanket up under a big shade tree. There's a soft breeze that makes the heat more tolerable.

"So we just exchange books and make our notes, right?" he asks.

"Yeah. I only made one entry so far."

"Me too." He hands me his notebook and I give him mine.

As soon as I see my notebook in his hands, I tense up and my heart starts beating faster. I quickly regret what I've done and I consider grabbing the notebook back, but he's already started reading it.

I look down at Garret's notebook and open it to the first page. He has nice handwriting. Way better than mine. I start reading.

Sept. 12. I met a girl last week who is the most interesting person I've ever met. I helped her move in and ever since then, I haven't been able to stop thinking about her. The next day I saw her out on the track. She started insulting me right away and for some reason I didn't mind it. I asked the girl to lunch that day, and after lunch I asked her to dinner because I didn't get enough of her at lunch. Later we went to a party. I've never left a party sober, but that night I did. Because of her. It felt good leaving with my mind still intact, still able to walk straight. I wasn't ready to let her go, so I took her for ice cream. I spent the whole day with this girl and then at night, I lay awake thinking about her, wanting to see her again.

I should have told her who I was on that first day we met. But I didn't. I should have told her the next day, or the day after that. But I didn't because I didn't want anything to change between us. Every moment with her was so real and so perfect. I didn't want it to end. But now it has. And I miss her. All I can say is that I'm sorry. But I know sometimes that's just not enough.

As I'm reading it, I feel wetness in the corners of my eyes. I turn my back to Garret so he won't notice the affect his English assignment is having on me. I read it again, mainly because I don't believe it. Nobody has ever expressed feelings for me like that. And I'm not sure I trust that they're real.

Garret is quiet and I wonder what he's thinking after reading my notebook. This is what I wrote.

I don't always understand people. Well, truthfully, I don't understand them because I don't trust them. I always assume people are lying because nobody wants to hear the truth. They say they do, but they really don't. But sometimes people need to hear the truth, even if they won't like it.

136

I met someone the other day. And after knowing him just a short while, I felt like I understood him. And that he understood me. I can't explain what this feels like exactly. There aren't really words to describe it. But I liked the feeling because for the first time in my life I felt like I made a real connection with someone. I started to trust this person, which doesn't make sense because I've only trusted two people in my entire life. But then I found out that he lied to me and I suddenly felt like I couldn't trust him or anyone ever again. But I want to be able to trust people, especially him. So I wish this person would tell me why he lied so I could trust him again. And so I could understand him again. And so that maybe we could be friends.

I turn back around to face him. Garret speaks first, holding up my notebook. "It's good. A few run-on sentences but other than that, I like it."

My heart rate returns to normal now that's he read it. I've completely exposed myself on paper and I can't take it back now.

"I like yours, too. It sounds like you really like this girl, whoever she is. But she sounds like too much work. You should just forget her and move on."

"I don't want to forget her. Or move on." He sets my notebook down. "I want to get to know her."

I put his notebook aside and look down at the blanket. "Maybe she doesn't want to get to know you." I don't know why I just said that to him. It's not at all true.

"Well, maybe you could talk to her and get her to change her mind. Convince her to hang out with me again. Maybe go on a run or watch a movie."

"I might be able to convince her to do that." My finger traces the circular pattern in the blanket which helps keep my emotions in check. "But I think she needs to hear what's really going on with you first. And why you lied."

Garret puts his hand around my wrist just as I start tracing the circles on a new section of the blanket. I look up at him and he releases my wrist and slips his hand into mine.

"Jade, I'm sorry. And I'm telling you again that I didn't have some hidden agenda. I just didn't want you judging me before you knew me. I assumed if you heard my name, you'd think I was just another spoiled trust fund kid and want nothing to do with me."

My hand tenses up as I consider yanking it away from him. He tightens his grip and I relax it again. I don't want him to let go of me and yet I fight him. And somehow he knows that and holds on. How does he understand me like that?

"You know about my mom, Garret. And I didn't want anyone here to know. I was counting on getting a fresh start and then I find out the person I want to hide my past from the most is the one who knows everything about it."

"But that doesn't make sense. You're mad at me because I didn't tell you about my family, but you didn't want *me* to know anything about *your family*."

"Because my family consisted of my mom. And she was crazy and then she killed herself. So, yeah, I really don't want people knowing about my past. But you have no excuse. There's no reason for you to hide the fact that you're a Kensington."

"Are you kidding? There's a million reasons why I'd want to hide that from someone." He lightly rubs the top of my hand with his thumb. That tiny movement makes my heart beat faster again. "I really don't know that much about your past, Jade. My dad told me that your mom had problems with alcohol and drugs. That's it."

"There's not much else to tell."

"What about your father? Do you ever see him?"

"I'm the product of a one night stand. He left that night and never came back." As I say it I realize that's the first time I've ever said that to anyone. I used to tell people at school that my parents were divorced and my dad lived overseas. "So what other stuff do I need to know about your family? Do they really have all these dark secrets?"

He lets go of my hand and sits back. "Yes. But I can't tell you what those are. I'm sure I don't even know half of them."

"Well, what did you mean when you said they had rules? What are the rules?"

"In families like mine, it's all about appearances and connections and being seen with the right people." He lies down on the blanket and stares up into the tree as the filtered light shines through. "I can't believe I'm telling you this, but—I've never had a real friend."

"What do you mean?" I lie down next to him, propped up on my elbow.

My dad's picked my friends for as long as I can remember. Like Blake. I hate the guy but his dad is Connecticut's attorney general and has a lot of connections that could be useful to my family or the company."

"So your dad's forcing you to be friends with that jerk?"

139

"That's how it works. Sometimes you get lucky and actually like the person. I like Decker, even though my dad made us be friends back in ninth grade."

"You're saying that your dad has picked every one of your friends?"

"Yes, and that's why I didn't want my family to know that we're friends. Well, I guess that's still up in the air until you decide. But I didn't want them interfering if we did become friends. Or more than friends."

"What are you saying? You can't pick your dates either?"

He rolls on his side so we're face to face. "No. That's an even a bigger deal than the friends thing. I go to a lot of big events and I end up in photos in the society pages of newspapers or online gossip sites. That means I have to show up with the right girl. And that girl is picked for me. I never get to choose. Like today I have to take Courtney to this party and pretend she's my girlfriend. I don't even like Courtney as a friend, but we have to put on this show for the cameras."

"So you've never been on a real date with someone you actually chose? You've never had a real girlfriend?"

"I've been on real dates and I've had real girlfriends. The fake girlfriend thing is mainly for when I'm at a public event, like a charity function or a big social function, like this party I'm going to later. Basically any place that photographers might show up. But still, when I'm dating someone for real I try to hide it, especially from my dad."

"Is this just something your family does or do other people do this?"

"Everyone at my prep school had a fake girlfriend or fake boyfriend. It's just something wealthy families do. It's stupid, I know. But it's all about image—who you're seen with and how it will benefit the family. So we all go along with it and try to secretly date other people on the side."

"Did your dad ever find out you were dating someone he didn't pick?"

"Yes, but in high school I dated girls at my school so my dad didn't say anything because they all came from rich and powerful families. If I screwed up and someone got a photo of me with one of those girls, it wouldn't be the end of the world. But he'd never let me take one of them to a public event. I always had to show up with the girl who was picked for me. I still do, which is why I'm stuck with Courtney today."

"Are you making this up?"

"Why would I make this up? I shouldn't even be telling you this. This is one of those secrets that's never supposed to get out. Don't tell anyone this, by the way. I'm serious. I'm only telling you this because I feel like I owe you the truth."

The wind blows and strands of my hair fall onto my face. He reaches over and brushes them behind my ear. "I want you to trust me, Jade. I know that won't happen overnight but if you give me a chance, I want to try to earn it back."

"So what are you proposing?"

"Let's just hang out like we did before and get to know each other. Hopefully you'll see that I'm not just a name. And that I really didn't mean to hurt you by not telling you the truth."

I'm quiet as I pretend to consider his offer. But I don't need to consider it because it's exactly what I want. I want to move past this and spend time with him again.

"If I agree to this, are you gonna make me watch one of those cartoon movies you love so much?" I smile at him.

He smiles back. "I told you to never bring that up again." He playfully wrestles me down on my back.

I fight him, laughing. "I don't care if you like talking dog movies. I am kinda curious to see what's so great about it. And I'd love to know how dogs fight crimes. Do they sniff for clues or—"

Garret's laughing, too. "Okay, you're done. No more talking about that movie." He has my arms pinned down and his face is hovering above mine. He catches my eye and I recognize the look he's giving me. It's the same one from the pool. He's asking me for permission and I really, really want to give him that permission but I can't. It's too soon.

I turn my head to the side. He gets my answer and releases his hold on me, then rolls onto his back.

We lie there next to each other, the warm sun filtering through the tree above us. I close my eyes and listen as the wind causes the leaves to make a soft rustling sound.

"So I talked to that girl you like," I say, keeping my eyes closed. "She said you could start hanging out with her again. Maybe even right now if you're not too busy. But if you need to head back to your room, that's okay, too."

"Tell her yes. I can hang out now. Or any time she wants." I glance over at Garret. His eyes are closed but a smile has grown across his face. "Maybe you could ask her if she wants to have lunch before I have to go."

My eyes close again. "She says lunch would be good."

He doesn't say anything else. But his hand slides across the blanket and he threads it with mine.

I guess I was wrong.

I guess it *isn't* too late to make a friend.

CHAPTER 14

I could stay there the rest of the day. There's a peacefulness to just being next to Garret, holding his hand, and not saying a word as the last moments of summer fade away.

After a couple hours, some of which I might have fallen asleep, I feel the blanket move as Garret gets up. "Ready to go to lunch?"

"Not really." I look up and see him sitting next to me. "I'm kind of enjoying this too much."

"Me too. But I have to be at my house at 1, so if we want to have lunch we should get going."

"Do you really have to go?"

He smiles as he lies back down on his side. "Why? Are you wanting more time with me?" He runs his hand down my arm, then loosely holds my hand. Just the touch of his hand on my skin stirs something in me. A desire. A need to be close to him. To be more than friends. I wonder if he feels it, too.

"Maybe," I say, freeing my hand and flipping on my side. "Or maybe I'm just curious why you're leaving so early."

His smile fades as he takes my hand back and rests it on the blanket between us. "This stupid party Courtney's family does every year is practically an all day event. They invite people over for food and drinks by the pool in the afternoon, then everyone comes back later that night for a formal dinner and dance."

"So do you drink at this event?"

"It's the only way I can get through it."

"And the adults don't care?"

"By dinner half of them will be drunk themselves."

We're quiet for a moment. All I can think about is Courtney and how she had her hands all over Garret at the party last week. In a few short hours she'll be all over him again, acting like they're a couple. And how will he act? Will he go along with it? Kiss her? Hold her hand like he's holding mine right now? If he's drinking he'll probably do that and more.

I sit up. "Would you do something for me?"

"Probably. What is it?"

"Would you try not to drink at this thing?"

He sighs and rolls on his back. "Come on, Jade. I need at least two drinks just to put up with Courtney."

"No you don't. Believe me. I've been through way worse things than that and I've never had a drop of alcohol. And as you can see, I managed to survive."

He sits up, facing me. "You've never had a drink? Not even a beer? Or a sip of wine? Nothing?"

I shake my head.

"Wow. That's impressive. But I don't know. I don't think I can go that whole time without a drink."

"Will you at least try?"

He takes a moment to consider it. "Okay, I'll try." He stands up and holds out his hands to help me up. I take our notebooks while Garret folds up the blanket.

"I don't want Professor Hawkins to see what I wrote," I say. "I'm going to rip out that page and write something else, okay?"

"Maybe we should get our own notebooks. Ones just for you and me."

"What for?"

"Sometimes it's easier to write stuff down than to say it out loud. We might need to do that again."

"Yeah. Okay."

I'm not sure what I'd write in them after today, but I have to admit it was easier to put my innermost thoughts on paper than to say them. There's no way I could have actually said those words to Garret. I could barely write them.

In the dining hall, I spot Harper sitting by herself eating lunch and reading a book. "Can we join you?" I ask, putting my tray in front of her.

"Sure." She closes her book and sets it on the seat next to her. "I was wondering where you—" She stops when she sees Garret come up behind me. He sets his tray down and gives Harper that perfect smile that seems to make girls go into some type of trance.

"Hi. We haven't met but Jade has told me all about you. I'm Garret by the way," he glances at me, "in case Jade hasn't mentioned me, which knowing her, she probably hasn't."

"Um, no. She's mentioned you," Harper says, staring at Garret like she can't get enough of him. "Nice to meet you."

"Harper, right?"

She doesn't respond. I kick her foot under the table.

"Yeah. Harper. Harper Douglas. I'm from LA."

"Is your dad Kipher Douglas? The director?"

"Yeah. How did you know?"

"Your dad's been at some fundraisers at my house. I've met your mom, too. You look just like her."

"All us girls do. I have two sisters." Harper has lost all interest in her lunch. She's too focused on listening to Garret's every word.

"So how do you like Connecticut?"

"I like it. I needed a break from the whole LA scene. I wanted to try someplace completely different than what I was used to. My dad actually suggested I apply at Moorhurst. They have a good communications program here, which is what I want to do. Plus they let me play on the tennis team."

"How long have you played tennis?"

"Ten years. But I'm not that good. Moorhurst doesn't exactly have the best team. I just wanted to be on any team." She picks at her salad with her fork but doesn't eat it. "So are you two going to that party tonight down on Beech Street?"

"Garret already has plans," I say.

"You should go to the party with Harper," Garret says to me.

"No, I don't feel like going."

Harper sets down her fork and pushes her tray aside. "I've asked her repeatedly to go to parties with me and she always says no."

"I have homework to catch up on and then maybe I'll watch TV."

"You don't even have a TV," Garret reminds me.

"I know, but I'll use the TV down the hall."

"I have to go." Harper gets up to leave. "I'll see you guys later."

"I've got an idea," Garret says once Harper is gone. "I'll give you my key and you can use my room tonight. Watch all the TV and movies you want. I have at least 100 movies in that box and my TV is brand new. Hi-def. Surround sound. The works. What do you think?"

"You don't care if I'm in your room without you there?"

He laughs. "Why would I care? Are you gonna trash it or something? Throw a party in there?"

"No, I just wanted to make sure it was okay."

"I'm the one who suggested it."

"Then, yes. I'd like that. Thanks for offering."

He glances at his watch. "I have to get ready."

"You're leaving already? You just sat down. It's only 11:45."

"I've got some things to do. I'll stop by on my way out and drop off the key."

In the afternoon I do homework, then go for a run and have dinner. By 7, I'm already bored and decide to go upstairs to watch a movie.

As I leave my room, girls race past me in their bathrobes getting ready to go out. When I get to the second floor I find a similar scene, only instead of girls there are shirtless guys with towels around their waists. I suddenly feel like I shouldn't be up here, even though I know girls are up here all the time. Some even spend the night on this floor. I hurry down to Garret's room and use the key he gave me to unlock the door.

When I get inside, I see that his laptop and books have been cleared off his desk and in their place is a pile of food. Not really a pile but an arranged assortment of snack items. There's a sign taped on the wall above the desk that reads *Concession Stand* and next to the words he's drawn those cartoon popcorn and soda people you see at the movies. On the table he has five full size bags of potato chips, some bags of popcorn, a bag of pretzels, a tall glass with red licorice sticking out of it, and at least eight boxes of candy like they sell at the theater. I spot a note next to the licorice that reads, *Sodas are in the fridge. Enjoy your movies!—G.*

I can't believe Garret made me a concession stand. That must be why he had to leave during lunch. I go over to the mini fridge and inside is an assortment of different sodas along with another note, *Wasn't sure what you liked so I got one of each.*

As I take a soda from the fridge I catch my reflection in the mirror and notice the huge grin on my face. I was already happy he let me use his TV but his homemade snack stand was a really great surprise.

Maybe I need to grow up and act like other people my age, but to me, this is the perfect Saturday night. Movies and junk food. It's so much better than being at some house party surrounded by obnoxious drunk people spilling beer all over me and vomiting on the carpet.

The box of movies is still on the floor where it was last time. As I'm going through it trying to decide what to watch, the phone rings. Do I answer it? It's probably the wrong number. Garret doesn't use that phone. In fact I'm almost certain I'm the only person on campus who uses the room phone. Everyone else uses their cell phone. The ringing is really getting on my nerves so I get up and answer it.

"Hello?"

"So you *are* there," Garret says. "What are you doing answering my phone?"

"Oh. Sorry. I shouldn't have, but it kept—"

"I'm kidding, Jade. I don't care if you answer it, although it probably won't ring again. Nobody calls that number."

"Hey, thanks for doing all this. I was so excited when I opened the door and saw this."

"Really? It's just some snacks."

"Yeah, but you went to all that trouble to buy them and set them up like this."

"Jade, it was no big deal. I just ran out after lunch and got some stuff. I've noticed your potato chip addiction by the way."

He doesn't seem to get how much I appreciate the gesture. People don't do stuff like that for me. I don't get surprises or presents. My mom ignored my birthday every year as well as Christmas and other holidays. That was fine with me because I figured she'd just use the holidays as an excuse to drink more.

"Well, it's a big deal to me, so thanks for doing it."

"You're welcome. Also, that key I gave you is yours. I had it made while I was out. That way you can watch TV or movies whenever you want."

"Garret, you shouldn't have done that."

"I had to. You don't have a TV. Plus now, if I ever lose my key, I can just come downstairs and get my spare."

"So that's the real reason you made an extra key," I kid. "How's the party?"

"Same as it is every year. Blake's here, but he's leaving soon to go to some party near campus. Sierra and Ava are here, too. You met them, right?"

"Yeah, they live on my floor. Is half the school there or what?"

"Not half, but a lot of them are. This is a huge event. The place is packed. Dinner starts in a few minutes, but I wanted to call you quick and see if you needed anything."

"I don't need anything. Thanks again for letting me use your stuff."

"You don't have to keep thanking me, Jade. What's mine is yours. Use anything in there. I gotta go. My little sister's pulling me away for dinner. I'll see you tomorrow."

I go back to the box of movies and pick out two, just in case I'm able to stay awake that long. Rather than sit in the bean bag chair, I watch from Garret's bed. It smells like him, with just the slightest hint of his cologne. By 11, I'm really sleepy but I put in one more movie. It's an action film so I figure it will keep me awake.

"Jade, I'm back." I hear Garret's voice and quickly sit up. He's sitting right next to me on the bed.

"What time is it?"

"It's 8:30."

"In the morning? Crap! I didn't mean to spend the night here. I must have fallen asleep."

"It's okay. I don't care. But you left the TV on all night."

You left the TV on! You think I have money to run that damn thing all night you ungrateful spoiled brat! I hear her screaming and I duck down knowing she's going to hurl the TV remote at me. I can almost hear it hitting the wall with a short loud thump.

"I'm sorry! I won't do it again! I promise! I'll never do it again!" I notice my own voice yelling in the room as I struggle to get free from whatever is touching me.

"Jade, stop." Garret is holding my shoulders, staring at me. "I was just kidding. I don't care that you left it on."

The voice in my head is gone and I feel my face heating up. "No. I wasn't talking to you. I was . . ." My voice trails off.

"Who were you talking to?"

"Nobody. I need to go." I try to get off the bed but he won't let me.

"Wait. What just happened? Why were you screaming at me?"

"I didn't mean to. I'm sorry. Now let me go."

"Something's wrong. You totally changed just now. You were all happy and smiling and then all of a sudden you changed. What happened? Was it something I said?"

"It has nothing to do with you."

He lets me up. "Then tell me what's wrong."

"I can't. I don't want to talk about it."

As I head for the door, Garret steps in front of me. He reaches around me and pulls me into a hug. I stand there with my arms stiffly at my sides.

He's laughing. "Jade, you're doing the exact same thing you did after the pool that night. Don't you know how to do this?"

"Do what?"

"Give a person a hug."

"I'm not much of a hugger."

"Well, you need one, so don't just stand there. Put your damn arms around me."

I wrap my arms loosely around him.

"What the hell? Tighten your arms. I'm not going to break."

I bring my arms closer to his body.

"That's better."

After a few seconds, I start to pull away. Garret tightens his hold.

"Nope. You're not done yet. You need more time."

"What? No. I'm done."

"You don't like this?"

"I like it, but I'm done." I'd have no problems being this close to him if we were making out, but this hug thing is totally different. It's too intimate.

"You need at least a minute."

"How do you know what I need?"

"I can tell. You were all tensed up before. You're starting to get less tense, but you're not relaxed yet so we're staying here until you are."

"You're crazy."

"Whatever, but I'm not letting go until you relax."

I sigh and resume the hug. My mother was not a hugger. Frank and Ryan aren't huggers either. Ryan's farewell hug when he dropped me off here was only the second hug he ever gave

153

me, the first one being at my graduation. I am not at all good at this.

"Are we done now?"

"Yes, we're done." He lets go. "See? You're way more relaxed now. Although I've never had to work so hard to get a girl to hug me."

I notice some candy wrappers and a couple empty soda bottles lying around and go to pick them up. "Why did you get back so early?"

"I was up at 7 so I left. Normally after one of those events I'm out until noon, but not today." He catches my arm as I drop a candy wrapper in the trash. "I was up early because I wasn't hung over. I didn't drink last night, Jade. I didn't drink the whole day."

"You didn't? Seriously?" I hug him again. I have no idea why. Maybe this hug thing is contagious.

"Oh, now you hug me?" He hugs me back. "Anyway Blake gave me shit for it. He was on my case the whole time trying to shove shots down my throat."

"Really?" I let go of him.

"Not literally, but he was holding them up to my face all night. He was so pissed. That boy doesn't like to drink alone."

"Well, thanks for doing that. I know it seems stupid but it's a big deal to me because of, you know, how I grew up."

"I know. And I don't think it's stupid. So how about breakfast? Let's go out. I'm craving a really big stack of pancakes."

"They have pancakes in the dining hall."

154

He rolls his eyes. "I want *good* pancakes. Light, fluffy pancakes. Not ones that stick to the wall when you throw them. I've tried that by the way. And they do stick to the wall."

"They're not that bad."

"If you like the pancakes at the cafeteria, then you've never had good pancakes. Allow me to introduce you to Al's Pancake House, the finest pancakes in Connecticut."

"I don't know. I think I should just eat in the dining hall."

"Because it's paid for, right?"

I don't answer, but I don't need to.

"Okay, here's the deal. I'm really craving the pancakes at Al's Pancake House, but I hate to eat alone at a restaurant, so if you went with me you'd be doing me a huge favor. And to show my gratitude, I will buy you breakfast."

I tilt my head as I consider it. "So I'm really helping you out here?"

"Totally helping me out."

"All right. Let me go shower. Come down in 10 minutes."

As I'm leaving I hear him talking. "I still can't believe you can get ready that fast."

"Okay, you were completely right about this," I say as I bite into the fluffiest buttermilk pancakes I've ever eaten. "This place *does* have the best pancakes. And I don't think it's just in Connecticut. They might have the best pancakes in the whole country. Maybe the world."

"I told you." Garret ordered the blueberry pancakes, which also look good. "You know, we should make this a Sunday thing."

"What do you mean?"

"Like every Sunday we'll come here for breakfast. It'll be like our own little tradition."

"I don't have money to eat out every week. And since I can't seem to find a job on campus, I don't see Sundays at Al's Pancake House in my future. Although that would be really good. I could eat these pancakes every day."

He sighs and sets his fork down. "Why won't you just let me pay for stuff? You know my family has more money than we can ever spend. And I'm not trying to buy you a car here. It's just pancakes."

"I've told you before. When people buy me stuff, I feel like I owe them. And I don't want to owe you anything."

"What if we were dating?" he casually asks. "If we were on a date, you'd let me pay, right?"

"I don't know. When I've let guys pay for dates in the past they expected sex. So again, we have the owing problem to deal with."

He smiles. "You won't owe me sex. We'll put that in the terms of our agreement."

"So we'll have an agreement?"

"Just a verbal one. You can set whatever conditions you want."

"We said we'd just be friends, remember? Spend time getting to know each other?"

"Then forget the dating idea and just go with the fact that you're doing me a huge favor because you know I can't sit here and eat by myself."

My plate of pancakes is now empty and I'm already craving more. "Hmm. I *would* like to come here again."

"And I would as well. But I can't without a dining companion."

"That's true. All right. I guess we can try it."

He reaches in his wallet and puts his credit card on the bill that's sitting on the table. "Week one of Sundays at Al's Pancake House. Our first tradition."

CHAPTER 15

"Our first? Are you thinking we'll have others?"

"We have four years here, Jade. I'm sure we'll come up with some others."

I'm surprised that Garret thinks we'll still be doing stuff together in four years. That's a long time. There's no way he'll be friends with me in four years. But I like the thought of it. And I love the idea of making traditions, something I've never had.

The waitress comes by and clears our plates and takes the credit card.

"So what are your plans for today?" I ask Garret.

"I'm playing football this afternoon. I'm on a flag football team and we play every Sunday. After that we're all going to this guy's apartment to watch some games. He has an 80-inch TV."

"I didn't know you played football."

"It's one of my many hidden talents." He gives me that cocky smile that I've seen several times now. I find it extremely hot. I love confidence in a guy and Garret's definitely got plenty of that. But so far, he hasn't crossed the line to arrogant. Plus, he always combines that cocky smile with a tone that implies he's just kidding.

"And what are *your* plans for today?" he asks.

"Probably go for a run. Call Frank and Ryan."

"You never say anything about them. Are you related to Frank? Is he like an uncle?"

"I thought you knew my whole life story. Didn't your dad fill you in about Frank?"

"My dad barely told me anything about you. I swear."

"Frank is my legal guardian. Well, he was until I turned 18. He and Ryan moved into my neighborhood when I was 12."

"So your neighbor offered to be your guardian?"

"He's more than a neighbor. He's been like a dad to me ever since I met him. And he knew my mom from college."

"Your mom went to college?"

"Yes. Why are you so surprised? She didn't get knocked up until she was 20. She had two years of college. Anyway, Frank took me in after she died. He has MS and now he's in a wheelchair. Well, he doesn't always use it but he's supposed to."

"That sucks. Is he going to be okay?"

"I don't know. It changes by the day. The day I got here he had to be rushed to the hospital and I thought he was going to die."

"Jade, why didn't you say something? I wouldn't have dragged you all over town that day if I knew that was going on."

"It was good you got me out. Otherwise I would've sat in my room thinking about it. But Frank's doing a lot better now."

"So is Frank divorced?"

"No, his wife died a long time ago. She got cancer when Ryan was just a baby. Frank was working at the paper and going to grad school at the time and he hired my mom to babysit Ryan so he could take his wife to treatments. That's how he got to know my mom. She was a freshman when he met her. Actually his wife met her first because she worked at the college. Anyway, around the time my mom got pregnant, Frank moved the family to San Diego to be closer to his wife's parents. She died a few months later, but Frank stayed out there so his in-laws could help take care of Ryan. Then when they died, he moved back to Des Moines."

"So your mom used to babysit Ryan." The way he says it I know what he's thinking.

"Yeah, I know. But apparently she was normal back then. She didn't turn crazy until after I was born." The waitress returns with the receipt. I scoot out of the booth. "Let's get out of here before I order more pancakes."

On the drive back to campus, Garret glances over at me. "You can take this if you want to go somewhere later."

"Take what? The car?"

"Yeah. If you want to get off campus, just take it."

"Are you kidding me? This car costs a fortune. I was scared to death to drive it the other night."

"It's insured, Jade. And I'm sure you're a safe driver. How many tickets have you had?"

"None. And no accidents."

"Then you're already way better than me. You have a key to my room, so if you need the car, there's an extra car key in my top drawer."

"I'm not taking your car, Garret. But thank you for offering."

"Hey, when we get back, come up to my room and take the food that's left. You didn't eat much of it."

"It's yours. You can have it."

"I'll never eat it. I'll just throw it away."

"Well, crap if you're gonna do that, then I'll take it."

"Or, if you plan on watching another movie soon, you could leave some of it there."

"I don't know. Am I invited again?"

"Jade, I told you to come by whenever you want to use the TV or any of my stuff."

"Okay, then leave the concession stand up. Maybe I'll watch something this afternoon while you're gone."

He smiles and shakes his head. "Well, I was kind of hinting for you to stop by when I was there, but whatever."

I spend the rest of the day with Harper, who keeps asking what's going on between Garret and me. I assure her we're just friends, but she refuses to believe me.

"So you two have spent all this time together and you haven't even kissed?" She asks it again for the third time. I keep lying and telling her we haven't but she doesn't buy it so I decide to fess up.

"Okay, fine. We kissed. One time. Are you happy now?"

"I knew it! You can't be around a guy that hot and not kiss him."

We're sitting in her room on her pink comforter-covered bed. She's leaning against the headboard, holding a pink pillow and playing with the fringe around its edges. I'm sitting at the end of her bed against the wall staring at the small chandelier she hung from the ceiling.

"So how was it? Garret seems like he'd be a good kisser."

"How could you possibly tell that just by looking at him?"

"Well, first, he has great lips. And second, I'm sure he's had a ton of practice." She hugs the pillow to her chest. "So how was it? I need details, Jade."

"It was good. That's all I'm saying."

"Did it go anywhere? If it did and you didn't tell me I'm going to kill you."

"It was just a kiss. Nothing more. And it probably won't happen again because Garret and I are just friends."

"I don't understand this friends thing. Did you take a vow of celibacy or something?"

She says it seriously and it makes me laugh. "No. I just want to take things slow and be friends first."

"And Garret's okay with that? Because from my experience, guys expect sex on the third or fourth date."

"He hasn't pressured me like that. Probably because we're not actually dating."

"And you're sure he's not dating someone else?" Her face scrunches up like she's afraid to even ask the question.

"No, but it's really none of my business. He can date whoever he wants." I say it like it doesn't matter, but it *does* matter. I don't want to even imagine him with anyone else.

She nudges my leg with her pink sock-covered foot. "Jade, I know you'd be hurt if he did that. You like him a lot. I can tell."

"He's just a friend, Harper. Nothing more." I change the subject to her own love life and the guy from her sociology class, who she's been out with twice now.

By early evening Harper takes off to play tennis and I decide to watch a movie in Garret's room. I figure if he's watching football with a bunch of guys, it could be pretty late before he gets back. Ryan and Frank are big football fans and would sometimes stay up until midnight to finish watching a game.

Just as my movie's starting, I hear the door open. I quickly jump off the bed.

"So I guess you decided to come back and visit your concession stand." Garret's smiling from ear to ear like he was actually hoping to find me in his room.

"I didn't know you'd be back so early." I grab the remote and shut the TV off. "It's only 7."

"The game was a blowout so I left. There's another game starting later but I didn't feel like watching it."

"I'll let you have your room back." I hurry past him but he catches me around my waist.

"You don't have to leave." He keeps hold of me. I don't squirm away because I like it. A lot. "Let's watch a movie."

My excitement over him wanting me to stay fades when the smell of beer hangs in the air between us.

I push him away. "You were drinking."

"Yeah? So?"

I glare at him.

"Jade, it was a couple beers. That's what guys do when they watch football. They drink beer. And I stopped at two. The other guys had at least six each and they're still drinking."

"I don't care what they do. I only care what you do."

He backs away and throws his hands in the air. "This is fucking college, Jade. I'm not gonna swear off drinking for the next four years. That's not even fair of you to ask. Do you know what a huge deal it was for me to not drink at that party yesterday? And people acted like something was wrong with me. Even my dad asked why I wasn't drinking wine during dinner."

"That's messed up. You're not even 21."

"That's how it is. I'm sorry if you don't like it, but I'm not gonna lie to you. There's gonna be times when I drink. And today I really wanted to drink more, but I held back because of you. And then you still get mad at me!"

"I understand why you did it. It's a social thing. People expect you to drink. I get that. But I don't have to like it. And I can't be around you when I can smell it on you. I'll see you later."

He doesn't say anything as I leave. We both need time to think about this. I realize that drinking is a part of college and I knew that any friends I made would drink. So maybe I'm being too hard on Garret. But being around him after he's been drinking is hard on *me*. So where does that leave us? No longer friends? Only friends on weekdays? I'm not sure and I don't think he
is either.

The entire week goes by and I don't hear a word from Garret, other than a quick hello during English on Tuesday and Thursday. It's the first full week of classes so I tell myself he's just busy. But I know that's not the real reason we're no longer hanging out.

I could just go up to his room and talk to him about this, but I don't. It's not like I've changed my mind, so what would I say to him? Sorry I got mad at you for drinking? I'm not sorry. I don't want him to drink. It's as simple as that. It's a lot to ask and I know he still wants to drink so we're at an impasse.

But that doesn't mean I don't miss him like crazy. I've been doing more stuff with Harper and some of her tennis friends, but it's not the same. Garret knows about me. He knows about my past and he's seen me in those dark moments I never wanted anyone to see. He may not understand what those were, but he still witnessed them and that brought us closer.

On Friday night after dinner, I do my biology homework because my useless lab partner refuses to meet with me to work on it. I can barely concentrate with all the yelling and running in the hallway as girls get ready to go out. Harper had a date and left an hour ago.

I search my backpack for my headphones so I can at least attempt to drown out all the noise.

"Jade?" The voice is followed by light knocking. "Jade? It's Garret."

What the hell does he want? To tell me he's heading out to a party to get wasted?

"What do you want?" I ask as I open the door.

"Well, that's a hell of a greeting." He smiles and flashes those beautiful aqua blue eyes. My heart skips a beat seeing him there. And my stomach gets a little fluttery. Are those butterflies? So that's a real thing? What the hell?

"I know it's short notice, but I wanted to see if you want to watch a movie upstairs." He leans against the door frame which for some reason is way hotter than if he just stood up straight.

I say nothing because I have no idea what's going on here. We haven't spoken all week and now he's inviting me up to his room?

"I have snacks if that sways your decision. I replenished the concession stand." He's still smiling and I realize that I'm smiling back. Why am I smiling back? I'm supposed to be mad at him. How does he do this to me?

My smile fades as I pull myself together from whatever spell he's put on me. "It's Friday night. Shouldn't you be out at a party?"

He shrugs with one shoulder. "Didn't feel like it. So are you coming or not?"

"I don't know. I—"

"Hey, Garret." I see a girl's red tipped fingers wrap around Garret's arm. I duck my head out into the hallway to see that it's Ava, wearing a tight red dress and black high heels. "Be my date for the party tonight." She sets her gaze on me as she puts her mouth up to his ear. "I'll make it worth your time."

A surge of jealousy courses through me even though I have no reason to be jealous. Garret's not mine. I have no claim on him. He's free to do whatever he wants with Ava.

"I already have plans," Garret says shifting away from her.

"Doing what?" Ava seems annoyed.

"We're going to a movie." I blurt it out, having no idea how or why those words just came out of my mouth.

Garret looks surprised but pleased. "Yes. Jade and I are going to a movie. But have fun at the party."

Ava glares at me. She makes a huffing noise, then spins around on her heels and storms down the hall.

Garret doesn't even notice. "What movie do you want to see? I'll check the times." He takes his phone from his pocket and starts swiping.

"What? No. I was just saying that to get rid of her."

His eyes remain on the phone. "Too late now. You told her and now it's public knowledge. We have to go. If she sees us around here she'll know we lied."

"I don't care if she knows we lied."

"Let's see. We missed the 7:30 show but there are four movies that start at 9 or a little after. Should I read them off?"

"Hold on." I cover his phone with my hand. "I never said I was going to the movies."

He moves my hand away from the phone. "You just said it. Like a minute ago."

"Yeah, but—"

"Never mind. You're taking too long to decide. I'll just pick one. Is that what you're wearing?"

I glance down at my t-shirt and running shorts, confused by this entire scene. "Um, no. I guess not."

Did I just agree to go with him? How did this happen?

He puts his phone away. "Can I come in? I'm kind of a target out here in the hall."

"A target for what?" I ask, moving aside to let him in.

"Girls fondling me." A smirk crosses his face as he waits for my reaction.

"Please tell me you're kidding. Because if you're not, then I need to start upping the insults again to bring you back down to earth."

He's trying hard to keep a straight face. "You saw Ava just now. Girls just can't help themselves. What can I say?"

I shake my head and start rummaging through my drawer for a shirt. "*I* can help myself. I'm completely immune to whatever you think you've got going on over there."

"Yeah, I know," he mumbles. "You need some help?"

"Why? You think I can't dress myself?"

He stands next to me, staring down at the open drawer. "Everything in here is black."

"Yeah." I close the drawer and open the one beneath it. "And everything in here is white."

"Where are your other shirts?"

"That's it. Well, I have a few in the closet."

He walks over to look. "You only wear black or white?"

"Uh, yeah. Are you just getting that? You've seen me how many times and you've never noticed that?"

"Huh. I guess not."

"It's just easier that way. Black and white go with everything." I take a black t-shirt from the drawer.

"You should wear purple sometime."

I almost choke laughing. "Purple? Are you joking?"

"What's wrong with purple?"

"I've never worn anything purple in my life. I've never even considered it. It's one of those weird colors that old ladies wear."

"Lots of people wear purple. And with your green eyes, you would look great in purple."

"I hate my green eyes. The last thing I want to do is draw attention to them."

He comes closer and lifts my chin up with his hand. "How could you hate your eyes? They're the most beautiful eyes I've ever seen. Why do you think I'm always staring at them?"

"Yeah, that's hilarious." I push him back. "Now get out of here so I can change. Wait in the hall. I'll be like two seconds."

"Jade, you know I'm not safe out there." He says it as if he's really in danger. "Did you see all those girls running around in towels and robes?"

I roll my eyes. "I swear. The insults are coming, my friend. So tell your ego to get ready."

He stands there.

"You're really not leaving? Fine. Then turn around."

I change into my jeans and black shirt. "Okay, I'm done."

He inspects me. "Yeah. You definitely need some color. The black and white thing is getting old."

"Well, I'm not planning on buying new clothes so you'll have to get over it." I search through my desk drawer for money. "How much are movie tickets? I haven't been to a movie in years, so I have no clue. Six bucks? Seven?"

"Don't worry about it. Let's go."

"Garret, you're not paying."

"You just saved me from being man-handled by Ava. That's at least worth the price of a movie ticket. Maybe even some popcorn, too."

I agree to his offer, thinking it's just a few dollars and not worth arguing about. Then we get to the theater and the tickets are $12 a piece! When did movies get so expensive? I tell him to skip the overpriced popcorn, but he sneaks out after we get our seats and gets a giant bucket and two sodas.

"You have to get popcorn when you go to the movies," he says when I scold him. "It's like presents at Christmas. It's tradition."

I don't bother telling him how presents were not a Christmas tradition at my house growing up.

"I can't believe you picked a romantic comedy," I say. "Do I seem like someone who would like that kind of movie?"

"No. That's why I picked it. I thought it might sweeten you up a little." He kisses my cheek. I ignore the comment. And the kiss. "So what's the last movie you saw?"

"I can't remember. I was like 15, so it's been a while."

"Why so long? You don't like going to the movies?"

"I do, but it's too expensive. And I didn't have anyone to. . ." I decide not to finish that statement. The truth is that after my mom's drug- and alcohol-induced suicide, the parents of the few friends I had didn't want me hanging around their kids outside of school. I guess they assumed I was just like my mom and would steer their kids down the wrong path. So social activities, like movies, ended from age 15 on. And Frank and Ryan never went to movies. They always rented them.

The movie begins, preventing any awkward conversation around my comment. An hour into it, I find that it's actually not that bad of a movie. It's more of a comedy with just a little romance. Garret's hand keeps meeting mine in the popcorn bucket which explains his insistence on getting the giant tub.

"We should do this again," Garret says when we're back in my room. "It could be another tradition, like the pancake place. We could go every Friday night."

"This was fun, but you need to go out like everyone else does on Friday night. Go to parties. I don't want you missing out on stuff because of me."

"I'm not missing out. If I wanted to go to a party, I'd go." He pulls on me to sit next to him on the bed. "I was planning on going to that party Ava was talking about, but then I thought about what it would actually be like when I was there and decided I'd rather be doing something with you. That's why I came down here tonight."

"What if I'd said no?"

That cocky grin appears as he points to himself. "Come on. Who can say no to this?"

"Goodnight, Garret." I point to the door.

"I'm kidding! Geez, you really think I'm being serious?"

Actually I did. He *is* incredibly hard to say no to.

"Well, next time you want to do something, you should give me more notice. You're just lucky I wasn't busy tonight." It's such an exaggeration. I'm never busy. I have nothing to do besides homework.

"What are you doing tomorrow night?" he asks.

"Laundry." It's the truth, but as soon as I say it I realize how pathetic it sounds.

"That's too bad because I was going to invite you up to my room for pizza and a movie marathon."

171

"Hmm. I do love pizza. And movies. But are you saying you'll be there, too? Because that kind of ruins the whole thing so—"

His nudges my side. "Okay, I guess I deserve that. So what's your answer?"

"Yes. I think it sounds fun, even if you *do* insist on being there."

CHAPTER 16

Before meeting Garret for our Saturday movie night, I do some prep work. I take a long shower, shave my legs, straighten my hair, brush and floss my teeth, and put on makeup.

I have no idea why I'm going to all this trouble to watch movies with a "friend." I attempt to rationalize it but come up with nothing other than the possibility that living with all these girls has given me an estrogen boost. My girly-girl side just can't help but come out when I'm living with a floor full of them. And frequent visits to Harper's exploding pink room certainly doesn't help matters.

I knock on Garret's door at 7, right on time. When he opens it, I'm greeted with a sea of sparkling blue lights hanging from the ceiling. They cast a soft glow as they're the only lights on in the room.

"What's all this?" I ask, walking inside.

"I wanted to add some atmosphere. It's cool, right? And now we don't have to use the harsh overhead lights or the bright desk lamp."

"I don't know," I say suspiciously. "This seems like some type of romantic mood lighting." I turn to him. "And I can tell you right now that you're not getting sex tonight."

He laughs and puts his hand on my shoulder. "Tonight? So you'd consider it some other night? Okay. That works for me."

"That's not what I meant. I meant that you're not getting sex tonight or any night. At least not with me."

Why did I just say that? It's far too bold a statement. I basically ruled out having sex with him for all of eternity which is not at all what I wanted to do. But it's too late now. I can't take it back.

"Well, if we're not having sex you might as well leave right now."

I stand there in shock as my anger rises. I should've known that's all he wanted from me. I try to push past him to get to the door, but before I can take two steps he scoops me up in his arms.

"I was kidding, Jade. Man, you can't take everything so seriously."

"Put me down."

"Only if you promise to stay."

I try to wiggle free, but it just makes him hold me tighter. I could use my self defense techniques on him, but that would hurt him and I really don't want to do that. Plus, I like being in his arms. He's really strong. Holding me up like this doesn't even seem to be any effort for him.

"Okay. I'll stay."

He starts to put me down, then stops. "One more thing. You have to give me a compliment. After all the insults you've given me, I don't think it's too much to ask."

"Just put me down."

"One compliment, Jade. That's it."

I sigh. "Fine. I like your stupid lights."

It makes him laugh to the point that he can no longer hold me. He sets me down on his giant bean bag chair.

His cell phone chirps. "That's the pizza. I'll be right back."

While he's gone I stare up at the twinkly blue lights. They *are* really cool.

"Did you pick out a movie?" Garret comes back with a large pizza balanced on his arm.

"Yeah. The crime-fighting dog movie."

"We're not watching that, Jade."

"Oh, we are *so* watching it." I crawl over to the box of movies and fish it out.

Garret doesn't bother trying to stop me because he knew we would watch it eventually.

After the movie, which isn't too bad for a cartoon, Garret takes the pizza box to the outside dumpster because it's stinking up the room. When he returns I'm searching the box for another movie.

"I'm picking the next one," he says. "After that last one, I'm starting to question your judgment."

"It's your movie!" I go to his fridge to get another soda.

"This one's good." He holds up a comedy.

"As long as it's not some sappy romance." I go back to my place on the bean bag chair, expecting him to sit against his bed like last time but instead he sits next to me on the bean bag chair. His change of seats has me wondering what's going on with him. Our friends-only agreement still stands and yet sometimes he tries to push its boundaries by holding my hand or kissing my cheek or getting really close like he's doing now. And as tempting as it is to take that next step, I feel like I shouldn't. But damn, it's tempting.

Midway through the movie I get sleepy. An hour later I wake up lying against Garret, his arm around me. He's asleep and the TV is now a blue screen.

"Garret, get up." I push myself off him and get up to take the movie out.

"The movie's already over?" He yawns. "How did that happen?"

"We fell asleep. You want to watch another one or do you want to go to bed?"

"It's only 10:30. It's too early for bed. Let's see what's on TV."

I grab the TV remote and return to the chair. I flip to an old movie from the eighties.

"My mom loved this one," Garret says. "It's about these two girls who—"

"You never mention your mom. Does she live around here?"

He gives me an odd expression. "My mom is dead. I thought you knew that. Don't you watch the news?"

I'm slightly offended by the comment, but I don't think he meant it to sound condescending. I turn the volume on the TV down.

"I'm sorry. I didn't know." I feel my cheeks getting warm.

"It's okay. It was long time ago. I was 10 when it happened."

"Why was it on the news?" I almost don't want to know. If it made the news, something really bad must've happened. The news only reports violent deaths like murders.

"She died in a plane crash. It was one of those small private planes."

That was my other guess. Some type of tragic accident. But I'm not sure why he thinks I would've heard about it on the news in Iowa.

"Did it happen close to here?" I put my hand on his arm. "I'm sorry, Garret. I shouldn't ask. I'm sure you don't want to talk about it."

"No, it's fine. I can talk about it. It, um, it happened in Virginia. My parents were down in DC for a political fundraiser. My dad had to fly back early for a meeting. Mom stayed behind to attend another event that night. She hated that political crap, but she was kind of expected to go because my dad was a big supporter of this guy's re-election campaign. Anyway, to say thanks, the guy offered to fly my mom home on his private jet. He had to do a speech in Hartford so the plane was supposed to arrive there and Dad and I were going to drive up and get her."

Garret pauses for a moment. I can tell that despite what he said, this isn't easy for him to talk about. "My mom didn't like private planes. She said they weren't safe. That's why we didn't have one back then. Anyway, soon after the plane took off it crashed. No survivors. It only made national news because that guy was a senator. And to this day, there's all these rumors on the Internet about how it wasn't an accident and how someone was trying to kill the senator. Crazy conspiracy shit. Just last year there was an hour long story about it on one of those news programs. It's like it never goes away."

I sit there not sure what to say. I had no idea Garret had this giant loss in his life. I get the feeling he hasn't shared this with many people. It almost seems like the topic hasn't come up in years. Maybe he tries to forget it. And then I go and open my big mouth asking him all about it.

I feel like I should say or do something, but I don't know how to respond. It proves once again that I suck at comforting people. Garret is sitting there quietly, likely reliving the event in his head thanks to me. His normally happy face is now sad. Even his eyes look sad. I feel terrible seeing him like this.

"Stand up," I say to him.

"Why?"

"Just do it."

He stands up.

I stand right in front of him. "Let's do that thing you taught me."

"What thing?"

"That thing with your arms."

He looks at me, confused.

"You know that day when you found me in your room after I accidentally spent the night here? That thing you did after the pool?"

He starts to smile. "You mean a hug?"

"Yeah. That. I need to practice that. Can you show me again?"

His smile grows. He puts his arms around me. I do the same to him.

"Tighter," he instructs.

I squeeze tighter, resting my head against his chest. We stay in that position for several minutes, the blue lights twinkling above us. As he starts to pull away, he stops briefly to kiss my forehead, then whispers in my ear, "Thank you."

Yes! I finally did it. I comforted someone. And it felt incredibly good.

The next morning, we meet for breakfast again for week two of our Al's Pancake House tradition. This time I order blueberry pancakes.

"I don't know what Al puts in these things but they are beyond amazing," I say, chewing slowly to make each bite last.

"I know, right?" Garret ordered the basic buttermilk ones this time, also an excellent choice. "Are you going to write about these in your English journal again?"

I laugh. "Yeah. Why? You don't like reading about pancakes?"

"It could get old by the end of the semester. And I think you're going to run out of things to say."

"Never." I close my eyes, savoring them. "These are so good that this week I might even make up a poem about them."

"Well, that's something to look forward to," he kids. "You really like pancakes, don't you?"

"What's not to love? They're basically a dessert but you get to eat them as a meal in giant stacks."

"You're funny." He takes a drink of his orange juice. "My mom used to love pancakes, too."

I almost choke hearing him mention his mom. I didn't think he'd want to talk about her again after last night.

"Katherine, my wicked stepmother, can't stand pancakes. She says it's poor people food. She won't even let Lilly have them."

"Lilly is your sister?" It seems odd that I don't know this by now, but we've both avoided talking about our families.

"Yeah. She's Katherine's daughter. And my dad's. So she's my half sister. Really sweet kid. Not at all like her mother."

"So Katherine's your dad's second wife?" I know she's the third but I'd rather let him correct me than try to guess how all these wives fit in relation to his mother.

"Third wife. My mom was his second. His first wife was kind of an arranged marriage so it doesn't really count."

"Arranged marriage?"

"My dad was only 22 and his parents made him marry this girl because her family was super rich and connected. Shocking, right? So they got married like they were supposed to, but it didn't last. The woman didn't want to marry my dad either so it was doomed from the start."

"And then he met your mom?"

"A few years later. Her family didn't have money and definitely didn't have any connections so my grandparents got really mad when my dad married her. They even took him out of their will. And my grandfather fired him from the company.

But they softened up after I was born. You know, first grandson and all. The grandparents wanted to be involved in my life so they reconciled with my dad, but they still didn't welcome my mom."

"What was she like? Your mom?" I'm not sure if I should even be asking him that but the words just came out.

"She was funny. She laughed a lot. She liked to play music really loud and drive my dad crazy." He smiles. "She loved to give hugs."

"So that's where you learned it from."

"Yeah. I really miss her." It's almost like I can feel his loss from across the table. "I know if she was still around, my dad wouldn't be the way that he is now. He totally changed after she died. He became a different person. And he got even worse after he married Katherine."

The waitress brings the check. I give her an annoyed look for interrupting us even though the woman is only doing her job.

"Ready to go?" Garret asks, back to his cheerful self.

"Yes." I look down at my empty plate. "But it's sad that I have to wait another whole week to eat these again."

He laughs as he drops some cash on the table and gets up from the booth. "We could always make a weekday trip if you're not able to make it that long."

When we get back to campus, Mr. Kensington is there waiting in the parking lot in front of our residence hall.

"Dad, what are you doing here?" Garret seems nervous.

Mr. Kensington gives me a quick smile. "Jade, nice to see you again. I hope your classes are going well."

I smile back. "Yes. Classes are going very well. I really like it here."

"Good. Very good." He nods, like he's signaling me to leave. When I don't, he seems annoyed. "I need to talk to my son now if you don't mind."

"No. Not at all. Goodbye, Mr. Kensington. I'll see you later, Garret."

I don't know what this is about, but Garret's dad seems kind of angry. When I get to my room, I peek out the window and see Garret and his dad in the grassy area just beyond the parking lot. His dad appears to be scolding him, making big hand gestures while Garret keeps his head down.

Garret finally speaks, looking like he's about to explode. His father interrupts and gets right in Garret's face. Garret looks like he's going to fight back but then gives up and puts his head down again. His dad turns and walks away, then gets in his car and drives off.

Garret walks over to a bench and sits down, his shoulders slumped forward. I feel like I should go see what happened. I didn't have to hear their conversation to know that something is definitely wrong.

When I get outside, he's no longer there. I race up to his room but he's not there either. I don't see him the rest of Sunday. I assume he played flag football and then watched a game or two at that guy's house again.

I don't talk to or see Garret again until Tuesday afternoon during English. He's late to class so I can't talk to him until it's over. He races out and I have to chase him down. "What's going on with you? It's like you're completely ignoring me."

"I can't spend every minute with you, Jade." His tone is harsh. He's never talked to me that way and I don't like it. "I'm behind on my homework. I'm not swimming enough. Blake's pissed because I haven't been doing stuff with him."

"But you don't even like Blake." I'm almost at a jog trying to keep up with him. "Garret, wait. Why are you acting like this? Is it me? Did I do something wrong?"

He stops abruptly and places his hands on my shoulders. "No, Jade. You didn't do anything wrong." His tone has changed to one that's warm and kind, like the Garret I'm used to. "Don't even think that, okay? This isn't about you."

"Then what is it about? Why are you avoiding me?"

There's something Garret's not telling me. I can see it in his eyes and the desperate way he's looking at me right now. It's like he wants to tell me the truth but can't.

"I just—we just can't see each other anymore. I'm sorry, Jade."

"Can't see each other? But we're just friends. You can't be my friend anymore?" Hearing myself say it, I realize I sound like a little kid on the playground. I try again. "You're saying that we're done being friends?"

"I have to go. I'm sorry. I really am."

He races off and I'm left standing there completely confused.

CHAPTER 17

I walk slowly across campus to my room. My mind keeps replaying Garret's words but they make no sense. Why would he shut me out like that when everything was going so well between us?

As soon as I'm back in my room, I change into my running clothes. Running is the only way I can handle the emotions I'm feeling right now. I sprint down to the trail that Garret and I ran on a few weeks ago. I'm a little afraid to go into the woods by myself but I do it anyway. My body gives out after an hour. I go back and shower, then lie on my bed and end up falling asleep until morning.

The next day, I go to class, run, eat dinner with Harper, do homework, and go to bed. I follow that same schedule the next day, and the day after that, just going through the motions. The routine becomes so familiar I lose track of the days, and the days turn into weeks. The weekends become all about homework and laundry.

Harper keeps asking me what happened with Garret and I just tell her we decided to stop hanging out. I don't give her the whole story because I don't like talking to people about my problems. I've always been that way, even with friends. I figure nobody wants to hear that stuff. They have their own problems to deal with.

Even though I haven't told her what's going on, Harper can see how depressed I am and she keeps trying to cheer me up. She offers to take me shopping or out to eat, but I have no money to do either of those things. Then she invites me to play tennis which we do, but I suck at tennis and she's really good so that doesn't work. I'm afraid that if I don't get out of this sad, gloomy state soon, Harper will stop hanging out with me and I'll lose her as a friend.

As if things aren't bad enough, my mom is haunting me even more now. The anniversary of her death is coming up and it's not like I sit around and cry about it, but it's not exactly the happiest time of year.

I keep hearing my mom telling me *I told you so* over and over again in my head. Telling me how boys are trouble and how they ruin your life. Maybe she was right. But I want so badly for her to be wrong. I know in my heart that Garret and I had something together that was real and good. I felt happy in the short time I was with him. Happier than I've ever felt. And even if I can't be with *him*, there has to be someone else out there who could make me feel that way again. Not every man can be bad. Frank's not bad. And Ryan's not.

The only time I see Garret is during English class, but he doesn't talk to me. We haven't even exchanged our notebooks. It's gotten to the point that I don't even look in his direction.

He never looks at me either. Since this happened, he just sits there staring at his laptop.

After the third weekend of moping around my room, I decide it's time to move on. I refuse to be one of those girls who remains depressed over a boy for months on end.

Despite whatever happened with Garret, I have plenty of other things to feel good about. It's early October and the leaves are brilliant shades of yellow and orange. The air is crisp and cool and perfect for going on long runs. I'm doing great in all my classes and Frank and Ryan are doing really well. So I'm not going to waste my time sulking over some stupid guy.

On Tuesday, I see Garret in English and ignore him as usual. When class is over, just as I'm about to leave, he drops two notebooks on my desk—small green notebooks that are unlike the big blue notebooks we were given for class. Garret quickly gets up and walks out before I can ask him about it. I stuff the notebooks in my bag and head home.

When I'm back in my room I plop down on my bed and open one of the notebooks. Inside it says, *Remember how we were going to get notebooks to write down stuff we couldn't say? I don't know if you want to anymore but if so, this is yours. The other one is mine.*

I set the notebook down and open the other one. The first page is the original entry he made in our official English notebook, the page we tore out so Professor Hawkins couldn't read it. I flip through and see several more entries. I read the second page.

I've been hanging out with this girl a lot now. She continues to fascinate me and I can't seem to get enough of her. Today we had pancakes at Al's Pancake House. I've never seen anyone get so excited about pancakes. Who knew that something so small could make someone so happy? I wanted to make her that happy again, so I told her we would go there every Sunday. Her eyes lit up like I'd told her I was taking her to Paris or something. But it wasn't Paris. It was just a promise of pancakes every week.

I read page 3. *Tonight I invited this girl to hang out in my room. I just thought we'd eat pizza and watch movies and that was it. But it became more than that. She asked about my mom so I told her the story. Talking about my mom was harder than I thought it would be. Maybe because I never talk about her or what happened to her. But I felt better when I was done because this girl actually listened to me like she cared. No one has ever listened to me like that. No one except my mom.*

The entry on page 4 says: *Today was one of the worst days I've had in a really long time. I was told I could no longer see this girl who I really care about and who was becoming my closest friend. My life is full of rules and even though these rules make no sense to me, for some reason I follow them. I told her to stay away from me and that I would stay away from her. It was the hardest thing I've ever had to say to someone. I ran off as soon as I said it because I was too much of a coward to see how much I hurt her. But now I feel like the worst person in the world.*

I turn to page 5, the last entry. *"I haven't talked to this girl in weeks and I miss her so much it hurts. I miss her smile and her laugh and even her insults. I miss having pancakes with her and watching movies and just sitting quietly together. I no longer care about the rules. They're someone else's rules. This is my life and I'll make up my own rules. If she'll let me, I need to talk to this girl again. If she hates me, I understand. But we shouldn't end it the way it ended. That was someone else's end. We need our own end.*

Jade, I miss you. I made a huge mistake. And I just want to talk. --Garret

I shut the notebook and throw it on the floor. This is the last thing I need right now. I'm finally feeling better and now he tosses this crap at me? Why does he keep doing this? He hurts me and then expects me to forgive him. It's just like when he lied about being a Kensington.

The phone rings. I get up to answer, then hesitate in case it's Garret. The ringing continues.

"Yeah. What?" I answer.

"Jade? It's Frank."

"I'm sorry, Frank. I didn't mean to answer that way."

"How are you doing? Are you okay?"

It's the anniversary of my mom's suicide and I've been trying to forget about it all day, but apparently Frank won't let me do that.

"I'm fine. Really. It's been four years. I've moved on."

"Honey, I just—"

"You don't have to worry about me, okay? I just want to forget about it. Can we talk about something else?"

He sighs and I know he's frustrated with me, but I really have nothing more to say about it.

"So anything new with you and Ryan?" I ask.

"No, not much, but I wanted to let you know that we sent you a package, so be sure to keep an eye out for it."

"A package? What's in it?"

"That's a surprise. It's for your birthday."

"You didn't need to send me anything. You know I don't celebrate birthdays."

"Everyone should celebrate their birthday." Frank's tone lightens. He's way more excited about my birthday than I am.

188

He always has been, probably in an attempt to compensate for my mom always forgetting it or ignoring it. "Now listen, Jade. I want you to go out with your friends on Thursday and have a good time. Don't eat in the dining hall and do homework all night."

"But I—"

"No, Jade. No excuses. You get out of that room and do something fun. It's on me, which you'll see when you get the box. And don't go spending that money on laundry or something practical. There's a separate envelope for that."

"Frank, I can't take your—"

"It's a gift. Now tell me what else you're up to. How are classes?"

"Good. I'm still getting A's, if that's what you're wondering."

"That's great, but not that surprising." I feel him smiling through the phone.

There's silence because neither one of us ever has much to say.

Frank finally speaks. "Well, Ryan and I will call you on Thursday, okay?"

"Okay."

"And Jade." Frank's tone turns serious. "There's something in that box I sent that you might want to set aside for later."

"What is it?"

"You'll see when you get the box. It was to be given to you on your 19th birthday but you'll have to decide what to do with it."

"Now I have to know what it is. Just tell me."

"Wait until you get the package and then we'll talk, okay?"

"Yeah. Bye."

That was strange. What did Frank put in that box and why was he so cryptic about it?

Wednesday night I'm reading a chapter in my psychology book when I hear someone knocking on my door. Assuming it's Harper inviting me to watch TV in her room, I jump up to answer it.

It's not Harper. It's Garret. He isn't his usual clean cut self. He's got a day's worth of stubble on his face and his eyes look tired. If he's hoping this disheveled look will make me feel sorry for him, it's not going to work.

"What do you want, Garret?" I keep the door open just a crack.

"Did you read my notebook?"

"Yes."

"So can we talk?"

"I have nothing to say to you. I'm finally moving past all this. Just go away. And don't come down here anymore."

I start to shut the door, but he puts his hand up holding it open.

"It was my dad, Jade. He made me do it. It wasn't me. You don't understand." He has that desperate tone again just like he had in the car that night after the dinner at his parent's house. "But I'm done taking orders from him. Especially about stuff like this. You and me. He has no right to interfere. None of them do."

"What are you talking about?"

"Let me in and I'll tell you. I can't talk in the hall."

I hesitate, then go back to my desk to grab my keys. "Let's go outside."

Sitting is out of the question. I've got the nervous energy thing going and I have to keep moving. We go outside and I take off, walking fast across campus with Garret trailing behind.

"Are you going to stop?" he asks.

"Nope. So start talking."

He runs a few steps until he's beside me. "There's rules, Jade. My family and every family like mine has these unspoken rules and if you don't follow them, they become spoken rules. If it gets to that point where they have to be said, then you're in deep shit."

"You're not making sense, Garret."

"When my dad showed up here a few weeks ago, he was here to remind me of the rules. Well, one rule in particular." He hesitates like he doesn't want to say it but then he does. "The rule that says I'm not allowed to have anything to do with you."

"And why is that? Because I'm poor? From a bad home? The rich can't associate with people like me?"

He's silent.

"Like I didn't know that already? I'm not stupid, Garret. I know how the world works. It's not like I was expecting you to put a ring on my finger and take me to live in your mansion. We were just friends. That's it."

"I know. But I told you. My dad picks my friends. Or at least he has to approve of them. And he doesn't approve of you."

"Big surprise there." I keep up my brisk pace. The night is chilly enough that I can see my breath. My bare arms are covered in goosebumps. "How did he even know about us?"

"Ava and Blake told him. Or they told their parents and word got back to my dad. I don't know exactly, but I know they were involved." He unzips his sweatshirt and takes it off. "Here." I stop briefly to let him put it around me, then continue walking across the open quad.

"Why do you listen to your dad anyway? You're 18, right?"

"I'm 19. My birthday was in August. And I don't know why I listen to him. I don't respect him or the things he does. I don't even like him."

"He's your dad. You must like him a little." The statement sounds ridiculous coming from someone who hated their mother, but Garret doesn't know how I felt about my mom.

"I used to like him before my mom died. But he's not the same person anymore. And he doesn't like me either. If he did, he'd let me make my own decisions and he'd stop taking away everything that's good in my life." Garret steps in front of me, forcing me to stop. "I'm not going to listen to him. We have something here. And I won't let my dad take this away."

"Maybe I want it to go away. Did you even consider that?"

"Of course I have. And I understand if you want nothing to do with me." His voice is soft, his eyes full of sadness and regret. "If that's what you want, I'll leave you alone. I'll see if we can get different partners in English. I'll never bother you again."

I don't know if I'm a glutton for punishment or have lost all common sense, but I don't feel ready to cut this guy out of my life.

"Tell me what you want, Jade." Garret takes my hand and holds it loosely in his, like he's afraid I'll yank it back if he holds it any tighter.

I glance away, hoping I'll come to my senses and tell him to get lost. I focus on the shriveled up leaves on the ground, their brilliant fall color now faded. I watch as even more red and orange leaves drop from the trees above us. I wait all year for the trees to turn color and within a couple weeks, it's over. Why does everything good have to end?

When I look back at Garret, his expression has changed. All hope is gone. He seems to assume that my long silence is an answer. He lets go of my hand and starts to walk away.

"I want pancakes on Sunday." I blurt it out without even thinking.

He turns back slowly. "What?"

"You asked me what I want. I want pancakes on Sunday. You said it would be a tradition. I've never had a tradition. You started it, but then it ended and I want it back."

A cautious smile comes across his face but he remains quiet.

"I want to see more movies from that box in your room. And maybe share another pizza."

He takes a few steps forward. "That could be arranged."

"But more than anything, I want a promise that you'll never do something like this to me again. Because I won't forgive you, Garret. This is it. I mean it."

"I know you do." He holds out his hand. "Friends?"

"Maybe. We'll see how it goes."

He puts his hand down.

I pull the sweatshirt tighter around me as a gust of wind blows. "So what happens if your dad finds out about us?"

"He'll stop putting money in my account and probably take my car. But I don't care about that. I need to make a stand. Otherwise he'll keep trying to control every aspect of my life."

"This is so stupid. I can't believe he won't even let us be friends. When I had dinner at your house he told you to get to know me."

"Yeah, but he didn't think it would actually go anywhere. He didn't think we'd end up being friends. Or more than friends."

"But he picked me for the scholarship. He can't hate me that much."

"He doesn't hate you, Jade. In fact I can tell that he likes you. But he's so focused on the Kensington image and what people think that he can't see past it. And Katherine only makes it worse. Plus it doesn't help to have people like Ava and Blake gossiping about us."

"Maybe you should go to more charity events or afternoon teas or whatever you rich people do. Then maybe everyone would see that being friends with me isn't that big a deal."

"I doubt it'll make a difference but I could try that." He smiles. "Although I don't go to afternoon tea, Jade."

The wind picks up again. "We should go inside."

"In a minute. First I need you to show me that thing I taught you." He holds his arms out in front of him. "It's been weeks now and you probably forgot how to do it."

I sigh dramatically. "Do I have to?"

"Yes. You need to practice."

I wrap my arms loosely around him. But he hugs me tight, his warm chest pressed against mine and his strong arms shielding me from the cold.

It feels good to be this close to him again. It feels right. I shut my eyes, breathing him in, listening to the pounding of his heart.

"Oh yeah, you definitely need more practice," he says. "We're gonna have to do this a lot in order for you to get it right."

I couldn't agree more.

CHAPTER 18

After class on Thursday I return to my room and find a note on my door telling me to go see Jasmine, my RA. When I get to her room, she hands me a big box.

"Care package?" she asks.

"Um, yeah. I guess." I take the box and quickly leave. I don't want her or anyone else to know it's my birthday. I've never liked my birthday. Growing up I had to watch other kids hand out party invitations and bring cupcakes to school while my mom acted like my birthday didn't exist.

Back in my room, I rip open the box. Inside there's a few small bags of potato chips, packs of gum, a box of snack cakes with candles taped to the top, colored pens, a couple wrapped packages, and three envelopes. I pop a piece of gum in my mouth, then open the wrapped gifts. Inside the first package are two long sleeve athletic shirts, one black and one white. The other package contains a pair of black running pants. It's exactly what I need for the colder weather. The sizes are even right.

Two of the envelopes have Frank's barely legible handwriting. I choke up just seeing it. I miss him so much. And knowing he went to all this trouble for my birthday causes that watery eye problem I can't seem to get under control.

The first envelope is a birthday card signed by both Frank and Ryan. It's a funny card about getting old with a picture of a wrinkly dog on the front. Inside is $50 cash and a note telling me to use it only for fun. The water escapes my eyes and runs down my cheek. It's too much money. I expected $10 or $15, not $50. Frank needs that money for his medical bills way more than I need it for my birthday. The other envelope contains $100 for expenses.

Just as I'm about to call Frank the phone rings.

"Happy birthday!" Frank and Ryan say it in unison.

"Thanks, guys." I wipe the tears off my face. "And thank you for all the gifts, but it was way too much."

"Nineteen is a big birthday," Ryan says. "It's your last year as a teenager. We couldn't cheap out on you."

"How do you like the gifts?" Frank asks. "You know how bad Ryan and I are with women's clothing. Do they fit?"

"I didn't try them on yet but you got the right sizes. I can't believe you two went shopping."

"Chloe helped me," Ryan confesses. "She's a runner, too. She said you'd want that stuff if you run in the winter. Something about how the fabric breathes. But I picked the colors. She wanted to get you pink shirts."

"Thank God you talked her out of that."

"Any plans for tonight?" Frank asks.

"No, not yet."

"Jade, I told you not to sit in your room."

"I know, but Harper has class on Thursday nights. I'll find something to do. Maybe I'll hang out with Garret." I regret saying it the second it slips out. Frank and Ryan don't know the whole story about Garret, but they know he's the reason for my depressed mood the past few weeks.

"You're seeing him again?" Frank's tone is more angry than concerned.

"We're not dating. We're just friends."

"It doesn't matter. I don't like that boy."

"You don't even know him."

"He hurt you," Ryan says. "You were miserable for weeks. And if he did it once, he'll do it again."

"Okay, let's change the subject. Thanks for the money but you really shouldn't have sent so much."

"Part of that money is only for fun," Frank reminds me.

"Yes, I know."

"I need to get to work," Ryan says, "but Happy Birthday, Jade. I'll call you later this week when I have more time to talk."

"Bye, Ryan." I hear the phone click as he hangs up.

"Jade, did you open the other envelope?" Frank asks.

"No, I forgot about it. Let me grab it." I reach over to my bed and pick up the long white envelope. "Okay. Got it. Should I open it?"

"I'm not sure. I wanted to talk . . ." Frank's voice trails off as my attention turns to the front of the envelope.

The phone almost drops from my hand when I see my mom's handwriting. Then it actually does hit the floor when I see what she's written. *To my sweet daughter, Jade. From your mother.* " I flip it over and written on the back over the envelope flap it says, *I will always love you, Jade.—Mom.*

"Jade? Are you still there?" I hear Frank's voice and pick up the phone.

"What the hell is this? Some type of sick joke? This isn't funny, Frank."

"It's real, Jade. It's a letter from your mother."

"Yeah, I can see that. But she's dead so how is this possible?"

"She wrote it when you were just a few weeks old. I'd already moved out of Iowa by then so she mailed it to me and said that if anything ever happened to her I was to give you that letter when you turned 19. When I moved in down the street from you I asked her if she still wanted me to hold on to it but she couldn't remember writing it. But she was pretty out of it by then."

"Why didn't you give this to me sooner? She's been dead for years."

"When she gave it to me she asked me to wait and I was respecting her wishes."

"I can't believe you had it all this time and never told me. Dammit, Frank. I'm really mad at you right now. And I hate being mad at you."

"I understand if you're mad, but your mother had her reasons for waiting and it wasn't my place to question that."

"Do you know what it says?"

"She just said it was a letter to you about her hopes and dreams for your future. Like I said, she wrote it right after you were born. It was one of those keepsake things she wanted you to have after you graduated high school. But then she wasn't here to give it to you."

"My mom had hopes and dreams for me? Yeah, right. You're thinking of someone else's mom."

"You don't have to open it if you don't want to." He waits for me to respond but I don't. "Just set it aside and if you decide that you never want to read it, that's fine. It's up to you."

"Yeah, okay."

"If you want to talk about it, call me. I'm always here for you."

"I know. And I didn't mean to yell at you. Thank you again for the gifts. And for remembering my birthday."

"I'll always remember. I wish I could be there with you to celebrate, but since I can't, you go out and have some fun tonight, okay? Promise me."

"I promise. Bye, Frank."

We hang up and I stare at the letter still stuck in my hand. Why would my mother write me a letter? When was she even sober enough to write this? Unless she wasn't drinking back then. I just assumed she was, but maybe she starting drinking later. The words she wrote on the outside don't sound like her at all. *My sweet daughter?* She never called me sweet. And on the back she writes that she loves me? She never once said those words to me, at least not that I can remember. I get up and shove the letter in my desk drawer. I can't deal with it right now. I'm not even sure I'll read it.

There's a couple short knocks on the door. "Jade? Are you in there?"

It's Garret. I haven't talked to him since our decision to attempt the friends' arrangement again.

I open the door. "Hey, Garret. What do you need?"

"I was just coming down to say hi. Can I come in?"

"Um, yeah, I guess." I wasn't expecting company and I definitely wasn't expecting Garret. We hadn't yet discussed the terms of this new friendship, like rules about stopping by unexpectedly.

"What's all this?" he asks, seeing the pile of stuff on my bed and the wrapping paper on the floor.

"It was for my birthday."

"Your birthday? When was your birthday?"

"It's today." I go over and pick the wrapping paper off the floor.

Garret stands in front of me. "Today is your birthday? Why didn't you tell me?"

"Why would I tell you?" I go around him and toss the paper in the trash. "It's just another day."

He blocks me again as I try to walk past him. "It's not just another day. It's your freaking birthday! Are you going out with Harper later?"

"No. She has class. I didn't tell her it's my birthday."

"Why didn't you tell her?"

I sigh. "Because I don't care that it's my birthday. It doesn't matter."

"It matters to me. And we're celebrating whether you like it or not."

"Garret, I really don't want to." I take a seat at my desk and open my biology book. "I'm just going to do some homework and go to bed."

He slams my book closed. "You are *not* doing homework on your birthday." He yanks me up from the chair. "I'm getting you out of here. It's only 6. We have all night. I'll take you to dinner, a movie, whatever you want." He pauses to think for a second. "I'll take you for pancakes at Al's. They serve them all day and we've missed all those Sundays. What do you think?"

"I think you've lost your mind. You're way too excited about this."

"Because it's your birthday. It's a celebration. And you're not spending it in your room doing homework."

I remember my promise to Frank. "Okay, I suppose I could go out for pancakes. But I'll pay for myself. Frank gave me birthday money."

"Al gives you a free meal on your birthday. You just have to show your driver's license."

"Really? That's awesome! You should have told me that before. I would have said yes right away."

He laughs. "I know another place that offers birthday freebies. We'll go there later tonight."

"What place?"

"It's a surprise. You ready to go?"

"Give me a few minutes to change clothes and do something with my hair."

"Okay. I'll be down in 10."

I walk him to the door. "You said you just came down here to say hi, not go out all night. Don't you have stuff you need to do?"

"This is way more important." He leans down and kisses my cheek. "It's your freaking birthday, Jade!"

His excitement over my birthday makes me laugh. It even puts me in a better mood. I decide to forget about my mom's letter. I'm not letting her ruin another birthday.

Garret takes me to the pancake house where I order the largest stack of pancakes on the menu. Then we go to the movies. I pick a teen horror film, Garret's least favorite genre. But it's October. It's horror movie season. And besides, he made me watch that romantic comedy.

After the movie, we go to the diner we went to when I first arrived on campus.

"Guess what you get free on your birthday?" he asks, as we're getting out of the car.

"The Boxcar whatever?"

"Jade! You ruined the surprise."

"You asked me! And it's the only thing I know on the menu since you never gave me a chance to look at it."

As we're eating the huge sundae, which I generously offered to share with him, his phone rings.

"Go ahead and answer it," I say, devouring the crumbled cookies.

"What do you want, Blake?" Garret leans back in the booth. "Yeah, I'll be there. But only if you keep your mouth shut." He looks at me. "It's her birthday. I'm out with her right now. You got a problem with that?" He listens. "Yeah. See you Friday." He sets his phone on the table.

"What was that about?" I ask.

"I made a deal with Blake. If I go to some parties with him, he'll stop telling my dad about us."

"I thought you weren't going to worry about your dad anymore."

"I'm not worrying about him. I'm just trying to make things easier for us. And things will definitely be easier if Blake stops talking to my dad."

"What about Ava?"

"She has a new boyfriend. She lost interest in me. She won't say anything." He leans forward again, grabbing his spoon and scooping some ice cream from the bowl. "So since you neglected to tell me that today was your birthday, I'll have to give you your present later. Is there anything you want or should I just surprise you?"

"No, don't get me anything. Really. This was plenty."

"You ate for free all night. I only paid for the movie. And it was bargain Thursday so I hardly spent any money."

"Gifts don't have to cost a lot, Garret."

"I know. But I like giving gifts and the movie doesn't count. I want to give you something."

"Then I'll let you spend $5. That's it."

"I can't buy anything for $5. That's nothing."

"That's your limit. If you can't make it work, then I don't want anything."

He nudges my foot under the table. "You're impossible. You know that, right?"

"I prefer to say I'm a challenge." I set my spoon down and push the bowl away. "I'm stuffed. You can have the rest."

He digs his spoon into the ice cream that remains on the bottom of the bowl. "You ate all the cookies."

"Because they're my favorite part. And it's my birthday."

"I know. I was just kidding. So you're 19 today?"

"Yeah. I'm kind of an old freshman."

"Me too. My birthday's in August. I guess I already told you that."

"What did you do for *your* birthday?"

"I went to Cabo for two weeks and learned to surf from this pro-surfer guy. And when I got back we had a big party at the house and I got the car."

"Is your birthday always like that?"

"They're all a little over the top. But it's not just me. Everyone around here has parties like that. Last year for Sierra's birthday, her parents paid $300,000 for her favorite band to come play a couple songs. That whole party had to have cost a million." He drops his spoon in the bowl. "I can't eat any more."

"It's getting late. We should go."

Back at campus, Garret walks me to my room and comes inside. "So I know it wasn't much, but did you at least have a little fun?"

"Yeah, I had a great time. Thanks for taking me out."

"I can't believe you were just going to sit here and do homework. Thank God I stopped by and took control of the situation."

I punch his arm. "You didn't take control. I'm the one who decided to go. And I almost told you no until you lured me in with the offer of free birthday food."

"Well, I was hoping my mere presence would convince you to go. When that didn't work, I had to pull out the birthday freebies." He smiles smugly. "I know how to get to you."

I roll my eyes. "Whatever."

"Do you want to watch a movie upstairs?"

"No, I think I'll go to bed. I have class early tomorrow."

"All right. See ya later." He gives me a kiss on the cheek and turns to leave.

"That was kind of lame," I say.

He turns around. "What was lame?"

"That kiss."

He looks offended. "What's that supposed to mean? We're friends, right? Nothing more?"

"Yeah, but it's my birthday. A birthday kiss has to be better than that. That was like a grandma kiss."

I've challenged him, knowing how much he loves a challenge. I'm sure I've confused him with my request, but I want him to kiss me. And I want a real kiss, not a friend kiss. I'm still committed to the friends-only agreement, but sometimes a girl just wants a damn kiss. Is that so wrong?

Garret stands there like he's unsure what to do. "So you're saying I can kiss you and you won't get mad? Even after—"

"Would you just kiss me before my birthday is over?"

He hesitates, then takes my face in both his hands and kisses me. It starts out as a gentle, sweet kiss and slowly moves into a deeper kiss that is so hot I find myself gripping the back of his shirt and pulling myself into him. Then, with his hands still cupped gently around my face, he ends with two soft, short kisses and pulls away. "Happy Birthday, Jade."

He's gone before I can critique the kiss. But it was great. It was beyond great. It was perfect. A perfect birthday kiss.

I'm sure Garret's upstairs wondering what the hell just happened. But let him wonder. He left me wondering what the hell happened when he told me to get lost a few weeks ago.

I clear my gifts off the bed and go over to the desk to put my envelopes of money away. When I open the drawer I see my mom's letter again. Part of me really wants to open it. But another part of me wants to burn it in the trash. Just having it suddenly appear like this makes me hate my mother even more. How dare she continue to haunt me from the grave. Isn't her voice in my head enough? Does she have to keep stepping in and destroying everything? I wish that Frank had waited to give it to me. If it weren't for that letter, this would have been my best birthday ever.

CHAPTER 19

Friday after class, I try out my new running pants and long sleeve t-shirt. The weather keeps changing from warm to cold and today it picked cold. I head outside and take the trail that leads into the woods. Yellow, orange, and red leaves cover the ground and the crunch of them under my feet almost sounds like popping fireworks. I alternate between steady running and sprints. The anger over my mother's letter still nags at me, but the steady running clears my head while the sprints burn off the anger.

When I get back to the residence hall, I feel empowered again. I refuse to let that letter take control over my emotions. I'm still on a high from Garret's kiss last night and that's the only emotion I want to feel right now.

I saw Garret at lunch and he was back to treating me like a friend, like the kiss never happened. But it's probably best if we keep the friends-only thing going. After what he did, part of me still isn't sure if I can trust him. And I'm still worried what his dad will do if he finds out I'm hanging out with Garret again.

What if he took my scholarship away? I'd have no way to pay for school.

"Jade, there you are." Harper slings her pink-sweater-covered arm around me as I walk down the hall. "We're going out tonight. You, me, and some other girls."

"I don't do the party scene. You know that, Harper." I wipe the sweat off my forehead. "I just ran. You might want to keep your distance."

She takes her arm away. "We're not going to a party. We're going to a nice restaurant for dinner."

"Why would we do that?"

"For your birthday. There's this great Italian place about 20 minutes from here. You like pasta, right?"

"Who told you it was my birthday? Garret?"

"Maybe," she says, smiling. "But don't get mad at him, Jade. You should've told me yourself."

"My birthday is over. I'm done celebrating." I open the door to my room and she follows me inside.

"You're going to dinner unless you already have plans. So do you?"

"No, I don't have any plans." I sit on the bed and yank my running shoes off. "So who else is going?"

"Katy, Rachel, Stephanie, and Madison." Harper's pink sweater is so bright it's blinding me. I wish she'd give the pink obsession a rest now and then.

"They all want to go out for my birthday? I don't really know them that well."

"What are you talking about? They eat with us all the time."

"They eat with you. They're not really *my* friends."

"They are, too. They like you. They think you're funny. And they'd invite you out more if you acted a little nicer to them."

"Nicer? I'm already nice to them."

"Yeah, but maybe you could talk to them more. You kind of ignore them and only talk to me when they're around. Anyway, we're leaving here at 6:30. And wear a dress because it's kind of a fancy place. I could do your hair if you want."

Harper's such a girly girl. She loves doing hair, makeup, nails—all that stuff. "Okay. If you have time, you can do my hair."

"Really?" She comes over and hugs me quick, keeping her distance from my sweaty body. "I didn't think you'd say yes. Come by my room in a hour and we'll get started."

She walks away, then turns back when she's halfway out the door. "Hey, what's up with you and Garret? Are you dating again?"

"No. We were never dating. We're just friends."

"He's so damn hot, Jade. I seriously don't know how you can just be friends with that guy. You sure you're not dating?"

I laugh. "Yeah. I think I would know that."

"Hmm. Okay. See ya."

I shower then let Harper do her magic on my hair. She has a gazillion hair tools, some of which look like medieval torture devices. She straightens my hair then curls it with giant rollers, making soft waves that look better than my hair's natural waves. Then I let her do my makeup because she insists I don't apply it right.

When she's done I put on my one and only dress and some sparkly earrings Harper let me borrow. As I'm leaving her room, she spritzes me with perfume.

Dinner is at a restaurant two towns over. It's a small place that overlooks a lake. It's very expensive and of course none of them will let me pay. Now that I know the other girls actually like me, I'm able to relax around them. I make a mental note to be nicer to them in the future. I could use a few more friends.

After dinner, three short, round Italian guys sing Happy Birthday to me and give me a cake. It's like I'm living someone else's life. Nobody's ever made such a big deal over my birthday.

We get back at 9:30 and Harper and her friends offer to skip the Friday night parties to hang out with me. But I insist they go. I know that's what they really want to do and I've had enough girl time for one night.

I go back to my room and when I open the door I notice a soft glow coming from the ceiling. I look up and see that it's covered in sparkly blue lights. I slowly walk inside unable to take my eyes off it. It's beautiful, like I'm looking up at the night sky.

"You like it?"

I turn back. Garret is leaning against the door frame.

"You did this?"

"I did." He comes inside and shuts the door.

"How did you get in here?"

"I have connections."

I look at him to explain.

"Jasmine let me in. When Harper told me she was taking you to dinner tonight, I took over your room for a couple hours. And no, I didn't go through your stuff."

He stands next to me and looks up at the ceiling as he casually puts his arm around my waist. It causes all kinds of sensations I probably shouldn't be feeling with someone who's just a friend. I glance over at him in his low-hung jeans and black t-shirt. His shirt is fitted and shows off his broad shoulders and lean abs. Harper's right. It's nearly impossible to be friends with a guy this hot.

He squeezes my waist. "You didn't answer me. Do you like it or not?"

"Yeah. I love it." More sensations fire off inside me as his hand slips down and rests on my hip.

"Good. Because I almost fell off the ladder getting that middle section tacked up." He points at the area above my bed where it looks like he tried to make some type of design with the lights.

"Why did you do all this?"

"It's your birthday gift. With your insane budget, I had to go to this store that sells everything for a dollar. These lights were so cheap they may not work for very long."

"I buy stuff at those stores all the time. I'm sure they'll last."

"I knew how much you liked mine, so I had to get you your own." He leans down and kisses my cheek. "Happy Birthday, Jade."

"Thanks." I look up at the sparkly lights again. "You see? You really can make someone happy with just a few dollars."

He turns to face me, placing both arms around my waist. "I made you happy? With these cheap ass lights?"

"Very happy. I love the lights. They'll make me happy every time I look at them."

He smiles. "It doesn't take much with you, does it, Jade?"

"Nope."

There's awkward silence. We're standing very close and his arms are still around me. Is he trying to test my willpower or something? He looks way too good. And he smells incredible. I feel like I should say something but I can't. I'm too busy trying to keep myself from kissing him.

Garret is staring at me. I'm wondering if I have marinara sauce on my face. Maybe it got on my dress. I glance down to check. He catches my chin with his finger and brings my face up to his. "You look amazing tonight, Jade."

"It's just a dress. You saw me wearing it at your parent's house."

"I know. And you looked nice then, too. But now you've got your hair like this and, I don't know, it's just different. Probably because you're not glaring at me from across the dinner table."

I laugh. "Yeah. That's probably it." He's still staring and it's making me self-conscious. I break free from his arms and go sit on the bed. "So you're going out with Blake tonight?"

"That's the plan." He sits down next to me. "But if you want me to stick around, I can skip the party and do something with him tomorrow instead."

"You should go since you told him you would."

"I guess, but I really don't want to hang out with him."

213

"Garret, you made a deal with the guy."

"And I shouldn't have had to. He should keep his mouth shut if he thinks we're friends." Garret kicks off his shoes and scoots behind me to lie down on the bed. "Hey, check this out."

Seriously? Is he trying to test every ounce of self control I have? He wants me to lie next to him on the bed under the sparkly blue lights? Like we're just innocently checking them out? Damn, he's good. Very smooth. He's clearly worked these tricks on girls before. And like the girls before me, I totally fall for it. But at least I'm aware of what he's doing. I give myself points for that.

I lie next to him, keeping a safe distance between us. "It's even better from this view."

"See that section right there?" He slides closer and points to the area above us. "I wanted to make a constellation with the lights but I ran out of time."

When he puts his arm down, we're so close the sides of our bodies are touching. I roll on my side facing him and putting some distance between us again. "You should really get going."

He turns on his side as well and removes the distance I created. He rests his hand on my hip, making my heart pound faster. "Are you trying to get rid of me, Jade?"

"No, but you have to go to that party with Blake. And I should get to sleep."

He leans in so close I can feel his breath. He lowers his voice. "It's not even 10."

"Really? It seems later." My heart's now beating out of my chest. I know I should back away but I can't do it. I keep imagining that kiss from last night and I just want him to kiss me again and end this torture. "It's probably 11 by now."

"It's 9:40. I can see the clock from here." His eyes never left mine. I'm sure he didn't check the clock. "So are you sure you want me to leave?" He gives me that cocky smile which I find so damn irresistible.

"Positive," I say in a tone that's not at all convincing.

He's so close to me now that I'm sure he's going to kiss me. I shut my eyes, preparing for it.

"Okay. Then I'll leave." The bed shakes as I feel him jump up. "I'll see you on Sunday."

I open my eyes and find him almost at the door.

"Sunday?" I get up from the bed, feeling the heat in my cheeks, which I'm sure are bright red.

"Pancakes. We're still going right?"

"Well, yeah. But what about tomorrow?"

"What about it?"

"Don't you want to do something?" I can't stop staring at his lips, wishing he'd just freaking kiss me.

"What do you have in mind?"

"I don't know. I haven't really thought about it."

"Well, think about it and if you decide you want to do something, you know where to find me. Goodnight, Jade."

Then he just walks out. Talk about mixed signals. What the hell was that? He touches me, compliments me, and gets all close like that and then doesn't even kiss me?

I can't be mad at him because it's what I wanted. He was being respectful of my friends-only request, waiting for me to decide when to take things farther. And tonight, I was very close to taking things farther. A lot farther.

We don't meet up again until Sunday morning. Garret tells me about the party Friday night. He says that Blake was so drunk that he didn't even remember him being there. And yet the jerk insists that Garret go to these parties. I guess Blake just wants to make sure Garret isn't hanging out with me. I know Blake hates me for taking up Garret's time and especially for cutting Garret's alcohol intake to basically zero. Even when Garret goes to these parties, he hasn't been drinking, which totally pisses Blake off.

Over the next few days and the weeks that follow, Garret and I become even better friends. On the weekdays we watch TV in his room, go for a run, have meals together, or just sit and talk. On the weekends Garret goes out on Friday nights, usually to a party with Blake, and on Saturday nights we do something together. Sundays are still pancakes followed by Garret's football game with the guys. So far, the arrangement seems to be keeping Blake, Ava, and anyone else who's watching us, quiet. We haven't had any unexpected visits from Garret's dad.

We've managed to keep our just-friends status going even though our attraction to each other is off the charts. Harper says she can feel it whenever she's around us. She keeps telling me to move out of the friend territory and I keep telling her I'm not ready for that, but I think I *am* ready for that. Actually I know I am.

But we still have the problem of Garret's family. Garret keeps telling me he's done taking orders from his dad, but then he goes along with the fake girlfriend thing. And he's doing all he can to make sure his dad doesn't find about us. So I don't need a psychic to predict where this is headed. It's clear that Garret and I will never be a couple. At least not a real couple. We can hang out and maybe even move past the friend stage, but it will always be in secret.

Knowing all this, I should probably keep my distance from Garret. I should spend less time with him and focus all my attention on school. But I can't do it. The more I get to know him, the more I want to be with him.

On the second to last Saturday of October, Garret and I plan a movie night in his room, which we haven't done for a couple weeks. It's cold and rainy and a good night to stay inside. We order Chinese food from a new place that just opened up close to campus.

"What are we watching?" I grab two sodas from the fridge.

"A sports movie." He holds up a movie that has a football player on the cover.

"Ugh. Really? Do I get a say in this?"

"It's a good movie. And it's football season. It's the perfect time to watch it."

"All right. Give it here." I take the movie from him. "The delivery guy's probably downstairs. You should go get the food."

When he's back we take our food and sit in the giant bean bag chair. I start the movie. A cartoon dog in a detective uniform appears on the TV.

Garret moans. "No freaking way I'm watching this again."

I tilt my head. "But, Garret, you love this one. It's your favorite."

He jumps up and searches the cardboard box for the football movie. "Where is it?"

"I don't know. Maybe it fell into the heating vent."

He stops searching. "The what? Jade, what did you do with it?"

My eyes remain on my chopsticks as I use them to pick up a chunk of sauce-coated chicken. "I don't know what you're talking about."

He snatches the Chinese food carton from me and sets it on the table. Then he kneels over me, putting his arms on each side of me so I can't move. "Where's the movie, Jade?"

"It's in the box."

He smiles. "It's not in the box. I just looked."

I smile back. "Maybe under the bed?"

He glances over there. "Nope. Try again."

"I really can't remember," I say innocently.

His hands start tickling my sides. I didn't think I was ticklish until now. Between the tickling and the howling dog sounds coming from the TV I can't stop laughing. I've never laughed that hard. It's making my stomach muscles tense up so much that I think I'm getting an ab workout.

"Okay. I'll tell you." I can barely get the words out.

He doesn't stop the tickling. "I'm waiting."

"The box. I swear."

"I already looked in there."

"Just let me up."

He moves aside. I get up and pick the movie up from behind the box.

"It was sitting on the floor *next* to the box." I plop back down on the chair, trying to catch my breath. "Here." I hand it to him.

"See? Was that so hard? A simple answer would have been so much easier."

"Yeah. But not as fun." I smile.

He looks at me, figuring out what that means. But he doesn't take the bait.

"You want your food back now?" he asks.

"No. I need a minute to breathe. That was a workout."

The cartoon dogs start howling again. I burst out laughing. That howling is too damn funny.

Garret reaches over me for the remote and turns the TV off. He tosses the remote on the floor and pins me to the chair again. "Jade, are you making fun of my movie?"

"No." It comes out as a laugh. "I love it."

He's working hard to hold back his own laughter. "Jade?"

"Garret?" I say in the same tone.

"You're a real pain in the ass sometimes."

"Just sometimes? I'll have to work on that."

Our eyes meet and I see that look on his face. He wants to kiss me but won't because of our strict friend agreement. To hell with the agreement. I can't take it anymore. I reach up to pull him toward me but he's already closed the distance between us and moved in for the kiss.

His lips just barely touch mine, waiting for my response. I kiss him back, making it clear that I want this. He shifts his body so that he's sitting next to me, taking me with him so that I'm on top of him. I straddle him and see a slight smile as he reaches behind my head and brings me in for a kiss. It's a slow, deep, intense kiss that is quickly moving us out of the friend category. His other hand reaches around my back and presses me into him.

It's just like that time in the pool. Only this time I won't let the voices interfere. I can't. I like this way too much and I won't let her ruin it for me.

CHAPTER 20

After several minutes I wonder why Garret's not taking this any farther. I love what he's doing, but I'm dying for more and he won't even go to second base. I guide his hand under the hem of my shirt and place it at the side of my waist, but he just leaves it there. He doesn't even attempt to make a move.

Finally I pull away from the kiss. "What's wrong?"

"What do you mean?"

"I'm not saying to go all the way, but we can do more than this."

"I didn't think I should after what happened, you know, the last time."

I look down. "Oh. Well, don't worry about that. I'm fine."

His hand moves up to the side of my face, brushing my hair aside. "Something happened that night in the pool and it scared me. I felt like I hurt you or something. You started screaming and kicking me."

"I wasn't screaming." Or was I? I don't remember screaming. At least not out loud.

"Yes, you were." He says it softly. "You said that you weren't me. I didn't know what it meant, but I assumed you were mad at me for touching you."

I'm not you. I'll never be you. I hear the words in my head. They're the words I say all the time.

"I wasn't talking to you. Or about you. That's not what I meant."

"Then who were you talking to?"

"I can't say."

"Then tell me what happened that night. And why it happened again when I found you in my room that morning. You got so freaked out when I joked about leaving the TV on."

All of a sudden tears are forming and despite my best efforts I can't make them disappear. My throat gets dry and I get this heavy feeling in my chest. I move off him and sit beside him on the bean bag chair.

"I don't want to talk about it. It won't happen again, okay?" A few tears run down my face before I can catch them.

Garret's watching me and spots the tears. "Shit!" He quickly takes me in his arms and pulls me into his chest. "Jade, I'm sorry. I didn't mean to make you cry. I was just trying to understand."

The tears come faster no matter what I do to make them stop. I bury my head in his shirt so he can't see my face.

"Jade, talk to me."

I can't speak. If I do, my voice will crack or be shaky and he'll know that I can't get this crying under control. And guys hate crying. *I* hate crying. So the fact that I'm doing this right

222

now is really pissing me off. A few minutes pass and the crying finally stops.

"Are you okay?" He gently lifts my chin up and I notice his shirt is wet from my tears.

"Yes. I'm fine." I sit up and wipe my face. "Sorry I messed up your shirt."

"I don't give a shit about the shirt. And you're not fine. Now tell me what's wrong."

"Nothing's wrong." My sadness turns to anger as I realize that I've shown him way too much of myself. "Just forget it."

"We're friends, Jade, and I don't like seeing you like this."

"Like what? Crying? I'm not allowed to cry?"

"It's more than that. It's something else. There's something you're not telling me. Just talk to me. Maybe I can help."

"You can't help, Garret. This is just something I have to deal with alone." I almost cry again saying the word. Alone. It describes how I feel all the time, because I can't tell anyone about this. And I'm so tired of feeling alone.

He rests my head back on his chest, then grabs a blanket sitting next to the bean bag chair and lays it over us.

We remain there in silence. And I wonder why I have to deal with this alone. Why I can't just talk to Garret about this. If I had to pick someone to share this with, it would be him over anyone else.

"It was my mother," I say barely above a whisper.

"What?" He moves my hair off my face. "Did you say something?"

"My mom." I say it louder. "I was talking to my mom."

There's awkward silence. I'm sure he thinks I'm deranged. I shouldn't have told him.

"Didn't your mom die?" he asks cautiously.

"Yes, but sometimes I still hear her."

"You mean like in your head," he confirms.

"Yes." Now he'll definitely think I'm crazy. "It started after she died."

"I hear my mom in my head sometimes, too. It's just the memory of her."

"This is more than a memory. It's like she's still alive, screaming at me. Telling me what a horrible person I am and how I'm going to screw everything up, just like she did. And I can't make it stop."

"Look at me, Jade." He waits for me to lift my eyes to his. "You *can* make it stop. You're incredibly strong. You're stronger than anyone I know. Look what you came from and look what you did with your life. You don't have to listen to her. You can shut her out."

"I can't. I've tried."

"Then I'll work on it with you."

"And how are you going to do that?"

"I don't know. Let me think about it and get back to you."

His offer makes me smile. His voice has so much sincerity, like he really does believe he can help.

I'm both amazed and confused at how Garret's responding to this. I thought for sure he would've called me a lunatic and kicked me out of his room by now.

"Can I ask you something about your mom?"

I nod.

"Did she hurt you? Like physically hurt you?"

"Sometimes. If I made her mad. So I learned not to make her mad. Or I'd get out of the house when she started to get angry. She got angry a lot."

"I'm sorry, Jade. I know that doesn't help, but I don't know what else to say."

"I don't want you to feel sorry for me. Like you said, I'm strong. I got through the hell of living with her all those years. And I'll get over whatever's going on now. I don't know why I broke down like that. It's just that I really like you and when you wouldn't even touch me it was like she was here again, controlling my life. Taking away everything I want. I keep trying to move on and pretend that she never existed, but I guess I need to try harder."

"Maybe that's the problem. You're trying to run from the past when maybe you need to face it."

"No, thanks. I lived it. I don't need to remember it."

"But dealing with the past can help you move forward. At least it did for me." He stops and I get ready to ask what he means but then he continues. "When my mom died, I refused to accept it. I kept thinking she would just come home one day. I'd wait at school, looking for her car to pick me up. I had dreams that she was still alive. Finally my dad made me see a counselor and after talking to the guy I realized that I couldn't say goodbye to my mom until I faced the fact that I was so damn pissed at her for leaving me. I hated her for it. And I hated myself for feeling that way. Because it wasn't her fault. She didn't want to leave. Eventually I figured out that I wasn't angry at her at all. I was angry that the plane crash even happened and that everything changed from that point forward. Once I accepted that, I could finally move on." He stops. "You don't want to hear this, do you?"

"I *do* want to hear it. And I've been listening to everything you said. But your situation is different than mine."

"Yeah, but what I'm trying to tell you is that to get past this you can't keep running from it. You have to deal with it."

"I'm not running from it! I just don't want to think about it!"

He lowers his voice. "It was just an idea, Jade. I was just trying to help."

"I know. And I'm sorry. I didn't mean to yell at you. I'll think about it, okay?" I run my hand along his shirt trying to smooth the wrinkles I created with my tears. "Garret, will you do something for me?"

"Of course." He takes my hand off his shirt and holds it in his.

"Don't treat me differently now that I've told you this. I'm not fragile. I'm not going to break. And I need you to promise you won't tell anyone what I told you tonight. Only you and Ryan know this about me. I haven't even told Frank."

"I won't tell anyone."

"Good. Now can we watch a movie and eat our cold Chinese food?"

He leans in and kisses my cheek.

"What was that for?"

"For trusting me enough to tell me." He gets up. "Okay, we're watching the football movie. I might even make you watch it twice after you hid it like that."

The rest of the night he acts completely normal, which is just what I wanted. He doesn't kiss me again and I wonder if he ever will. What I told him probably totally freaked him out. No guy wants to date a girl who still hears her dead mother's voice in her head. But at least he listened and he seemed to actually care, which is more than I expected.

Surprisingly, things aren't weird at all between Garret and me after that night. Sunday we go out for our usual breakfast and the rest of the week goes on as normal. He doesn't bring up what happened and neither do I. But I do think about what he said. Facing the past may be the only way to make the voices go away. Ignoring it sure hasn't gotten me anywhere. It's only made it worse.

Friday night I decide it's time to open the letter that's been sitting untouched in my desk drawer since my birthday. I'm not afraid of it anymore. Why should I be? Frank said it's just my mother's hopes and dreams for me. Coming from her, that should be comical.

Garret is at a house party a few blocks from campus. Halloween is tomorrow so it's a costume party. Earlier I saw some girls leaving in their costumes, which looked more like lingerie. But apparently if you add a witch's hat or strap on some angel wings, it's a costume. Harper wore a sexy bunny costume, pink of course.

I think the entire college went to that party or at least everyone in my building. It's completely quiet. I don't even hear footsteps from the floor above. Garret asked me to go with him tonight, but I still have no interest in parties, especially this one, which will be packed with people.

Even though I decided to open the letter, I've been avoiding it. Now it's 9 and I feel like I should just get it over with. I sit on my bed staring at the handwriting on the front, which still freaks me out. It's like my mother is truly visiting me from the grave.

I tear open the envelope and inside is a full sheet, front and back, of my mother's handwriting.

Jade, If you're reading this it means that you're 19 years old, which doesn't seem possible as I look at you now, my three-week-old baby girl sleeping soundly in your crib. My little Jade, with your beautiful green eyes.

My mother gave me a jade necklace for my 13th birthday and I thought it was the most beautiful stone I'd ever seen. When your little eyes looked up at me for the first time, I knew that Jade would be your name.

I stop to examine the handwriting again. It's definitely my mother's but this doesn't even sound like her. It's like someone else wrote it. Someone who actually cared about me. I continue reading.

If I still had that necklace, it would be yours now. But I no longer have it. I lost it on the night that I'm going to tell you about. I wish I didn't have to tell you any of this, but you have to know. Because if you're reading this, then something bad has happened to me and I'm no longer there to tell you the truth."

What does she mean by 'something bad'? It almost sounds like she's blaming someone else for what happened to her, which isn't possible. Her overdose was her own doing. I keep reading.

"Last year, when I was still in college, I got a job as an intern for one of the candidates for the presidential nomination. Caucus season was in full

swing and I was so excited to be part of it. When I wasn't in class, I worked day and night with the other interns at the campaign headquarters.

One night we were helping out at a speech and I met a man there— about ten years older than me and very attractive. He worked on the campaign in a different state and was in Des Moines for the speech. We started talking and he asked me to dinner and I said yes. But he never took me to dinner. Instead he drove me outside of town and parked near a cornfield. It was dark and cold and I was so scared because part of me knew what he was about to do. He proceeded to do what I thought he would and when he was done, he left me there on the side of the road in the freezing cold. I was in such bad shape I thought for sure I would die there, but I woke up the next day in the hospital. The police asked me questions and I told them who did this to me. They said that no person matching that name or description worked for the campaign. They said what happened to me was a random crime. But I knew who did this to me and I refused to let him get away with what he'd done.

A friend of mine worked at the newspaper and I told him what happened but he couldn't run a story about it because there was no evidence to prove it. The next night I got a call from someone telling me that if I repeated my story to anyone that something bad would happen to my parents. It scared me but I didn't believe it. That week I began seeing a counselor at my college. I told her what happened. A few days later, there was a gas explosion at my parents' house, killing both of them. I knew it wasn't an accident. When I went for my next counseling session, the woman accused me of lying. She said I made the whole story up. And then she refused to see me.

The man who did this to me was determined to silence anyone who knew what really happened. Somehow he was able to silence the police, the hospital staff, my counselor—anyone who knew the truth. But he knew my parents wouldn't keep his secret so he killed them. I thought for sure he'd kill me, too, but for some reason he left me alone and I don't know why. Maybe he figured his threats were enough to keep me quiet.

I never spoke of the incident again. But out of that horrible night came the best thing that ever happened to me. You, Jade. I learned I was pregnant with you two months after this happened. I was so devastated after your grandparents died, but then I learned about you and it was like a miracle. I was actually feeling hopeful again. Then he called. Your father. He somehow found out. He ordered me to take care of it saying he would have money sent. I told him I would, but I never did. I dropped out of college and went to live with a friend in a small town just south of here. The past few months I haven't left the house. I've been hiding out until you were born.

Just yesterday, I heard from him again. He knows about you. I told him I'd never tell my story if he agreed to leave us alone. And surprisingly he agreed. I don't know if he'll really leave us alone, but I can't worry about it now because I have to take care of you. You're all I have, Jade, and I'm being the best mother I can. I'm seeing a counselor at the free mental health clinic downtown. There's a doctor there and he gave me medication to help with my depression and anxiety. I'm working so hard to get past this, Jade.

I know you want to know who this man is but I can't tell you. I promised him I never would and I have to keep that promise. I'm only telling you this because someday he might try to contact you. Maybe he'd pretend he just found out about you or tell you he wants to be part of your life. Be a father. I don't know why he would do that, but there's always that chance, especially if I'm gone. So I wanted you to know the truth about this man. If he ever shows up, don't believe anything he says. Stay away from him. He's dangerous and although I don't think he would ever harm you, I can't be sure given what he's already done. You're probably living on your own now and I need you to be safe.

I'm so sorry I'm no longer there for you. I hope I was a good mother to you until my passing. You're all that I care about and the only thing that matters in my life. I love you, Jade, with all my heart.——Mom

CHAPTER 21

My head feels dizzy and I have a sudden urge to throw up. I toss the letter on the floor and sprint down the hall to the bathroom. After I get sick I hang my face over the sink and splash cold water on it. I can't stop shaking. I'm not sure if it's from the freezing cold water or the shock from what I just read.

It can't be real. The letter has to be some sick twisted joke my mother is playing on me. Now she's telling me I'm the product of a rape? The one night stand story wasn't bad enough? And she thinks my own father might try to harm me?

I hurry back to my room and search for a towel. As I'm drying my face, I see the letter still there on the floor and I'm tempted to tear it into a million pieces.

My mind is spinning as I think back to the few things my mom told me about her past. She did say she worked on a political campaign back in college, but she never went into details about it. And I remember her telling me about the small town she lived in before I was born. The one and only time I asked her about my grandparents, she went hysterical. She started throwing things and told me never to ask again. I was only 5. When I asked Frank about it years later, he told me they died in a house fire. I guess an explosion is similar to a fire.

Frank! He would know if any of this was true. I race to the phone. My fingers are shaking so much that I keep pressing the wrong buttons. After the third attempt, I get the number right. It rings and rings but nobody answers. Where the hell is Frank? He never leaves the house. Now when I really need to talk to him, he's not home?

Even though I don't want to, I force myself to read the letter again. And one more time after that. It was definitely written a long time ago. The mom I knew wasn't coherent enough to put multiple sentences together on paper like that. Plus, she would never say I was all she cared about or anything like that.

What if it was all true? What if my mom became addicted to alcohol and pills because of what happened to her? Maybe my father threatened her again. Maybe it was all too much and she couldn't deal with it. Just like I can't deal with stuff. We're exactly alike that way. But the shitty stuff I've had to deal with isn't even close to being as bad as what she's written here. I don't know what I would do if something like this happened to me. I'd probably turn to alcohol and pills, too.

I call Frank again. Still no answer. I have to talk to someone and the only person I can talk to about this is Garret. I throw on my coat and go outside. I run to the main road that goes into town. The road is dark and I could easily be hit by a car but I have to get to Garret. I turn down a side street and from a block away I can see the lights and hear the noise coming from the party.

I finally reach the house, sweaty and out of breath. The party is so crowded that people have spilled out onto the lawn, which is littered in red plastic cups. Most of the girls are wearing Halloween costumes and the guys are dressed normal. People are making out on the front porch and one couple is blocking the front door. I push them aside but they're too drunk to notice or care.

Inside the house, the music is blaring and the smell of sweat, perfume, and beer permeates the air. The place is packed. I squeeze between people as I make my way through the room, searching for Garret.

"Look who's here." I feel a heavy arm drape across my shoulder and smell that disgusting woodsy cologne. "What's up, Ohio? You look like you could use a drink."

I notice that we're standing right next to the bar, which explains why Blake's there. He's completely wasted and reeks of alcohol.

"I need to find Garret. Have you seen him?" I have to yell to be heard above the music.

Blake leans down near my ear and yells back. "He's busy. You like vodka, Ohio?"

I back away and shove his arm off me. "What do you mean he's busy? Is he here?"

"Yeah, he's here."

"Then where is he? I need to talk to him, Blake. It's important."

"Get in line, sweetheart." He points to a closed door on the other side of the room.

"What's that supposed to mean?"

"Garret's in the boom boom room." He laughs as he thrusts his hips at me.

"No, he's not. Tell me where he's really at."

"Go in there and see for yourself. He's in there with Ava. I don't think Ava's that hot, but shit, the guy's gotta get it from somewhere because he's not gettin' it in Ohio." Blake laughs so hard he starts coughing, then grabs a bottle of vodka and takes a drink.

"You're so disgusting. Just tell me where he—"

The door to the room Blake was pointing at opens and Garret walks out followed by Ava.

I'm sure my heart has stopped because I can no longer feel it beating. I'm too overwhelmed by shock, hurt, loss, betrayal, and every other horrible emotion. Even if Garret and I aren't officially dating, I never would've guessed he'd be sleeping with Ava. He hates Ava. He told me he can't stand even being around her and yet he took her in that room. So was he just lying to me? Have they been sleeping together this whole time? He promised me he wouldn't lie anymore. He said he wouldn't keep stuff from me. And I believed him. I confided in him. I told him things. I trusted him.

"See? I told you, Ohio. Need a drink now?"

With my eyes still on Garret, I grab the vodka bottle that Blake is holding out in front of me. I lift it to my lips and tilt my head back. It burns like fire as it moves down my throat. But for that brief moment, I don't feel any other pain. I take another big gulp. It burns again.

When I bring the bottle down, I see Blake out of the side of my eye, waving over at Garret and pointing at me as he laughs. I catch Garret's eye across the room. He spots the bottle in my hand and I see his mouth saying my name, his eyes frantic. He starts pushing his way through the crowd. I shove my way to the outside, drop the vodka bottle, and run as fast as I can back to campus.

It's all too much. My mom's letter. Garret with Ava. Drinking for the first time. I don't understand any of it.

When I'm back in my room I rip off my coat, shirt, and jeans and put on my running shoes, shorts, and a t-shirt. I sprint to the track at the edge of campus.

I need to run.

The lines on the track are like a map telling me where to go. I follow their orderly path, my arms and legs moving in a rhythmic pattern. My body repeats the motion effortlessly, leaving my mind to replay what just happened.

I see a girl at a party. She's drinking. She never drinks. Ever. But there were no other options. It was history repeating itself. Like the script had already been written and she just had to let the scene play out. For 18 years, she promised herself this would never happen. And then it did. She lost all control within a matter of seconds.

That girl was someone else. I will never be her. And I will never be her mother. I refuse.

My legs take longer, quicker strides as I become aware of my body again. I pump my arms because I'm not going fast enough. I still feel all of it. The confusion. The rage. The pain. And I just want it to go away.

The cold night air clings to my skin, cooling the sweat and sending an icy chill through me. My arms and legs ache and my lungs burn from inhaling the frigid air. But I keep going. Because I like feeling this pain. I understand it. And it keeps my mind off the pain that I can't understand.

A drop of rain hits my face. Then two, then three. Soon rain pours from the sky, stinging my skin.

"Jade, what the hell are you doing out here? I've been looking everywhere for you! Jade!"

It's Garret, the boy who made the girl live out that scene at the party. The scene that was never supposed to happen.

My eyes remain on the lines in front of me and I run past him like he's not even there.

"Jade, stop! Wait!"

I make another loop around the track as he continues to call out my name. As I approach him again, he moves into my lane and I veer to avoid him.

There's a sharp tug on the back of my shirt and I stumble forward to a stop. I'm gasping for breath as Garret turns me around and holds me against him so tight I can't move despite my efforts to break free.

"Stop." He says it quietly now as he presses my head against his chest. "Just stop running."

I give up trying to fight him and let my body collapse into his.

A minute ago I never wanted to see him again, but now I don't want him to let me go.

"Tell me what's wrong," he says. "If it's something I did, I'm sorry. I'll fix it."

The cold rain continues to pour down in a steady stream. My shorts and shirt feel heavy against my skin and I shiver as the wind blows around us.

He runs his hand along my arm. "What are you doing out here? It's freezing and you're soaking wet. Let's go inside."

My legs aren't ready to move. My entire body is aching, leaving my emotions numb, just the way I want them.

"Jade, talk to me."

I look up and see him watching me, waiting for some kind of answer. Before he can speak again, I reach up and press my lips to his. I shouldn't be kissing him so I don't understand why I'm doing this. But I don't understand anything right now.

Garret gently pulls away. "Tell me what's going on. Why are you out here? Why were you at the party? And why were you drinking?" His voice is filled with so much worry and so much concern. After seeing him at the party I don't know why he even cares. But I know he does. I can feel it and I can see it in his face and it pisses me off. I don't want him to care about me. Not now. Now after what he did.

I push away but his arms tighten around me. I won't look at him. Because when I do all I see is the image of him coming out of that room. With her. And then I see the vodka bottle and it reminds me of my mom and that letter she wrote.

It's too much. It's too many emotions. I want the numbness back.

The rain continues to pour and I shiver again.

"We're going inside." Garret's tone is forceful. He finally lets me go but grabs my hand, pulling on me to go with him. "Jade, come on. I'm not leaving here without you."

My mind is still racing, trying to make sense of things that make no sense at all.

When I don't move, he picks me up and carries me up the hill to our dorm.

He takes me to his room and wraps towels around my soaking body, sitting me down on his bed. I'm shivering and my teeth are chattering. He takes a blanket from his closet and covers me with it. Then he kneels down in front of me and holds my ice cold hands between his warm ones.

"What happened, Jade?" He sounds even more concerned, desperate to help. "What's going on?"

"My mom." I find it hard to talk with the shivering. "She was raped. He almost killed her."

I keep my head down, not wanting to see his reaction. I'm not sure why I'm telling him this. I shouldn't even be speaking to him after what I saw at the party.

"What are you talking about?"

"She left me a letter. She was raped. That's why I'm here."

"What letter? I don't understand what you're saying. Where did you get this letter?"

"It doesn't matter." I finally look at him. "That's why she hated me, Garret."

He gets up on the bed and forces me into his arms. "She didn't hate you, Jade."

"She did. It all makes sense now. I was a constant reminder of what he did to her. And she hated me for it. That's why she drank and took pills." Saying it out loud, my life is finally beginning to make sense.

My shivering continues. Garret removes the blanket and wet towels from me. "Let's go to your room and get some dry clothes."

"I can't go down there right now. I'll read the letter again and I can't do that."

"You can't sit here in wet clothes." He goes over to his drawer and takes out sweatpants and a sweatshirt, then holds them out in front of me. "Put these on."

I remain seated on the bed, staring at the blank TV screen.

"Jade, come on." He pulls me up to standing. "I'll turn around while you change. You need to get these wet clothes off."

I don't move. I'm not even really listening to him. My mind is too busy with a million other thoughts.

Garret sighs and walks behind me. He peels my wet t-shirt and sports bra off and slips the sweatshirt on. It's so big it goes to my knees and hides my hands.

He stands in front of me again and holds out the pants. "Now put these on."

"I don't need those."

"You'll never warm up in wet clothes." He waits while I stand there shivering. "If you don't do it, I'll do it myself."

I don't move. I'm so cold and my legs are so tired that putting those pants on is far too much effort.

"Fine." He reaches under the long sweatshirt, being careful not to let it ride up so he doesn't see too much. He slides my shorts and underwear off. I don't even care that he's undressing me. It's the least of my concerns. Besides, I'm sure he just saw Ava naked and has no interest in seeing me that way. He puts

240

the sweatpants on me, one leg at a time but they're so big he has to hold them up as he walks me to his bed.

The dry clothes feel good but I'm still cold. I get under the covers and he tucks me in, putting extra blankets on top. I close my eyes and hear Garret taking his own wet clothes off and putting dry ones on. Then he gets into bed and pulls my body against his, keeping his arm around my middle.

We lie there quietly for a few minutes and his warmth finally stops my shivering.

My thoughts return to the party.

"Are you dating Ava?" I ask him so quietly I'm not even sure he heard.

He sits up slightly and moves the blanket away from my face. "Ava?"

"I saw you in that room with her. Blake said it's where people go to, you know."

"No! Jade, you know I'd never do anything with her. I was just asking her if she'd said anything to my dad. The music was so loud I couldn't hear her so we went in that room. Did you really think we were doing something? Is that why you ran out of there like that?"

"Frank wasn't home. I had to talk to you. I don't have anyone else. And then I saw you in there with her."

"Nothing happened. I swear. You should never listen to Blake. So is that why you were drinking?"

"I lost control. I never lose control. But that drink took everything I was feeling away. I guess that's why she drank. I get it now."

"Jade." He lies down and rests his head against mine. "You need to stop trying to make the feelings go away and just feel them."

He leaves a kiss below my ear and whispers something, but I don't hear him. I'm so tired. And now that I'm warm, I drift off to sleep.

CHAPTER 22

Loud noises in the hallway wake me up. People are stumbling back from their night out, laughing and banging into doors. Garret's body is nestled close to mine, my back against his chest and his arm around my waist. I lift my head to read the clock. 3:30.

"I should go," I whisper.

He tightens his hold on me. "Just go to sleep, Jade."

I don't argue with him because I want to stay. I just wasn't sure if he wanted me to.

As we lie there, I realize that I've never felt this close to another person, not just in the physical sense but in every way. And that scares me. Just the idea of Garret being with Ava sent me over the edge. I lost control. That's why I keep people far away. Caring about someone the way I care about Garret screws with my judgment. I no longer think rationally. But I'm not sure what to do about it.

"Hey." I hear Garret's voice and open my eyes to see him lying there facing me. "Did you get some sleep?"

Light is filtering through the curtains. "What time is it?"

"It's 9. You can sleep some more if you want. I'm going to take a shower. I just wanted to let you know in case you woke up and I wasn't here."

I sit up on my elbows. "Why would I care if you weren't here?"

He kisses my cheek. "Because you'd miss me. That's why."

I smile and turn away from him. "I probably wouldn't have even noticed you were gone."

He turns me back toward him. "You'd notice. You'd at least wonder where your portable heater went. Don't think I didn't know you were just using me for my body last night."

"Damn, you're on to me. But it worked. I stopped shivering. I'm actually kind of hot now." I kick the blanket off and shove the giant sleeves of his sweatshirt up. They fall right back down.

"You look ridiculous in my clothes." He starts feeling for my waist. "I can't even find you in there."

"I like these sweats. They're really soft. I think I might keep them."

"No way! Those are my favorite."

"Then I'm definitely keeping them. You can come visit them downstairs."

"Sorry, but you're not getting them. Besides, they're gray. They're not even your color."

"Yeah, that's true. All right, you can have them back."

He smiles. "That was easy. Guess you're not much of a fighter first thing in the morning. I'll have to remember that." He gets up. "I'll only be a few minutes. Don't go anywhere."

While he's in the bathroom I stare up at the blue lights hanging from his ceiling. I just want to stay in his room all day, sleeping in his warm bed and comfy sweats. But I can't. I have to call Frank and deal with what was in that letter. Or maybe I should pretend I never read it. I could rip it up or burn it, act like it never existed.

I spot the remote on the floor and reach down to get it. I turn the TV on.

". . . live from Des Moines, Iowa, today where we'll be interviewing local residents about their feelings toward the current presidential hopefuls visiting their state." A white-haired old man is speaking. He's standing downtown Des Moines bundled up in a long coat and scarf, looking like he's freezing to death. Poor guy. Why do they make these reporters stand outside like that? Last time I talked to Frank he'd said it was like winter already in Iowa and that they'd already had a snowstorm.

"What are you watching?" Garret comes back, bare-chested and wearing only a towel on the bottom half. He glances over at the TV. "Do you follow politics?"

"No. I hate politics. I was only watching because they're in Des Moines. It's caucus time, the only time Iowa makes the news."

He grabs some clothes from his drawer. "My dad is obsessed with politics. He spends a fortune supporting those campaigns. I don't even want to know what he's getting in return."

"What do you mean?"

"That political shit is all bribes and corruption. And my dad's there waiting with an open bank account along with every

245

other person with money." Garret turns to the TV where four men are lined up on a stage. "See that guy right there?" He points at a middle aged guy with dark, slicked back hair and a phony grin on his face. "My dad's having a campaign fundraiser for him at the house in a few weeks."

"I don't anything about the guy but he looks like a liar with that fake smile and those overly white teeth. Well, I guess they all do."

Garret puts a t-shirt on, then stands there holding the towel at his waist. "This is coming off so you might want to turn around."

"I'm watching TV. I'm not even looking. And even if I saw something, it's not like I'd care."

"Okay." The towel drops and I quickly turn the other way. He laughs. "I knew you wouldn't look." I hear him pull his jeans on. "All right, I'm done."

I look back again and he's fully dressed. He comes over and sits on the bed. "What do you want to do? Sleep some more? Get some breakfast?" He pauses. "Or do you want to tell me what happened last night? Because I think we should talk about it."

"There's not much to say."

"You wouldn't show up at that party unless it was an emergency. Last night you said something about your mom and a letter. Where did you get this letter?"

I hesitate, not sure if I want him knowing what's in the letter. But I already told him part of the story last night so he might as well know the rest. "The letter was in that box Frank sent me for my birthday. My mom wrote it when I was just a baby. I was only supposed to get it if something happened to her."

"Why would your mom even plan for something like that? Why would she think she'd be dead in her thirties?"

"If I tell you this, you have to swear you won't tell anyone, okay?"

"Yeah. Go ahead."

"In that letter my mom said she was raped and then she found out she was pregnant with me."

He nods. "Yeah, you said that last night. So she never told you that?"

"No. Never. But that's not all. She said the man who did it got the police, the people at the hospital—basically everyone to cover up what happened. And then someone called my mom and threatened her. When she told her story to a counselor, her parents died in a house explosion a few days later. She was worried she'd be next."

Garret sits there quietly, so I continue.

"I don't even know if I should believe any of it, but why would she make up something like that?"

"How did she meet this guy? Did they know each other?"

"She was an intern working on a political campaign. She was a political science major in college. The guy was just a campaign worker from another state. She wouldn't tell me his name."

Garret is silent again.

"What's wrong, Garret? You're too quiet. Say something."

"I think you should forget about this letter. I mean, what happened is a crime and the guy shouldn't have gotten away with it, but there's nothing you can do about it now."

"I know there's nothing I can do, but I have to talk to Frank. He was friends with my mom back then. I have to know if he knew anything about this."

"Why? How does that help you, Jade?"

"Because maybe she didn't mean to be that way. Maybe my mom didn't know how else to deal with what happened to her. I need to know that. My mom hated me, Garret. She looked at me every day with disgust and I never knew what I did wrong." I feel tears forming but I hold them back. "I couldn't understand how a mother could hate her own daughter like that."

Garret finds my hand within the oversized sleeve of his sweatshirt. "It was her addiction. It wasn't you. She didn't hate you. You didn't do anything wrong."

"I have to know the truth. You told me to face the past so I can move on. And that's what I'm doing."

"I know but—" He stops.

"But what?" I sit up and lean against the headboard.

"I don't like this. I don't like the fact that this guy was able to quiet the cops. You don't mess with people like that."

"I'm not messing with anyone. I'm just asking questions and trying to see if what she said in that letter is true."

"Asking questions just leads to more questions and then you'll want to know even more. Trust me, you don't want to go digging up the past. It's dangerous."

"Why would it be dangerous? I'm not going to try to find the guy."

"Whoever this guy is, I guarantee he's got people he pays to keep that shit buried. To take care of anyone who starts asking questions. That's how it works."

"And how do you know this? Do you run a crime ring on the side? Are you part of the mafia and you forgot to tell me?"

He sighs. "This isn't funny. I'm being serious. I told you back when we first met that my family does shit that I don't want any part of, remember?"

"Yeah, but I still don't know what that means."

"It means that they get what they want. Just like this guy. They do whatever they have to do to cover up stuff they don't want people to know. They'll do anything, Jade. Anything."

"Okay, stop it. You're freaking me out."

"I just want you to think about this before you go talking to Frank or looking up stuff on the Internet. Think about if it's really going to help you."

"Fine, I'll think about it." I swing my legs to the side of the bed and sit next to him. "I guess I should go."

He puts his arm around my shoulder. "Hey, I'm sorry I wasn't here for you last night. Next time, call my cell. I'll be right over, okay?"

"Why were you talking to Ava anyway?"

"My dad called the other day and was asking all these questions about you and if I'd seen you lately. I asked Ava if she'd been spying on us again and reporting back to my dad. She claims she hasn't but I can never tell if she's lying or not."

"I really screwed up last night, Garret. I promised myself I'd never drink and then I did. I wasn't even thinking."

249

"You had one drink. That doesn't mean you'll be an alcoholic."

"I have the genes for it. I can't risk it. I don't want to end up like her."

"You won't. So stop thinking that way."

I get up and the sweatpants start slipping off. I hoist them back up, laughing. "I think I need to put my clothes back on. I can't walk to my room in these."

"Your clothes are still damp. I'll go down to your room and get you some dry ones." He takes my room key and leaves. He comes back with jeans, a black sweater, underwear, and a bra.

"Garret, you went through my underwear drawer?"

"Would you rather put on wet underwear from last night?"

"No, but still. That's embarrassing. Turn around while I change."

When I'm done, he looks me up and down. "Much better."

"At least I can walk to my room now. But I need to shower. I feel gross."

"Then go shower and I'll take you out for breakfast."

"I can't go. I need to call Frank. I know you don't think I should, but I have to ask him some things."

"Come here." He's seated on the bed and waits for me to stand in front of him. "I wasn't trying to tell you what to do. I just want you to be careful." He smiles. "And I think Frank can wait until after breakfast."

"I guess. I'll go get ready. Come down in 10 minutes." I turn to leave but he grabs my hand.

"One more thing. Do you think we could do this again?"

"Do what again?"

"This sleepover. I kind of liked it."

"How could you have liked it? The bed's so small you probably didn't get any sleep with me in there."

"You're not very big, Jade. You barely take up any space. And I've never slept better. I could use a good night's sleep like that again. I'd let you wear my sweatshirt."

"Maybe. I need to think about it." I really don't need to think about it, but I don't want to sound too eager.

"What's there to think about?" He pulls me down to sit on his leg.

"Well, for one, it kind of goes against the whole friendship agreement. You don't usually spend the night with your friend in the same bed."

He considers it. "Well, what if you weren't just my friend?"

"What do you mean?"

"What if we were more than friends?"

"We're not allowed, remember?"

"I don't give a shit about that anymore."

"Garret, you made this big deal about how your dad has to approve of any girl you go out with."

"I'm sick of playing by the rules. My dad. Katherine. His society friends. They can all go to hell." He picks up my hand and kisses it. "So what do you say? Will you go out with me?"

"I go out with you all the time."

"Never on a date. We've only gone out as friends. I'm asking you out on a date."

"Is this just your way of forcing me to let you pay for breakfast?"

"I already pay for breakfast per our agreement."

"That's only on Sundays. Today is Saturday."

He sighs. "Fine, you can pay for your own breakfast. But breakfast doesn't count. I want to take you out on a real date."

"And you think that'll make me spend the night here again?"

He throws his head back. "How many questions are you going to ask before you answer me? It's just a date. It's not that complicated."

I pretend to give it some thought. "Okay. Yes. I'll go out on a date with you. One date. That's it. If you're not too annoying or I'm not bored out of my mind I might consider another one after that. But I'm not making any promises."

He rolls his eyes. "I'll do my best."

"And I might consider sleeping next to you again, you know, if I get cold, which is possible because it's almost winter."

"You just can't give a straight answer, can you? You have to have conditions along with an insult or two."

"I'm just keeping your ego in line, pretty boy."

"Pretty boy?"

"Yeah." I laugh. "That's what Ryan calls you by the way. I don't think he's ever used your real name."

"I'm not a pretty boy. What the hell?"

"Yeah, you are. Perfect face, perfect body, perfect teeth. It's annoying."

"Huh. That almost sounded like a compliment."

"It wasn't meant to be. See? Your ego's still too high." I get up from his lap. "I need to eat. I'm really hungry."

"Okay, I'll be down in a few minutes."

When I return to my room, the letter is sitting there on the floor where I left it. I'm tempted to read it again but I don't want to. Reading it will take away how good I feel right now. I've just had one of the best nights of my life after one of the worst nights of my life. I don't know how that's even possible.

Last night at the party I was at an all time low and somehow Garret made it better. More than that, he made me feel something even after I tried so hard to feel nothing. He made me feel wanted and needed and not at all alone. I don't understand how someone can affect me that way, but I don't want that someone to go away.

CHAPTER 23

Precisely 10 minutes later, Garret shows up at my door holding my wet clothes. "You forgot these." He tosses them to me. "And here, you can have this, too." He holds out his sweatshirt.

I throw the wet clothes on the floor and snatch the sweatshirt from him. "But you said I couldn't have it."

"I was joking. Come on, Jade. Like I really care if you take my sweatshirt."

"Thank you." I give him a quick hug. I can't seem to stop this hug thing. It's happening without my control.

"You're welcome. So where do you want to have breakfast? Do you want to go to Al's? I know we're going there tomorrow but—"

"No, Al's is only for Sundays. Otherwise it ruins the tradition. Let's just eat here. We don't have to go out."

"Ugh. I hate the cafeteria, especially at breakfast. Their eggs are like rubber."

"The food there is good. You're just spoiled."

He spots the letter on the floor. "Is that it? Is that the letter?"

"Yes." I pick it up and shove it in my desk drawer. "I'm trying not to think about it right now. Let's just go eat breakfast."

Despite Garret's protests, we eat in the dining hall. A few minutes after we sit down, Ava saunters over wearing black yoga pants and a pink tank top, her hair pulled back with a thick white headband.

"What happened to you last night?" She takes a seat next to Garret, acting like I'm not even there. She moves over until she's so close she's touching him. "You left the party and never came back."

"I had better things to do." Garret pushes the eggs around his plate with his fork, not even glancing Ava's way. "Why do you care if I left? Did you have something else you wanted to tell me?"

Ava's eyes wander over to me and remain there as she leans over and whispers something to Garret.

He quickly shifts away from her. "We're done here, Ava."

She gets up, leaning over so that the cleavage from her fake boobs is practically in his face. "This goes both ways, Garret. You want me to keep my mouth shut to your dad, you better start acting like a real boyfriend."

"What's your problem, Ava?" The words shoot out of my mouth before I can stop them. Seeing her hanging all over Garret that way just set me off. "Why do you care if Garret and I do stuff together?"

She tilts her head and pouts her glossy pink lips. "Aww. The poor little orphan girl doesn't understand. Garret, you should

255

really explain how things work around here. You shouldn't keep leading her on this way. It's just sad."

Garret stands up and gets in her face. "Go. Now."

Ava smiles, pleased with herself. She takes her time walking away.

I lean across the table. "How does she know I don't have parents? Did you tell her that?"

"You think I'd really tell her anything about you? Or us?"

"Then how does she know?"

"Everyone knows. It's not some big secret. The people around here live for gossip. They always try to dig up whatever they can about people. Not just you. Everyone."

I glance over at Ava's table. She's sitting with Sierra checking messages on her phone. "She really hates me, doesn't she? Sierra does, too."

"Just be glad they've left you alone. Normally if they decide they don't like you, they make your life hell. But I'm sick of them pushing people around. They did it in high school, but they're not freaking doing it here. And they're definitely not pulling that shit with you."

"Are you saying they had something planned?"

"When you first got here they were going to take you out for dinner pretending to be all nice and then leave you out in the middle of nowhere. In the dark. And that was just day one."

"And they told you this?"

"I overheard Sierra talking about it at that party I took you to. I told her and Ava if they did anything to you I'd come after them."

"You didn't have to do that, Garret. I can handle myself. You should've just told me what they were up to and I would've taken care of it."

"You can't just take care of it. It's like I keep telling you. It's all a game. Bribes. Blackmail. That's the only thing that gets them to back down."

"So you bribed them or what?"

"I didn't have to. My family practically runs this school. They donate a ton of money. My dad and grandfather are on all these boards and committees. They have a lot of influence here." He glances over at Sierra and Ava. "If I wanted to, I could get those two kicked out of school. Well, maybe not Ava. At least not now."

"Why? What did she say to you? And why was she telling you to act like her boyfriend?"

We hear Ava laughing from across the dining hall. Garret picks up his tray. "I can't sit here anymore. Let's go."

On the walk back to my room, he's quiet. Too quiet.

"Okay, I know you're hiding something from me, Garret, so what is it?"

He sits down in my desk chair, leaning back and tapping a pencil on the desk. "My dad, or more likely Katherine, thinks it's time for me to get a new fake girlfriend. Apparently Courtney isn't getting generating enough press for the Kensington name so she's been replaced by Ava."

"Why Ava?"

"She was on some stupid reality show last year so she gets photographed a lot at events."

"When did you find this out?"

"Ava told me at the party last night. I didn't believe her so I called my dad and he confirmed it. He said it was both his and Katherine's idea but I know it was all Katherine."

"Do Ava's parents get a say in this?"

"They were all for it. In fact they want me to go out with Ava for real. For some reason they like me. I have no idea why. I barely know them."

"Why didn't you tell me this last night?"

"We had enough going on last night." He sees the distrust on my face. "I swear I was going to tell you about this. I just wanted to wait until after you had your talk with Frank."

I'm not sure I believe him. "So you still didn't tell me what she said to you just now."

"Why do you have to keep talking about this? Just forget it."

I stand in front of him determined to get answers. "I didn't like the way she was whispering in your ear and whatever she said seemed to really piss you off. Just tell me what she said."

He sets the pencil down and folds his arms across his chest. "You heard what she said. She wants me to act like a real boyfriend or she'll start telling my dad about us again."

"What does that mean? Take her out on a date?"

"Uh. No. She has plenty of guys who will take her out. And those guys can take care of her other needs as well because I'm sure as hell not doing it."

"Wait. So she wants you to have sex with her?"

"It's blackmail, Jade. Ava can get sex anywhere. She doesn't need me for that."

"Hold on. Let me get this straight. So if you sleep with her, then she won't tell your dad about us. But if you *did* sleep with

258

her, there would no longer be an us. So that logic makes no sense."

He laughs, easing the tension that Ava has built up between us. "Yeah, she's not that smart. She's just being a bitch because she doesn't like the fact that I'm with you."

"Doesn't she know we're not dating? Tell her we're just friends."

He smiles just slightly and gazes at me with those gorgeous blue eyes. "Ava can see that you and I are more than friends."

"What do you mean? It's not like we're making out in the hall."

Garret unfolds his arms and holds both my hands. "Jade, aside from you, everyone on the planet can see that I'm completely crazy about this girl from Iowa who runs constantly and as is addicted to potato chips."

"Have I met this girl? Because she sounds really cool. I think we could hang out." It's a dumb response, but I wasn't expecting to him say such a nice thing and I got nervous.

"I don't know what you do to me, but whatever it is, I guess it shows on my face because everyone knows how I feel about you. Not just Ava."

"Is my face showing anything?" I turn it right and left.

He holds it straight again, his hand cupping my chin. "No, because you're not into me yet. I haven't won you over. But I'm working on it." He gives me a quick kiss.

Garret has totally won me over. I'm just trying desperately to hide it and I don't even know why. Maybe because I still don't trust him.

I go over and open the drapes in my room, letting the light in. "When does this fake relationship start?"

He sighs. "Next week there's a charity event we have to go to but it's during the day and it's just for an hour, if that. They'll get some photos of Ava and me together and then I'll leave. But I'll probably be forced to take her to that political fundraiser at my house in a few weeks."

"That sounds fun," I say in my most sarcastic tone.

"Yeah, I know."

I lie down on the bed and gaze up at the lights. They aren't even on and yet they still make me happy because Garret went to all that work to tack them up there. "She'll probably get you drunk and have her way with you."

Garret joins me on the bed, staring up at the ceiling. "I don't get drunk anymore." He reaches over and holds my hand. "And the only person getting her way with me is the one who's lying next to me right now."

My lips curl into a smile and I get that strange feeling inside that I can't quite explain. A feeling I'm still not used to, but one I crave to have again and again.

"Jade?" He keeps looking up.

"Garret?" I say, mimicking him.

"Just in case I haven't made myself clear, I like you. I like you a lot."

My smiles grows. "I like you, too."

We lie there quietly. I know I should call Frank but I also know that doing so will take away how good I feel right now and I just want a few more minutes of this.

"I think we fell asleep." Garret sits up and checks the clock by the bed. He nudges me. "We just slept for an hour."

"Really? It didn't feel like an hour." I get up from the bed. "I need to call Frank. I can't keep putting it off."

Garret comes over to me. "Do you want me to stay here while you talk to him?"

"No, I need to do this alone."

Alone. There's that word again. It's the only way I ever do things.

"Okay. I'll be right upstairs if you need me." He holds his arms out. "But first, practice time."

"Ugh, not again," I groan, slumping my shoulders and pretending to be annoyed.

He picks up my arms and drags them around him. "I think you're getting worse at this, Jade. Now tighten your arms up."

I hug him and keep hold of him because now I'm really getting nervous about talking to Frank. What if he knew about my mom and never told me? But he wouldn't keep something like that from me, would he?

Garret waits for me to end the hug, like he always does, but several minutes go by before I finally let him go.

"Still needs work," Garret says, kissing the top of my head. "Come upstairs when you're done with your call."

When he's gone I shut the door and get the letter from my desk drawer. I sit down at the desk and call Frank.

"Hello?" His voice sounds tired.

"Hi, Frank. It's Jade."

"Hi, Jade. Do you have any fun plans for tonight?" Frank coughs loudly into the phone.

"No, I don't have any plans. Are you sick or something?"

"Yes, I woke up with a cold this morning. Probably from too much activity."

"Did you go out last night? I called and you weren't there."

"Ryan's girlfriend insisted I go to the movies with them. I told her it would ruin their date night but she kept insisting I go so I did. Chloe's a very nice girl. Very considerate. I hope it works out with those two."

"Wow, you haven't been to the movies in years."

"Yes, I know. Chloe's right. I should get out more. I had a good time. So did you do something with your friends last night?"

"Um, yeah." Technically, Garret is a friend so I'm not really lying.

"What did you do?"

"We just hung out here."

"You and Harper? I thought she went out on Friday nights."

This small talk is making me anxious. I just want to get this over with. He either knows about my mom or he doesn't. I stand up and start pacing the floor, but my movement is limited by the short phone cord so I stand in place, twirling the cord around my finger.

"Harper was at a party so I hung out with Garret."

He's silent for a moment. "Well, as long as you had fun." I can tell that Frank still hates Garret for ignoring me all those weeks. And he isn't too thrilled with me, either, for letting Garret back in my life.

"Frank, I have something to ask you." I'm so nervous. But I shouldn't be. It's just Frank. He's practically my father.

"Go ahead. What do you need to ask me?"

"I, um, I opened that letter you gave me. The one from Mom."

"Yes." He moves away from the phone to cough again. "So what did it say?"

"Well, it wasn't about her hopes and dreams for me. It said something really strange. I'm not even sure I believe it." I hold up the letter with the familiar handwriting. Just seeing it makes me shudder. "She said that a man attacked her back in college when she was working on a political campaign. She said he, um, he raped her. And that's why I'm here."

There's a loud noise as the phone on Frank's end drops either to the table or the floor. "Frank? Are you still there?"

Jumbled sounds fill the line, then I hear his voice again. "What else did the letter say?" His tone is almost angry.

"She said that the man left her almost dead on the side of the road and that when she woke up in the hospital nobody believed her story. Not even the police. Or the doctors. No one. And then she got threatening phone calls."

Frank remains silent. All I hear is his labored breathing.

"She said somebody purposely caused an explosion at my grandparents' house. But I thought you said they died in a fire. Isn't that what you told me?"

His breathing gets faster, causing him to cough again.

"Frank, did you hear me?"

"Yes." He clears his throat.

"So what do you think?" I feel a giant knot forming in my stomach when he doesn't answer. "Why aren't you saying anything?"

The silence continues. I wonder if he passed out, but then I hear him breathing hard again.

"Frank, did you know about any of this?"

After another long uncomfortable silence, he finally speaks. "Yes, Jade. I knew about all of it."

"What?" I slump down on the floor, leaning my back against the wall, the letter still in my hand. "What do you mean?"

"Your mother and I were friends back then."

"I know you were friends, but in this letter she said she didn't tell anyone. Well, she told the police and the hospital workers, but they didn't believe her." I quickly scan the letter again. "She said the only other people she told were her parents and a counselor and—" I find the section and read it again. "And a reporter from the newspaper." It finally hits me. "Were you the reporter?"

"I was her friend first, Jade. That's why she told me. But yes, I was the reporter. I was working at the newspaper covering the caucus. Your mother was hoping I could convince my editor to do a story on what happened and maybe get the guy to confess. But I couldn't do it. There was no evidence. I never told anyone your mother's story. Even after all these years."

"But everyone who knew either kept quiet or was . . ." I flip the letter over.

"Killed." His tone is cold. It doesn't even sound like Frank.

The phone is silent until I'm able to speak again.

"So my grandparents—it wasn't an accident?"

"No. This man knew your grandparents wouldn't keep his secret. Plus their deaths were a warning for your mother to keep quiet."

"Why didn't he just kill her? I don't understand."

"I don't either. I've never understood that. And luckily he never found out that she told me. If he had, I probably wouldn't be here right now."

"You're scaring me, Frank. What really happened back then? And why didn't you ever say anything to me?" My hands are now shaking and I drop the letter on the floor.

"I didn't think your mother would ever tell you about this. If I'd known that's what she wrote in that letter, I never would've—" He stops.

"Never would've what? Let me see it?" I get up from the floor, my anger building again. "Why would you hide something like that from me?"

"It's the past, Jade. And you need to leave it there." His tone is stern and somewhat threatening.

"What is wrong with you? Why are you acting like this? Tell me what happened. My mom was crazy so half of the stuff in this letter probably isn't even true, right?"

"It's all true. And your mother wasn't crazy when she wrote that. She didn't even drink back then. She was as normal as you and me."

CHAPTER 24

"Then what happened to her? How did she become the person I grew up with? Was it because of what he did to her? Or because they called her a liar and threatened her if she told the truth? Because I kind of understand that. It almost makes sense why she acted that way. She just couldn't deal with it."

"That wasn't it. Your mother was one of the strongest women I've ever met, at least she was back then."

"If that were true, then why did she start taking those pills and drinking?"

"Just let it go. It's over now. Your mother is gone. There's no need to dredge up what happened nearly 20 years ago."

"Frank, how can you say that? You know I've struggled my whole life trying to figure out why she was that way and if I would someday—" I don't have to say it.

"You won't turn out like her, Jade. What made her that way wasn't her fault. There were bigger forces at work. She couldn't help what happened."

I take a moment to try to figure out what he means. "Nothing you're saying makes any sense. I don't even know what you're trying to tell me."

"Honey, I know you've always felt like your mother didn't care about you or didn't want you, but nothing could be further from the truth. I've told you that before many times."

"Yeah. And it was a lie. You saw how she treated me. She hated me. And now I know why. I just reminded her of what happened that night."

"Listen to me." He sounds angry again. "Your mother risked her life to have you. If she didn't want you, she would've taken his money and had it taken care of like he told her to. Instead she hid out for nine months so she could have you. She wanted you more than she wanted anything. She just wanted to be a mother. And they took that away."

"Who took it away? My father? Who is he? What do you know about him?"

"Nothing."

"She would've told you, Frank. When she told you what happened, she would've said his name."

He's coughing again. "I need some water. I'll be right back."

A giant lump has lodged in my throat and immense pressure is building behind my eyes as I force myself not to cry. Frank has just admitted that he's lied to me all these years. All those times I ran to his house, asking him to explain why she was that way, he could've told me. But all he did was listen, never saying a word. And he still isn't explaining it now. If anything, he's making me more confused.

He's gone so long I'm sure he's not coming back. Then I hear the phone pick up again. "Okay, I'm here. What else do you need to know?" He sounds calmer now, but I can tell he's had enough. He doesn't want to talk about this anymore.

"I want to know everything. I want to know who my father is. I want to know what else you know about my mom."

Frank takes a deep breath, then coughs again as he lets it out. "The answers won't make anything better, Jade. You have a good life, now. You're moving on. There's no reason to dig up the past."

Dig up the past. His words remind me of Garret's earlier words . . . *you don't want to go digging up the past. It's dangerous.*

"What are you not telling me? Am I in danger?"

"If you keep searching for answers," he hesitates, "then yes. You could be in danger."

His words and the way he says them cause a cold chill to rush up and down my spine.

"Then why won't you just answer me so I don't have to go searching? Talk to me, Frank. I don't like the way you're acting all cryptic like you know stuff but won't tell me. It's not fair and it's freaking me out. I have a right to know the truth about my mother. She wouldn't have wrote this letter if she didn't want me to know these things."

"I don't know why she wrote that letter. It was careless of her. She should've known better. If someone had found—" He stops suddenly.

"Found what?"

"Did you hear that?" Frank's voice turns frantic.

"Hear what?"

268

"That clicking noise on the phone just now."

"No, I didn't hear anything. Now what were you saying?"

He pauses, listening for whatever clicking noise he thinks he hears.

"Never mind. I want you listen to me. Leave this thing with your mother alone. Just let it be. Don't go searching for answers. They won't help you."

"Why does everyone keep saying that?"

"What do you mean by everyone? Did you tell someone about this?"

"I told Garret. Why?"

"Dammit, Jade! Why would you do that?" Frank scolds me as if I should've somehow known not to tell anyone. "You are not to talk about this with him or anyone else. Do you understand?"

"No! I don't understand! You're not telling me anything and it's really pissing me off!" I yell it at him, then immediately feel bad for doing so. Even though I'm furious with the way he's acting, I feel like I can't get mad at him. I always feel that way with him. Like I can't possibly get mad at someone who has done so much for me.

"I'm sorry, but you need to trust me on this. You need to let this go."

We both get quiet and I know if I stay on the phone a second longer I'll say something I'll regret.

"I have to study. I'll call you later. Bye, Frank."

I hang up the phone. My body is aching to move. It needs to release the anxiety and confusion and rage that's bottled up inside me. Why would Frank lie to me like that? Why would he keep that from me? And if I'm in some type of danger, why wouldn't he at least tell me what *kind* of danger or who's after me? I thought Frank cared about me. But I guess he doesn't, at least not enough to tell me the truth. It's just like I always say. You can't trust anyone in this world. Not even the ones closest to you.

Garret is upstairs waiting for me to tell him how my call went, but I can't talk to him right now. Instead I change into my running pants and long sleeve shirt. When I get outside, it's colder than I thought it would be. It's probably only 40 degrees, with an even colder windchill. But that's good. The cold will keep my mind focused on my body and not Frank or that stupid letter.

I hurry down the hill to the track which is still damp from the rain we had earlier. Wet leaves are scattered on the surface and as I run I have to keep dodging them so I don't slip and fall.

The dark, gloomy sky reminds me that today is Halloween. Soon everyone will be drinking and partying even more than at last night's Halloween Eve parties.

Garret hasn't said what he's doing tonight. I wonder if he'll go to another party. Saturday is usually our night to hang out, but it's such a huge party night that I'm sure Blake will force him to go out, threatening to tell Garret's dad about us if he doesn't.

The thought of Garret hanging out with Blake makes me run faster. I really hate that guy. I've dealt with assholes before, but something about Blake really bothers me. It's one of those gut feelings that doesn't make sense but nags at you, telling you something isn't right.

The biting wind eats through the fabric of my clothes. My muscles tighten up, signaling me to go inside. But it's not time yet. I'm still so angry at Frank that even my run isn't helping get rid of my rage. I counted on him. He's all I have. In a few years, Ryan will move on and get married, maybe have some kids. He'll forget all about me. Frank is the only person I'll have left in my life. And now I can't trust him.

I focus on my breathing, trying to calm down. *You can't count on people, Jade. They'll only let you down.* She's there again, talking in my head. And she was right. I can't count on people. And the fact that she was right infuriates me.

My mother's world was dark and sad. I used to tell myself that her words were a reflection of that. That her words weren't true. That the world was a better place. It had to be. I couldn't live in the world my mother described. But now I'm realizing it's exactly what she said. Dark. Lonely. Dangerous.

"Jade." I look up and see Garret on the side of the track, bundled up in a coat and scarf.

I run over to him. "I can't talk right now. I'll see you tomorrow for breakfast, okay?"

I'm mad at Garret, too. I'm not even sure why.

I turn to take off again but he holds onto my arm. "Tomorrow? What are you talking about? I thought we were spending the day together."

"Let go of me." I tug on my arm.

"Did you talk to Frank?"

271

"Yes. Now let go of me!" The bitter wind is drying my sweat, making me shiver.

"So it didn't go well. Is that why you're out here freezing your ass off?"

"I don't want to talk about it. I need to run. We'll talk later."

"You're done running. You're not even dressed right. It feels like winter out here. Come on." He puts his hand firmly around mine and starts dragging me off the track.

I yank my hand back. "Dammit, Garret! Would you just leave me the fuck alone? I'm sick of this!" I scream it at him as the wind howls around us. My cheeks are so frozen it's hard to even form the words.

"Sick of what?"

"I'm sick of you trying to rescue me all the time! I'm sick of you interfering! I'm sick of you thinking you know what's best for me!"

His eyes search my face, trying to figure out what's going on. I can see that I've hurt him and I feel horrible about it. There's no reason for me to yell at him. So why am I doing it? Why am I screaming at the one person who is the only glimmer of light in my life? Why am I like this?

"Just go! Leave me alone, Garret! I need to be alone!"

It's not at all what I need. And it's definitely not what I want. And yet I ask for it. Beg for it!

I stand there, waiting for him to scream back at me. Waiting for him to tell me I'm not worth it. Waiting for him to turn and walk away, vowing never again to involve himself with the crazy girl standing before him. But instead he takes his coat off and puts it around my shoulders, zipping it up in front. He takes his scarf and wraps it around my neck. Then he plants his arm firmly around my shoulder and starts walking back, pushing me forward. I go with him, confused but also incredibly relieved that he's taken charge of the situation that I've lost all control over.

On the walk back, he says nothing. I can't tell if he's angry or frustrated or just wants to drop me off in my room and never speak to me again. I'm convinced it's the latter.

When we're back at my room, he waits for me to unlock the door, then follows me inside. I can't figure out why he's still here.

He takes his coat and scarf off me, then starts going through my dresser drawers. He pulls out some clothes and shoves them into my hand. "You're freezing. Go take a hot shower and get dressed. I'll wait here."

I take the clothes and leave for the bathroom, unsure why I'm listening to him. The hot shower feels good so I linger a few extra minutes letting it thaw my muscles and warm my skin.

When I'm done I get dressed and head back to my room, certain Garret will be gone. But he's not. He's sitting right there on my bed, waiting.

"Feel better?" he asks.

I slowly walk over and stand in front of him. "What's going on here?"

"What do you mean?"

"Why are you still here?"

"Why wouldn't I be? Am I supposed to be somewhere else? Because last I checked my day was pretty much open."

"But didn't you hear me out there? Screaming at you?"

He shrugs. "You didn't mean it. You're just pissed about something."

"I told you to leave me alone."

"You don't want to be alone. You just say that."

"How do you know? Maybe I really do want to be alone."

He smiles and pulls me onto his leg to sit. "Why would you want to be alone? Alone sucks."

I can't argue because it's true. Alone does suck. But it's all I know. When you lose faith in people, alone is your only option.

"So do you want to talk about what happened now?" he asks. "Or later?"

"I don't want to talk about it."

"Okay, then later it is." He loosely holds my hand. "So here's what I was thinking. I have to get at least an hour or two of swim practice in and I thought you could come with me. You don't have to swim, but you could bring a book or music or whatever and just hang out. It's nice and warm in there."

"I guess I could do that."

"And then after that is the Halloween party."

I look at him confused. "I'm not going to a Halloween party. That's like a regular party on steroids. And after the vodka incident last night, I can't be around all that alcohol right now."

"We're not going anywhere. The party is upstairs. I've got my room all ready. We're having a horror movie marathon."

"We are?" I find myself smiling like an idiot. "But you hate horror movies."

"I know. But what the hell? It's Halloween, right?"

"So what else is going on at this party?" I try to act cool but I can't hide the excitement in my voice.

"Well, I've loaded up on candy, of course, and your other favorite junk foods. I thought we'd order a pizza for some real food. That's about it. It's not that great but—"

"Are you kidding? It's totally great! I can't believe you did all this." I have to hug him. I can't stop myself. I don't know how it's possible, but he's somehow turned my anger and sadness into pure joy and happiness.

"Wow. A hug. Thanks. I'm glad you're excited about it."

"But I thought you were going out tonight like everyone else."

"It's Saturday. That's our night, remember?"

"But it's Halloween. It's a major party night. Isn't Blake gonna get mad?"

"Blake's already drunk off his ass. I talked to him earlier. He didn't even know who he was talking to."

"So when does this party begin?" I say it with such enthusiasm it doesn't even sound like me.

He gets this huge smile on his face. "It starts as soon as I get some swimming in. I'll go grab my stuff upstairs and then we'll go."

My enthusiasm seems to be spreading to Garret. I know it makes him happy to see me this excited about something he did. And I like that. I like making him happy. It's so much better than yelling at him.

CHAPTER 25

Watching Garret in the pool, I can't help but check out his body. It's total perfection. Muscular arms, sculpted chest, six pack abs, broad swimmer shoulders. Every part of me wants to get in the pool with him and replay the scene we didn't get to finish.

I told myself I wouldn't get involved emotionally or physically with a guy in college. But I'm already emotionally involved with Garret and am more than ready to be physically involved with him. We're not even technically dating, so I know it's too soon for that and it might ruin what we have going on between us, but that doesn't make me want it any less.

As I watch him swim laps, I wonder how many girls he's been with. It's got to be a lot. From the few physical encounters we've had together, he definitely knows what he's doing. I, on the other hand, have no idea what I'm doing when it comes to that. Back in high school, I didn't have a ton of experience with guys. That said, I have had sex. One time.

It happened after homecoming last year. The guy went to a different school. I met him at a knowledge bowl tournament which I participated in only because I have a better than average ability to remember random trivia. Plus, I thought it would look good on a college application.

A really cute guy from the opposing team asked me out. We went on a few dates, then he asked me to go to homecoming at his school. For the week leading up to it, I kept hearing my mom's voice in my head, saying how girls always got pregnant at school dances. Because of that she told me I'd never be allowed to go. But since she was no longer around, I went. And for a reason that makes no logical sense at all, I decided to challenge her theory and have sex, proving to her and myself that I wouldn't get pregnant. And I didn't. I've been on the pill forever and he used a condom.

It was over in a minute. Okay, maybe not a minute. I wasn't timing it, but it was over really fast. After that, the guy never called me again. So much for remembering your first time. I try to forget it ever happened.

"You bored yet?" Garret is hanging off the edge of the pool, smiling at me with those yummy wet lips that are begging to be kissed.

"No, not at all." I've been pretending to read a book but I've spent the entire time staring at his nearly naked body.

"We can go soon. I just need to do a few more laps."

"That's fine." I glance up at the clock. We've been here for two hours? I didn't realize it'd been that long.

A few minutes later, he jumps out of the pool. "I'm done. I'll go get dressed and be right back."

He's in such a good mood. He's almost always in a good mood. I don't know how he does it. My mood changes from hour to hour and it's usually not a good one. Except I'm finding that the more I'm around Garret, the more good moods I have.

We get back to the dorms and Garret goes upstairs while I go to my room to drop off my book. It's early afternoon and girls are already getting ready to go out. Harper has a new guy in her life and she's been staying at his apartment all week. I've barely seen her.

I head upstairs to Garret's floor. Some guy at the end of the hall has the door to his room propped open. About 20 guys are stuffed inside, watching a football game on a giant TV. I can smell their beer from the hallway.

One of the guys stumbles out, nearly falling on me as I walk by. "You know, you're kinda hot," he says, slinging his arm around my shoulder. "You wanna come back to my room and—"

"Get off me." I push his arm off, but he puts it right back.

"Come on." He pouts. "I promise I won't bite. Unless you want me to."

Garret comes out of his door and sees drunk boy hanging on me. "Shane, get the hell away from her." He comes over and shoves the guy's arm off my shoulder.

Drunk boy looks offended. "I was just being friendly. Shit, can't a guy be friendly?"

"Go be friendly to someone else." Garret takes my hand. "Come on, Jade."

"Where did you find her?" Shane yells from behind us. "Does she go here? She's got a nice ass on her." He continues his drunken rambling as he stumbles down the hall.

"Ignore him," Garret says as we walk to his room. "He's been drunk for hours. He doesn't know what he's saying."

"Are you saying he was wrong about my ass?" I smile. "Because I took that as a compliment."

He smiles back. "You do have a nice ass, but I don't want him looking at it. That's my job."

"Oh, really? Because I don't think you should be checking out your friend's ass."

"Speak for yourself, there, Jade." He flashes that cocky smile. He totally caught me checking him out at the pool.

He stops in front of his door. "Okay, are you ready?"

I nod and he opens the door. His whole room is decorated for Halloween. The blue lights along the ceiling have been replaced by bright orange lights. Cobwebs are draped along the walls, the windows, the dresser, his desk, and around the TV. Ghost and witch cutouts are taped to his closet door. And the infamous concession stand is filled with more candy than any trick or treater could ever want.

"I told you it wasn't that great, but it's Halloweeny, right?"

"Totally Halloweeny! I love it! This is way more than I was expecting." I lie down on his bed and stare up at the bright orange lights. His drapes are closed but it's such a gray, dreary day outside that even with the drapes open, it would still be dark in here.

"I'm glad you like it." He lies next to me, propped up on his side, resting his hand on my stomach as if it somehow belongs there. It immediately takes my focus off the ceiling lights. "Do you want to look through the movies I rented? I don't know anything about horror movies so I got like 10 of them. You can pick what you want."

I turn to face him and his hand moves to my hip. "Garret, thanks for doing all this. The movies. The decorations. The food. The lights." I can't stop smiling as I glance around the room. "This is so great."

He leans in to kiss my cheek. "I love how excited you get over stuff like this."

"What can I say? You combined junk food and movies, my two favorite things." I tug on his shirt, a black thermal henley that fits snugly over his chest. "You even wore Halloween colors."

He looks down. "Yeah, I guess I did. I wasn't even thinking about that when I put it on."

That shirt looks really good on him. His hair looks good, too. Actually everything about him looks really good. I have this major urge to kiss him right now in a non-friend way and see where that leads. I need to take control and stop waiting for him to make a move. Just as I'm getting the courage to do it, he gets up from the bed. Damn!

"Okay." He picks up a stack of movies and brings them over to me. "We have zombies, ghosts, vampires, witches, or the classic psychotic killer who lives next door. What do like?"

"Zombies."

He sighs. "I was afraid you were going to say that. Don't you think it'll be boring? I mean, zombies don't even talk, right?"

"Then how about witches instead?"

"We have all day and night to watch these, so if you want we can start with zombies."

The zombie movie is so dumb that we make fun of it for the whole 87 minutes, making up lines for the zombies to say. Next we watch the witch movie, followed by a vampire one. After that, we get our pizza and watch a ghost movie which turns out to be way scarier than I thought it would be.

At 10, we're still sitting there on his giant bean bag chair and I've completely stuffed myself with pizza and candy.

Just as movie number five, the psychotic killer movie, begins, someone knocks on the door.

"Kensington, get your ass out here," a guy yells.

"Just ignore him," Garret says.

"We know you're in there. Hurry up," another guy yells.

"Just talk to them," I say. "Otherwise they'll never go away."

Garret gets up and opens the door and the smell of strong cologne wafts into the room. He walks out into the hallway, closing the door behind him.

"What do you want?" I hear Garret say.

"We're leaving for the party. Let's go."

"I'm not going. I told you that earlier."

"What do you mean you're not going? Do you know how many girls are gonna be at this party? I just talked to Aiden and he said the girls are all wearing costumes and they're practically naked."

"I told you I'm not going." Garret's voice is more forceful.

"Why? You got some girl in there? Well, finish up with her and let's go."

"Don't be an ass. Just get out of here." I hear Garret's hand on the doorknob.

"Who's in there? Ava?"

"It's none of your damn business," Garret says loudly. "Just go."

"Whatever, man." I hear them walking away. "You used to be fun, Garret. Now you're just a fucking loser."

Garret comes back in the room and sits next to me again. "Sorry about that. They've been drinking so were even more obnoxious than usual."

I turn the volume down on the TV and scoot closer to him. "You know, those guys are right. You should be out at one of the gazillion parties going on right now. You're missing out on all those girls in sexy nurse costumes, not to mention all the half-naked angels, witches, devils—"

He puts his finger to my lips. "This is where I want to be, Jade. Right here."

I pull his hand away and look up at him, practically begging him to kiss me. He leans down and gives me a quick friend kiss, then looks up at the TV. "So what's going on with this one?"

"The psychotic killer met this girl on an Internet dating site." I shudder. "It's totally freaking me out. Look at that guy. Look at his eyes. I feel like he's watching me."

He laughs. "I'll protect you. Come here." I snuggle up next to him. A few minutes into the movie I fall asleep.

I wake up when I feel Garret move his arm off me. "Jade, I can't sit here any longer. I need to move."

The clock on his desk says it's 1 a.m. "Have you been awake this whole time?"

"Yeah, the movie ended and I've been watching TV."

"You should've woke me up."

"Nah. I like it when you sleep on me, but my arm was starting to go numb."

"Oh. Sorry about that." I sit up. "I should go."

"Do you really want to go?"

"Well, it's kind of late to start another movie." I yawn and rub my eyes.

He turns the TV off. "I wasn't going to watch another movie."

I'm sleepy and it takes a moment for me to figure out what he means. "Are you inviting me for another sleepover?"

"The night's practically over. You might as well stay."

"Yeah, because my room's so far away. It'll be morning before I make it back."

"I'm not trying to get you to have sex with me, if that's what you're thinking. I just want to sleep next to you again. Sleep. That's it. But if you don't want to, that's fine."

"Okay, I'll stay." I'm happy he wants me there, but I'm a little concerned that he thinks I've totally ruled out the idea of having sex with him. I made that one comment and now he assumes I'm not at all interested.

I get up from the chair, take my jeans off, and climb into bed.

"What are you doing?" he asks, standing over me.

"Going to sleep." I pull the covers up.

"But you're not wearing anything."

"I'm wearing a shirt."

"Yeah, but nothing else. You want a pair of my shorts?"

I prop up on my elbows. "I'm wearing underwear. I'm not going to wear my jeans to bed. What's your problem? You can't sleep next to me like this?"

"Uh, no. Definitely not."

I tilt my head and smile. "And why is that? We're just sleeping, right? Nothing else? You won't even notice what I'm wearing because you'll be asleep."

"Trust me. I won't be sleeping if that's all you're wearing. I'll go get you something from your room."

"You're being crazy. Just go to sleep." I lie back down with my back to him and close my eyes. I hear him sigh as he changes into his pajamas.

The mattress sinks in as he gets in behind me. The bed is so small our bodies can't help but touch and I can tell my lack of clothing is affecting him. He keeps trying to move away from my lower half, but can't because he'll fall off the bed. I love torturing him like this. I try not to laugh when he attempts to move again.

"What is going on back there?" I ask, feigning annoyance. "I'm trying to sleep."

"I'm sorry. I can't do this. You need to put something on." He gets up, goes to his drawer, and comes back with a pair of fleece athletic shorts.

I can't hold in my laughter anymore. "Are you saying you can't resist me?"

"That's exactly what I'm saying." He throws the covers off and drags my legs to the side of the bed, pausing a moment to look. "Damn. And then you have to wear sexy underwear? Did you do this on purpose?"

"Nope. This is my normal underwear." I pull my shirt up more to show off my silky black bikinis.

He slips my legs into the shorts. "You were *not* wearing underwear like that when you were running last night."

"Oh, yeah. I forgot about that. For someone who isn't dating me you've sure seen me naked a lot."

He pulls the shorts up to the top of my legs. I stand up and yank them the rest of the way on.

"There. That's better," he says, looking at the oversized shorts that go past my knees.

We get back in bed, the orange lights glowing above us. He's lying on his back and I sneak under his arm, making myself comfortable. "You know, I wouldn't care if you tried some stuff."

He kisses my forehead. "I know. But that will lead to other stuff. And I want us to start dating first, like a real couple."

"Then let's go out on this date you keep talking about."

"Okay, next Saturday night we'll go on real date. As in go out, not sit in my room."

"Saturday? But that's so far away." I don't mean to sound desperate but it almost comes out that way.

"Are you in a hurry or something?"

"Um, no. I guess not." I actually *am* in a hurry. I'm finding him hard to resist and now he's holding out on me. I don't know why he's so insistent on having this official date. It seems like we've been dating this whole time.

"So I think it's time to make another tradition."

I lift my head up to look at him. "Like what?"

285

"I think we should have one of these sleepovers every Saturday night."

"Hmm." I lower my head back down on his shoulder, hiding my smile. "But we already have a tradition for Sunday morning."

"Yeah? So?"

"I'm just saying if we did this, we'd have two traditions in a row, really close together."

"We could add another one during the week if you feel the need to even things out a little."

"Yeah, I guess we could do that." My smile keeps growing. He wants more traditions with me? So he thinks we can really be a couple? Even with his rules and his family? I'm not going to question it. At least not tonight.

"Then it's settled. Saturday night sleepovers are our second tradition. You figure out the midweek one since I made the other two."

The way he says it makes me laugh. "Okay. I can do that."

I turn over on my side and he does the same, my back against his front.

"Goodnight, Jade." He moves my hair aside and kisses the nape of my neck, sending a tingle through my body. It makes me want to flip around and have my way with him, but I don't. I'm sure he did it to get back at me for my underwear trick.

He pulls me closer to his chest and tucks his arm around me. It makes me feel warm and safe and happy. I've never felt so at peace.

Being with Garret all day, I haven't even thought about my mom's letter or my argument with Frank. He took all of the bad stuff away, at least for a little while.

CHAPTER 26

We wake the next morning to loud knocking on the door. "Garret. Open the door! Right now!"

"Shit!" Garret quickly gets out of bed. "It's my dad."

"Your dad?" I whisper. "What is he doing here? What time is it?"

He checks the clock. "It's 8. I don't know why he's here. Maybe there's some kind of family emergency." He takes his pajama pants off and puts on a pair of jeans.

"What do you want me to do?" I hurry out of the bed.

He tosses me my jeans. "Put these on. We'll tell him we were heading out for breakfast."

"Garret, are you in there?" his dad yells as the knocking continues.

"Yeah. Just a minute."

I take his shorts off and pull my jeans on, then try to brush my hair with my fingers.

Garret opens the door just a crack. "Dad, what's wrong? Did something happen?"

Mr. Kensington shoves the door open and storms into the room, stopping when he sees me. "What is she doing here?" he asks Garret.

"We were going to breakfast."

"At this hour? You seriously think I'd believe you two got up this early on a Sunday to eat breakfast?"

"It's not that early, Dad. Now why are you here?"

Mr. Kensington comes over to me. "Jade, my son and I need to talk. You need to leave."

I glance at Garret.

"I'll be right down, okay?" He says it, but he doesn't sound confident.

"Don't wait for him, Jade," Mr. Kensington says. "He's not going down to your room. He's not having breakfast with you. He's not doing anything with you anymore. This thing you have going with him is over."

"No, it's not." Garret tries to keep his tone positive. "Just ignore him, Jade."

I look at him, not sure what to do.

"Just go. I'll be down later," he assures me. But I don't believe him.

I slowly walk out the door and down the hall. Garret's door slams and I can hear Mr. Kensington yelling. "What did I tell you about that girl? From now on you're seeing Ava and only Ava. You understand me?"

When I get back to my room, I collapse on my bed, trying to figure out what just happened. Who talked to Garret's father? Blake? Ava? Those guys who came by Garret's room last night? Why are all these people so obsessed with keeping Garret and me apart? Can't they mind their own business? Why do they keep interfering?

I feel a tear run down my cheek and I quickly wipe it away. This is not worth crying over. It's not a big deal. Garret's dad got mad before and it didn't stop us. This time won't be any different. Except part of me fears that it will. This didn't seem like just a warning. Mr. Kensington was furious. Last time he at least tried to hide his anger from me. This time he wanted me to see it.

My phone rings. I'm sure it's Frank but I'm not in the mood to talk to him. I'm still angry at him but I'm getting over it. I don't understand why he never told me the truth about my mom but I don't want to fight with him about it. I just want to pretend the conversation never happened.

The phone continues to ring. I reluctantly get up and answer it.

"Hello."

Nobody answers.

"Is that you, Frank?"

There's silence again. I start to put the phone down, then stop when I hear a man's voice.

"What did you do with the letter?"

I put the phone back up to my ear. "What?"

"The letter, Jade. What did you do with it?"

The voice doesn't belong to Frank. It doesn't belong to Ryan either. It's a really deep voice and the man is talking slowly.

"Who is this?" I ask, trying to hide the fact that this person is scaring the crap out of me.

"Answer me. The letter from Julia. Do you still have it?"

A chill runs down my spine as I hear my mother's name. My mother always went by the name Julie, not Julia, her real name. Frank said only her parents used to call her Julia.

"Tell me who you are or I'm hanging up."

"If you hang up, I'll just call back. If you don't answer the phone, I'll show up at your door. I won't go away, Jade, unless you cooperate."

My heart is banging against my chest and I'm sure all color has drained from my face. For a second, I think this is some cruel Halloween joke, but this man doesn't seem to be joking.

"What do you want?"

"I want you to destroy the letter. I want you to burn it until it's nothing but ashes. Do you understand?"

"Why? Why do you care about a stupid letter? I don't even know what letter you're talking about." My voice is shaky. I take a deep breath hoping to steady it.

"Don't play games with me. Do as I say and burn the letter. When you're done, you'll never speak of the contents of that letter again. You'll forget that it ever existed. Now do you understand?"

"I'm not listening to some anonymous caller." I try to sound confident even though my hands are shaking.

Silence fills the phone line for a few very long seconds. Then he speaks again. "It's a shame about Frank's condition. I'm sure you wouldn't want him to take a turn for the worse. Or for Ryan to have an accident."

My legs give out and I have to sit down. "You're threatening me? Over a letter? Please. Just tell me what this is about."

"I've told you what to do. Now be a good girl and do what you're told. We're watching."

The phone drops from my hand. It hits the top of my desk, making a loud thud. I quickly pick it up again. "Hello? Are you still there?"

The man is gone. I hang up the phone and drop to the floor. I hug my knees to my chest as my whole body shakes.

I need to see Garret. I need to talk to him and have him tell me that everything will be all right. I need to be close to him so I can feel safe. But he hasn't come downstairs and after seeing his dad's outburst this morning, I'm sure Garret will never appear at my door again.

Now someone I don't even know is after me. Calling me. Watching me. Threatening to hurt the people I care about. But why? Why is this happening?

Just when everything was going so well, life smacks me in the face knocking me back down. Reminding me that I can't be happy. For some reason, I'm not allowed to be.

My past continues to haunt me.

And this time, I can't run from it.

Made in United States
Orlando, FL
21 May 2022

18059558R00176